THE
MERCER ISLAND MURDERER

T. A. AUGUST

THE MERCER ISLAND MURDER

by T.A. August

Copyrights

Copyright © 2021 by T. A. August

All rights reserved. No part of this book may be reproduced or used in any manner without written permission of the copyright owner except for the use of quotations in a book review.

This is the work of fiction. Names, characters, places, and incidents either are the product of the author's imagination or are used fictitiously. Any resemblance to actual persons, living or dead, events, or locales is entirely coincidental.

First paperback edition February 2021

ISBN 978-1-7360478-0-4 (paperback)
ISBN 978-1-7360478-1-1 (ebook)

Published by T. A. August

www.taaugust.com

PART I

CHAPTER 1

"Rachel?" I said softly.

"I'll be fine. It's just hard seeing Joelle go to her first day of kindergarten. It seems like just last week we were picking her up from the hospital, holding her in my arms for the first time, and taking her home to her beautiful new life," Rachel said as a tear ran down her cheek.

"I know, Peaches, but this is a good thing. Now we will be able to watch her grow and learn new things with her. Also, it'll be good for her to make new friends, especially after the recent move," I said, trying to ease her mind about our only child reaching another one of her big milestones, schooling. Of course, we wanted her to get the best education possible to set up her future, so we sent her to a private, nonprofit school close to our house. It wasn't an academy that had a dress code, and it was well diversified, which Rachel thought was important in a school.

I wiped the tear off her cheek and reached over to hold her awkwardly as we sat in the car outside of Joelle's new school. After a few minutes, we were able to have a conversation about what we planned to do for the rest of the day. As Rachel was a therapist, and I worked in IT, we rarely had the opportunity to take time away from work together. However, this was an emotional day for us – we knew that it would be – so we both decided to take the entire day off.

We decided to go for lunch at a nearby restaurant that we had never been to. Since moving to Mercer Island in Washington, we hadn't had the chance to try a lot of the restaurants on the island, or even in downtown Seattle.

We were careful when designing our home to not make it too extravagant. We didn't want to draw attention from criminals. The crime rates were also relatively low, compared to Seattle city, except for theft and property damage. Those things were unavoidable in a wealthy neighborhood like this one, though.

Our house was right on the water, and the only thing on the property when we'd bought it was a grove of trees. We left a good portion of the trees and built a dock for a boat, which would come in handy if Rachel ever decided that I could get one. Our home was larger than any home I lived in previously, with five bedrooms and six bathrooms. Almost everyone else who lived on the waterfront had a deck outside the back of their house, looking over the ocean. Since we left many of the trees on the land, ours was somewhat tucked away, so we could only see a small portion of our neighbor's decks.

The restaurant was quiet, as it was only 9am and most people were either just arriving to work or already at work. With it being the start of the school year, there weren't as many tourists in the area as there had been only a few weeks ago. Yet the streets still seemed busy for school and work to be in session. Rachel ordered a healthy salad that had an unhealthy amount of Caesar dressing on it. Although it was still so early, she'd started her day many hours ago and had eaten breakfast after her morning run and workout. I, on the other hand, was nowhere near ready for lunch. I ordered a couple of scrambled eggs, white toast with grape jam, and a good-sized slab of ham. I would have preferred eggs over-easy so I could dip my toast in the yolk, but many places just don't cook them as I would.

After our meal, we took a walk around the nearby park. Exploring parks had become something of a tradition for our family – the way some families go to the movies every '$5 Tuesday'. Back in Chicago, we'd find the closest parks, and stroll around them, or play frisbee when Joelle was along. It was a tradition that we hadn't resumed since we'd moved to the island.

"Have you gotten any more clients?" I asked her. Getting clients was a big deal when you're a therapist. Rachel had to leave her practice in Chicago when we moved, but I wasn't worried. I knew she would fill spots up fast; she was good at what she did.

"Yeah, I'm up to fifteen every week and a few ad hoc clients too."

"That didn't take you long. You must be good." We looked at each other, and I winked at her. She smiled at me and nudged my arm. As we were looking at each other, a person ran straight into us. Moving at speed between the pair of us, he slammed right into both of our shoulders, causing us both to grab them while they throbbed from the impact. By the time I registered what had happened and turned around, he was already a long way down the path.

The man was rushing, nearly running, in the opposite direction. Light brown hair, nondescript features, average height; nothing about him stood out, aside from the fact that he'd almost knocked us over. He wasn't dressed in running clothes or even running shoes, which could indicate why he was plowing through us in a hurry. His jeans were worn out, and his plain black sweatshirt had seen better days.

"That was so bizarre. I wonder what that was about," Rachel said, puzzled and still rubbing her shoulder.

"It really was. It almost seemed like he was running from something. He certainly didn't look like he was simply jogging in the park," I observed.

"Yeah, I agree. Weird," she said, ending the conversation.

We continued to walk in silence until we reached the next parking lot, then we turned around and walked back to our vehicles.

After whiling away the morning in each other's company, we retraced our steps. We decided to take Joelle to get ice-cream after school while she told us all about her first day.

~

I first met Rachel in college; it was my second year and her first. She looked so mature for her age, and I was far from it. We met at a football tailgating party. One of her new girlfriends was sleeping with Mark, a friend I'd known since we were still in diapers. When I approached her, she seemed shy at first, but I offered her a beer, and she gladly accepted it. We sat at the end of Mark's old pickup truck and got to know each other that day. She said that she knew right away that she wanted to study psychology. I told her I wasn't sure what I wanted to do, and I had till the end of the year to figure that out.

As the game started, we quickly ran up to the bleachers and sat on a blanket she had brought. I was glad she had the blanket; I underestimated how chilly it would be on that fall night. We spent the rest of the game talking about our hobbies and sports. I was surprised to learn that she enjoyed football but followed Lacrosse more closely. I decided that day not to tell her that I was actually on the Lacrosse team. I'd let her figure that out the next time she went to one of our games and saw me on the field. We sat next to our friends as they made out the entire game. Just like the previous year, the football team threw a party every time they won. With victory in our sights, we all knew there was a party to follow. I asked her if she wanted to go with me. She told me that she wanted to stay in and study but agreed to meet for brunch the next morning.

That evening, Mark and I got ready for the party and left a little later than normal. The later we went, the more entertaining it seemed to be when we got there. Of course, we were right, especially tonight. The three football houses were packed. All three houses had people spread out across the lawn, laughing, drinking, and acting foolish. Inside the first house, there were mostly drinking games, like beer pong. The second house was where most of the stoners were. They tended to stick together and stay glued to their couches. The third house was where all the entertainment was. The best drinks, hottest women, and the loudest music, which was where I usually gravitated.

Mark quickly spotted his latest hookup. Following him into the crowd, I was surprised to see Rachel holding a beer and standing next to her friend. I quickly tossled my chestnut brown hair, that I had just gotten cut the day before.

"I thought you were staying in to study tonight?" I asked in the gentlest yet loudest way I possibly could.

"Yeah, I was. But then Sally told me that I had to come out with her and get some *fresh air*," she said with air quotes, as she smiled and rolled her eyes. We both knew that there wasn't going to be much fresh air in this house. She turned to our friends, realized they had already disappeared, then turned back at me. "So much for that. She said she wouldn't leave my side."

"What did you say?" I said, holding my finger to the ceiling to let her know that the music was too loud for me to hear her. She leaned in very close to my ear, and I could feel her breath on my neck. It made the hairs prickle up.

"I said my friend ditched me. Do you want to go dance?" she asked, already swaying to the beat.

I was never much of a dancer, but for Rachel, I could be. I let her grab my hand and lead us through a crowd of people; we got very close to the DJ.

It was hard for me to look away from her. At the football game, in her Chicago State football sweatshirt and a pair of Levis, she'd been naturally beautiful. Waves of shoulder-length auburn hair framed a face that was lit up by bright brown eyes and rosy cheeks that needed minimal make-up. Now, at the party, she looked like a beauty queen. Her make-up was noticeably heavier. Her same outfit was casual yet very sexy, and her smile was bright beneath the colored lights. It was almost as if the lights were created for her.

She started to move effortlessly but also rhythmically. It was hard to take my eyes off her body. Not just her body, her smile too. We danced the night away, side by side. She looked to be five feet and nearly three inches, which matched perfectly with my five foot, eleven inch muscular body. Women around her height have always been my weakness.

That night, she never let me get too close to her, but she never strayed too far away either. She kept me guessing and waiting the entire night. By two o'clock in the morning, the lights began to turn on, and the music became less vibey, and everyone knew it was time to go home. She gave me a hug and said she'd had a really great time.

I was speechless. The only thing I could say was, "Do you still want to get brunch with me?"

"I would really like that, but I must apologize, I don't know your name," she laughed. That's when I realized I'd never introduced myself. If I'd told her my name, I would have felt offended that she didn't remember. But I let it pass because I couldn't be offended by that smile.

"It's Timothy; Timothy Cardington, but you can call me Tim if you'd like." Truthfully, she could call me anything, for all I cared.

"Okay, Timmy," she said with a huge smile, undoubtedly seeing if I'd let her get away with the name, which I did. "I'm Rachel, and it's nice to meet you…again." She stuck her hand out, and I took it in mine. She smiled as we shook hands, and I grinned because I was smitten and because I couldn't wait for our brunch, to see her beautiful face again.

CHAPTER 2

We weren't in the habit of giving Joelle ice-cream and treats, but we wanted her to be happy if school didn't go well. We also wanted to coax her into telling us about her day. Thankfully, she'd enjoyed it. She'd made three new friends and asked if she could have a sleepover with some of the girls. We thought this was too soon but told her we would talk to their parents.

That night, Joelle had a hard time falling asleep and ended up crawling into the middle of our bed. Rachel slept right through it, but I woke up the instant she walked into the room and asked, "Daddy, can I come sleep with you tonight?" Of course, I let her in. We tried not to baby Joelle, but it's always difficult not to indulge your first child. Especially for us, not knowing if we were ever going to be blessed with a second. Joelle might end up being an only child.

The next day came around, and it was time for us to get into our new routine. We'd decided that we would take turns dropping Joelle off at school. That day, it was Rachel's turn, so I had a few extra minutes to get ready. Rachel often woke up earliest in the family, probably because she seldom slept well. She had cooked breakfast before she left with Joelle, and I headed out to the balcony to eat mine while reading the morning paper. We'd chosen this land partly because of the view of the open water, but also because of all the full trees that offered an element of privacy. I looked around and didn't see any of our neighbors sitting out on their balconies, watching the water move around in what felt like slow motion.

I'd recently taken up reading the paper in the mornings to learn more about the island. They had already started talking about who would be running for mayor. Currently, there was only one candidate, the same one as the last few years. It didn't seem like a popular position around here.

On the bright side, it did seem like the mayor did a good job. The grass along the highways was always cut, not much trash laying around, and the roads didn't have potholes everywhere, unlike some roads that we used to drive when we lived in Chicago. This island seemed to be well-maintained, which was a big factor in deciding to plant our roots here. We'd considered other options, but many weren't ideal for our family situation, especially since Rachel loved extra space.

After sitting there and enjoying the view for a few minutes, I decided to get up and get ready to leave for work. I was a project manager for a company that created outsourced software. My job provided a comfortable salary but didn't demand that I keep regular hours as long as the work got done. At that point, we didn't have very many projects, which made for a boring day. I had time to spare in the morning until we got the clients and the funding and started planning the next big assignment. Once that started, it would be a long few weeks until the project came to an end, and I'd be able to go back to a relaxed schedule.

~

After that first night when we met, Rachel and I spent the next week hanging out together every chance we could. Going to the movies, taking walks, going for dinner; just about anything you can do with someone, we did together. The only thing we didn't get to was sex. It was just never the right moment, and I wasn't one to push sexual activities on a woman.

This might have bothered some men, but I felt that having a chance with someone like Rachel was worth the wait. All of my friends made fun of me over my infatuation with Rachel. I simply couldn't get enough of her.

Many couples will tell you about their 'love at first sight' or how they just fell in love over time. With Rachel, I was blinded by love. Call it what you want; I was deeply, madly in love with her. Every smile or giggle deepened my feelings.

A little over a month after we met, I was talking to Mark when he mentioned that Sally, his steady 'friend with benefits', had said something about

Rachel being excited to sleep with me. I asked him if he knew when, but he said he didn't get the specifics; it sounded like it would be very soon. I was ecstatic, and I could hardly contain myself. I went to the grocery store and made sure I had condoms handy and everything else that she could possibly ask for…drinks, snacks, and even paper towels. Thinking back to it made me chuckle at the awkwardness of those youthful moments.

Later that evening, when she invited me over, I couldn't say no. I arrived five minutes late to make it seem like I didn't know what was about to happen. Her room was lit with just a few candles, and no other lights were on.

She kissed me and spoke very softly. "Hi, Timmy, how was your day today?" She acted so casual, like there wasn't about to be some serious sex going down in just a few minutes.

I gave her a shy smile and said, "It just got a lot better now that I'm here with you." Cheesy, but that was the extent of my skills back then. "What is going on here? Did your lightbulbs burn out? I can change them for you if you need me to." If she was going to play it cool, so would I.

She giggled and gave me that smile that made me come apart at the seams. "No, silly, I was just planning a special night with you. I hope you came prepared." With a swift and positively brazen move, she reached into my back pocket and pulled out the condoms I'd tucked in with my wallet. I was surprised that she was capable of something so bold yet so sexy. I couldn't help but lean in and kiss her softly.

She was wearing jeans and a sweatshirt, her classic 'go-to' outfit. It only took a few minutes until she wasn't wearing anything. We made love that day, for the first time, and my life would never be the same.

CHAPTER 3

Two weeks into our daily routine, Joelle had a dentist appointment. Ever since she was young, we would get our teeth cleaned and checked as a family to make her feel less nervous about it. First, I went, then Joelle, and finally, Rachel. It doesn't take long for things to become a tradition in our family. Afterward, we went to the park and tossed around the frisbee for a good hour. Then it began to rain, and we left the park to go to the pizza spot close to our house.

Choosing pizza was always a battle in our family. Rachel and Joelle liked pineapple and ham, the classic Hawaiian pizza. I liked everything but the pineapple. We usually compromised by getting one of each because even when you pick the pineapple off and throw it to the side, there's still a hint of the sweet juice that stays behind. The juice would ruin an entire pizza for me. The girls, however, would eat whatever kind of pizza combinations remained when it came to leftovers. They simply preferred the Hawaiian.

"What are we doing for my birthday?" Joelle had asked. It was still a month away, but she was the type of kid who liked to remind everyone of the upcoming festivities.

"What would you like to do, dear?" Rachel asked.

"Can I have some friends over? We could get one of those party things and have a sleepover and do our nails and watch movies and stay up all night!" Joelle said with a little too much excitement as if she'd been planning this for the last year.

"Well, that depends, hon'. How many friends were you thinking of inviting?" I had to ask.

"Well, just Jenny, Juniper, and Amy," she said, with a little less excitement. "Those are the only friends I've made so far anyway."

"Give us a day or two to think about it, and we will give you an answer, so you can get invitations out. How does that sound, Joe?" Rachel said while looking at me with a little bit of worry in her expression.

"Okay, Mommy," she said with a smile.

Later that evening, as Rachel and I were getting ready for bed, Rachel brought up her concern about Joelle. "I'm just worried that she's not going to make as many friends as she had back in Chicago."

"Okay, my love, why don't we let her three main friends stay over, but for the party portion, we invite the entire grade to the party? That way—" She cut me off by kissing me and smiling broadly all at the same time.

"I knew there was a reason I married you. So handsome, wonderful, and smart," Rachel said, still smiling and kissing me. "A smart man like you deserves a reward for your quick thinking," she continued. There was no more talking after that.

She grabbed me close and straddled me. It took but a split second for my body parts to register what was about to happen, but once they were ready, they were ready.

We were lucky that Joelle didn't have any nightmares that night.

~

Joelle was adopted, but the story of how she became our child was a sad one that I tended not to share with many people. Often people would ask about our family because Joelle had bright blonde hair and fair skin. With my Australian heritage and Rachel being half Hispanic and half white, it was fairly evident that she wasn't our birth-daughter.

The period leading up to Joelle's adoption was one of the hardest times for us, personally as well as for our relationship. There were countless hours spent crying and embracing each other for comfort. It was really a dark time.

The trouble began when Rachel was 22, and I, 23. She was often sick. She felt like she was getting hot flashes, and she often went to the doctor to treat urinary tract infections, but the medication never seemed to help. Eventually, she decided to see a specialist, who told her that she had started early menopause. At this age, neither of us really knew the challenges we would face after hearing this. She didn't get the answers she wanted from the doctor, so she spent hours in the library doing research until she came across the worst sentence she could ever read.

Once we found out from the professionals that she was infertile, we spent a lot of time having sex. We were upset and trying to make a baby, trying to prove that there was nothing wrong with her fertility. After a few months, Rachel broke down and spent a lot of time by herself. She wasn't sure how to handle the information, and I wasn't sure how to handle her in such a fragile state.

There was a lot of yelling, screaming, and crying. We spent a lot of time apart and doing our own thing. It was as if we were living together but had completely separate lives. Eventually, Rachel started sleeping in our bed again. She started crying less and smiling more. It was almost as if a switch flipped inside of her.

She told me that she'd started to see a therapist and was feeling much better about the situation. She told me that the therapist recommended finding a different way to express what she was feeling and going through. Out of all the options, she decided that poetry would be the way to move on from this terrible ordeal. She became more and more like herself, and our relationship began to heal. The only significant difference was that she spent a lot of time writing.

I never minded that she wanted to write in her journal. It was amazing to see all her pain and hurt transformed into beautifully written words. Often, she would be having a moment and need a second to write down her thoughts that might become a poem later on. They were all thoughtful, relating to her situation, yet broad enough that they could be applied to many other people's situations.

She went to therapy for a while after that, getting a little better each time. Her therapist thought it was a good idea for us to talk about what the future would look like for us. At that time, it didn't look like there was going to be a future. It was something we'd stopped talking about altogether. Rachel was still distant, but gradually things became better.

Together, we decided that we wanted to adopt a child. To us, it didn't matter what race or where the child came from. Just as long as we were able to still have a family together. We spent months gathering the necessary funds, finding a child to adopt…and then watching as that child's birth parents decided to keep them. We tried four times, and each one fell through. It seemed like the luck just wasn't there for us; like we weren't meant to be parents.

Throughout all of this, Rachel kept writing and seeing her therapist. It was almost as if it didn't faze her, but it took a toll on me. I never mentioned it to her because I was too self-conscious to expose my emotions to her. I was proud of her for trying so hard and for pushing through, but I was simply sitting in the background, filled with my pain and hers.

Before we decided to proceed with the planned adoptions, we reached out to the local fire station and told them we wanted to take a child if one came in. We'd learned that safe-haven laws permitted indigent parents to surrender infants to facilities such as fire stations and hospitals. In desperation, we'd tried every option. Over time and distracted by the heartbreak of so many unsuccessful adoptions, we'd forgotten that we even contacted the fire station.

One day, we got a call. A firefighter gave us the news that there was a child dropped off and ready to be adopted. We picked her up the moment we could. We never saw her before the day we took her home, but the minute we gazed into her deep, beautiful brown eyes, we knew that this was our daughter. The beginning of our family.

CHAPTER 4

The Saturday of Joelle's birthday dawned. We got up early because even though guests wouldn't start arriving until mid-afternoon, we still had a lot of setting up to do. It took longer than we expected, but after the table and chairs were in place and the bouncy house arrived, we still had a few hours to kill. We decided to pick up Joelle's best friends and take them to her favorite pizza joint before heading to the mall for a little bit of birthday shopping.

We got home in the nick of time. People started arriving only ten minutes after we got back to the house. This was expected within this neighborhood. We lived in a suburb where people prided themselves on not being busy. So they were either out on their boats or sitting at home watching morning cartoons. There was no doubt that this party was the only thing on these people's agenda for the day.

We weren't sure how many guests would arrive, but there was a good number who ended up coming. Every child brought a gift, and our present table soon filled up with perfectly-wrapped boxes. Joelle didn't seem to notice the large pile of presents that were all for her; she was surrounded by friends and family, and that's all she wanted.

After a few hours, all the kids were exhausted from playing and almost ready to go. There was only one thing left to do, and that was eat the cake. Joelle chose strawberry, but we had a small vanilla cake made in case some people weren't fond of strawberry. Mermaids had become Joelle's favorite topic, so there was a mermaid on the top of the cake made from frosting. It had a long, scaled tail that started blue from the bottom and transformed into a deep purple. We put candles on the top, and she blew them all out with one large breath. Joe named the beautiful, majestic mermaid Joelle Junior, after herself.

Eventually, her classmates all left, except for the three who were spending the night. Soon after, the bouncy house people gathered their equipment and left, saying we should be receiving the bill within a few days. Rachel and I sat down on the couch, absolutely exhausted. It was only sunset, but we'd had a long and busy Saturday. Joelle and her friends sat down right in front of us while she opened all her birthday presents.

She had gotten a wide range of toys. Some of them she already had, and some she got more than one of from her classmates. She gave all the duplicates to her friends, which we both thought was sweet. Joelle led her friends down to the basement to play. We had cameras down there, so we could see what they were doing and make sure they were behaving. We were far too exhausted to play with them ourselves.

Rachel laid her legs across mine and sat up. Her face was bright, and a broad smile played about her lips.

"What is it?" I asked while a smiled crept up onto my face to match hers. Her smiles had always been contagious.

"Nothing, I just love you so much," she said as she stretched the word 'so' out for a few seconds longer than necessary.

"I love you too, my love bug, always and forever." We sat there silently staring into each other's eyes, and soon she came in close for a warm, loving kiss. We only got a few good kisses in before the kids started running up the stairs, looking for something sweet and strawberry-flavored.

Two hours later, they were just as tired as we were. We all decided to call it a night. The kids lay around the living room. Joelle was lying in the curve of our wide gray sectional, and two of her friends by her side. The remaining friend had flopped onto the matching gray loveseat beside the couch.

I brushed my teeth and took a shower. By the time I was crawling into bed, Rachel was fast asleep. I stared at her for a little while, beyond amazed that I was still with someone so perfect, even in sleep. I gave her a kiss on the forehead, turned out the lights, and wrapped my arms around her before falling asleep.

~

Family had always been the most important thing to Rachel. I couldn't give two shits about family coming together. However, this was due to our extreme differences in growing up. Rachel had been given almost anything she could dream of. From a fancy house with a pool in the backyard, to a new Cadillac on her 16th birthday. It wasn't that her family spoiled her...or perhaps, it was that a little. It was simply that they were able to splurge money on her and not ever need that money back.

Truthfully, that's why we lived in the house on Mercer Island. Her parents had bought the land and paid for the construction of the house. They even went as far as to furnish it with whatever Rachel liked. Rachel had been used to this; she didn't think anything of it. To me, it was insane. Never would I imagine my in-laws to be so rich and yet not stuck up about it.

Her family had an interesting background. Her dad worked for the state of Illinois doing construction, and he'd served in the Army for twenty years. Her mom was a social worker who dealt with scheduled visitations to separated families. They also happened to be lucky enough to win the lottery – $37 million. Instead of being foolish and spending it on lavishing things, they saved it. They invested it so well that they could retire early and give their only child the best life possible.

Family wasn't something I was used to; in fact, it was rather foreign. I grew up in a home where my father beat my mother while they were shooting heroin all day long. I remember having two other siblings in my house until my mother's sister had called Child Protective Services. We were instantly put into foster care. I was only seven years old. I was continually going in and out of different homes, getting beaten, sleeping on dirty floors, and cleaning an entire house instead of doing homework after school. Most of the people who took me in were only there for the small paycheck that I brought in. I never got to stay anywhere for more than a few months.

However, eventually, I had some luck in my life. When I turned 17, I changed foster homes yet again because my previous house didn't want me, knowing I was closer to 18 and hard to handle at times. I went to a nice couple, Louis and Angela, who took me in, gave me a bedroom, and fed me well. They couldn't have kids themselves, but they raised me for the last year of my childhood, and they paid for me to attend our state college. It was almost a dream come true; the only thing better that happened to me was Rachel and Joelle.

Thinking back, if I had never been put into that house, I would never have gone to college. I probably would have been homeless, doing crack on the street, while businessmen walked past me and threw change at my feet so I could get my next fix. Instead, I ended up on the beautiful Mercer Island, with my gorgeous wife and sweet daughter.

Of course, I did return the favor to my last foster parents. I paid them back for my college, with what I thought was a reasonable amount of interest. The last time I spoke to them, they had just gotten another foster kid and were planning on spending the money I returned to put that child through college as well. They were always generous like that, taking in one child at a time and focusing on them until the child was old enough to venture into the world. I wasn't their first foster child, and I was glad I wouldn't be the last.

CHAPTER 5

My love,

My love.

You came to me in my wildest dream,

Just like a bright white dove.

To you, I owe everything good in my life,

And I sure am happy to be your wife.

As I walked down the stairs, I saw something sticking to the refrigerator. Normally, Rachel kept this spot clear, so I knew right away what was sitting there. A poem she had written on the typewriter for me.

It was beautiful, as always, and I put it in my office drawer where I kept the rest of them. I knew that the only reason I had gotten one was because I went above expectations last night. After our first couple of weeks together on Mercer, work had picked up. We hadn't been seeing much of each other lately, as I had been working late and Rachel had been getting more clients. So the previous night I planned a surprise with a bunch of candles lighting up the room, and rose petals spread across the bed and floor.

As soon as she walked in, I had called her to the bed, where I sat naked. Waiting. She must have been prepared, because she immediately took off her clothes. Letting her skirt fall right off her hips, slowly unbuttoning her black-and-white striped button-down. If I wasn't already hard, it wouldn't have been a problem getting there. She slowly crawled onto the bed, like a lion hunts its prey. Within a second, she pounced. Pushing me back as she put her head down and started sucking me. It only took a few brief minutes for her to finish her job.

She could tell once I was reaching my moment of fulfilment, as I let a out a low moan and succumbed to her. I lay there for a few seconds until she joined me. She curled next to me, and once I came back to my senses, I murmured, "My turn," as I gave a devilish smile.

I got up, pinned her to the bed, and put my face between her legs. I could hear her breath getting heavier, turning into moans. I could tell that she was reaching the top, but I wasn't ready for her to release this fast.

It didn't take long for me to get hard again, so I teased her until I was ready. Then with a swift move, I flipped her over on her stomach, grabbed her hips and pulled them up till she was on all fours. Then I grabbed her ass with my hand and stuck my dick right inside her, thrusting until she cried out in sweet, sweet release. She came apart right around me. She was finished and we were happy.

We both fell to the bed, on our backs and spent a few minutes cuddling until it was time for us to get up and get something for dinner.

We were all sitting around the dining room table, eating our dinner. We laughed about our day and talked with food in our mouths. We did this normally, but tonight just felt different, like there was something added that made everyone a bit happier than usual.

~

Rachel didn't write me poems often, just enough to keep me constantly guessing. I loved them, and they were always something special and close to the heart.

The poems were never random. They always emerged after something happened. A few times, she even wrote me an apology poem after an argument.

When she first started to write the poems, she had a notebook that she quickly filled. There were enough to get them all published in a book. I'd always thought she should do something like that, but I never brought it up, thinking it might be too sensitive of a subject still.

One Christmas, though, I did buy her a typewriter. One of the old-fashioned ones that you couldn't erase or go back after a mistake; you had to start over from the beginning. It came in a large box. Every year we'd try to guess what gifts were in the boxes, and we usually were pretty good. For this specific gift, she was completely off. Which made the unwrapping all that much better.

She tore off the red paper with its green polka dots. She stared at it in shock for a few seconds, then a single tear trickled down her left cheek. She looked up towards me just as the second tear fell. These were tears of joy, ones she couldn't stop once they started.

"How did you know?" she asked me, trying to contain her tears and excitement as she stared at her old-fashioned typewriter. It had the raised keys that you had to push down hard on to get the letter to appear on the paper. It was obviously used, but in great condition, an authentic antique, some would call it. She was like a little kid that Christmas, full of smiles, joy, and appreciation.

"My love, I always try to pick special gifts for you. I'm surprised you didn't guess this one; you do almost every year."

"I could never have guessed this. It is just beautiful and must have cost a fortune. I thought we agreed that we weren't going to spend money like this on each other." We did, but knowing that her family had money, I felt that the only way I could get a good gift was if it was something both expensive and meaningful. Plus, I knew she was the one for me. The happiness it brought was worth it to me.

"Right, like this mini-vacation to Seattle for your spring break didn't cost you a fortune either," I said to her, knowing that what I was saying was very accurate. "Besides, you never would have bought this for yourself, and I felt that you needed it. All good poets love an antique typewriter."

We shared an intimate moment at that time; it was one of the best Christmases we had as husband and wife. Not only because of the gifts we got, but also the fact that we were happy after such a long period of unhappiness since finding out about Rachel's infertility. It was the first time in a while that we felt at peace.

CHAPTER 6

Joelle had plans to spend the night at Juniper's house that Friday. Rachel and I decided we would go downtown and do some sightseeing. The first thing we did was go out to eat. We'd put our names on a waiting list for an exclusive restaurant in town and were thrilled when we were called due to a cancellation just hours before dinner. The alternative would've been a fast-food burger house. Rachel was ecstatic to go to this place. She had heard a lot of good things about it from her receptionist, who had been talking about it for the last few weeks.

"Please follow me to your table, Mr. and Mrs. Cardington," our host said, guiding us to our booth after we'd sat in the waiting area for at least thirty minutes. "Your server will be with you in just a moment. Please look at the menu and the wine list. We have a few wines on special tonight, but you must buy it by the bottle to get the deal," she explained, as if that was going to be a problem for us.

"Thank you," Rachel said. The host walked away with a polite smile. Rachel crossed her legs and pressed her left leg against my right leg. She looked stunning in sleek black pants, a vibrant red high-neck top, a matching black blazer, and black high heels. The diamond necklace she was wearing was one I'd bought for her in Italy on our honeymoon.

"You look absolutely gorgeous," I spilled out.

"Well, you don't look so bad yourself," she said with a smile and a wink.

"What are you thinking about getting?"

"I'm not sure, dear. I think we should get some wine, though. It's been so long since we've enjoyed a good glass of wine," she said, sounding a little irked.

"Of course, whatever your heart desires. Although, I do prefer a nice glass of sweet Riesling over a merlot." I acted as if I cared about the wine when all I cared about was keeping that brilliant smile on her face the entire night. She grinned, knowing that I was joking, and let a small giggle slip from her lips.

We spent a few minutes in silence, going over the menu until the waiter came to get our drinks order. We knew the wait would be longer if we didn't order our food with the drinks, so we did. Rachel got a large salad topped with steak, strawberries, and a *tarte vinaigrette*. I ordered a traditional 10-ounce steak, garlic and cheese mashed potatoes, and grilled asparagus. We got our wine quicker than expected.

"I loved the poem you left me the other day; it was beautifully written."

She smiled wide. "It was typed actually. On the typewriter," she said playfully. She seemed to be in a sassy, sexy mood.

The food came and went. It was delightful, in my opinion, but Rachel seemed keener on the idea of dessert. We got a chocolate cake with ice-cream, and I gave most of it to her. For me, it was just a little too rich in chocolatey flavor.

"Shall we go for a walk?" Rachel proposed. I thought it was a great idea. I pointed my hand in front of her as if to direct her forward.

"Ladies first."

I stuck my arm out, and she wrapped her hand around it, holding near my bicep. We started walking but only made it a few blocks before we hit the Space Needle. "You know we haven't been there since moving to Washington," Rachel mentioned.

"We have all night, my love. Would you like to?"

"I would love nothing more," she said with a smile, then reached up on her tiptoes and placed a kiss on my right cheek.

We bought our tickets and went to the top. The view was simply breathtaking and beyond beautiful. "Rachel, would you like me to take your picture with the view in the background?"

"No, thanks. But can we take one together? I want to remember this feeling for the rest of my life."

We asked a kind passerby to take our picture, and she said yes and took several. Rachel returned the favor by taking a photo of her and her girlfriend. We sat on the bench, held hands, and stared out at the view for a few minutes, just taking in the scene.

Rachel smiled, looked at me, and said, "This is so beautiful. I cannot believe we live here."

"Yes, you are. You're so beautiful, and I cannot believe I live here. With you by my side every day," I said while returning the favor of her smile.

For the rest of the night, we walked around the town and went into little shops that were still open, not buying anything, but just enjoying the Seattle culture by taking it all in. We ended the night in a small all-night coffee shop. Rachel loved a good cup of joe; it was one of the reasons we chose Seattle. I, on the other hand, preferred tea. We ordered our drinks – her black coffee and my Earl Grey with cream and sugar – and picked a table in the corner to observe the place. Rachel always said that a good cup of coffee never needed anything mixed into it. If she had to add anything like sugar or cream, we knew that we would never be returning to that coffee shop.

We got our beverages and scanned the rest of the room. There were younger people, most likely studying, and older people who probably thought clubs were a boring place to be on a weekend night.

The shop was somewhat dark inside, but it had just enough light surrounding the counter where all the employees huddled and gossiped. It had a homey feeling to it; the seats were comfortable yet fashion-forward with their mix of colors and funky patterns. The environment was pleasing and welcoming, yet somewhat reserved, as if the place had many secrets hidden inside. We sat in the corner, but we were still close to the windows on both sides of the corner. There was a pleasant view of the street out one of the windows and a distant view of city lights out the other window. It seemed like everywhere we went tonight just made the city more inviting and beautiful.

We sat in silence as we drank, taking in the views out both of the windows. Rachel's phone dinged to let her know that she had a notification. She pulled the phone out of the front pocket in her purse and instantly froze.

"What is it? Is it Joe? Is she okay?" Rachel could hear the worry in my voice. I hadn't seen Rachel look this shocked in a long time. It felt like hours that I sat there waiting for her to respond, even though it was probably only seconds. A million things ran through my head, about our daughter, then about her parents and her family.

She opened her mouth slowly, and I could tell that she was slightly shaken as she turned the phone in my direction. It was an article posted by the local news station. It took me a split second to read the headline, and I was frozen just the same as she was.

UNIDENTIFIED FEMALE FOUND DEAD OFF INTERSTATE

It was the heading of the online news article for Mercer Island.

Woman found dead and dismembered off busy Island highway. Most of the current details are unknown, and police are still at the scene. Stay tuned for the next update.

~

Rachel had never been one to react well to bad news. Some people, like myself, can easily process it and then move on. Unlike me, Rachel would dwell on bad news. It almost seemed to consume her for a short time. As if her life revolved around that tragic instant, suffocating her happiness.

One night, when we were in college, sleeping in the same bed, we were woken by police sirens. When we heard the noise, Rachel and I went to the hallway to see what was happening. Apparently, we weren't the only ones since the hallways were full of students. Everyone was still in a groggy blur from just waking up, but we all came to very quickly. The sirens weren't quiet, and there were more than one as if they wanted to wake up the entire campus. At that moment, nobody knew what had happened, but people had a pretty good guess. Being college, most assumed that it was some drunk person doing something that only a drunk person would do, and then getting hurt.

Rachel was either more curious than the rest or just more awake. She convinced me to go outside and see what was happening. We walked down to the main level and met the others who were out there at the time. There were only three others outside near the scene.

It turned out to be a woman, a young freshman, who went home with the wrong man. The man ended up killing her and leaving her out in the open for everyone to see. The coroner hadn't had time to take the body away yet, and Rachel saw the entire thing. From the body, to the blood. It really shook her up, and for weeks afterward, she was terrified to even leave her dorm and refused to go anywhere alone. I was closer to her than ever. I stuck by her side because I never wanted her to feel alone when there had been a murder just yards away from the dorm buildings.

I never blamed her for having such harsh reactions to tragedy, but she was never one to experience any real tragedy firsthand. On the other hand, I was young when I was beaten continuously and had to go into foster care. Yet when I thought of tragedy, that night always seemed worse.

That experience made me love Rachel even more deeply and gave me insight into how she processed trauma.

It would start with denial, where she couldn't believe what was happening and tried to put the event out of her mind. This would be followed by a lot of talking to fill the void that she would otherwise fill with stressful ruminations. The talking would stop just as soon as it started because then she'd go into a period of silence. This was the troubling part because it could last just minutes or as long as several days. It all depended on how tragic or triggering the event was for her. The first time it happened, I thought she was breaking up with me because of something I did, but it didn't take her long to snap out of it and return to normal.

CHAPTER 7

A body was found on September 28th, on the side of East Mercer Way. According to police reports, the female's remains were dismembered and contained in black garbage bags. The discovery was made by a homeless man, who claimed that he thought the bags held mannequin parts.

There is reason to believe that the body may be that of a local woman reported missing by her parents on September 8th, who has since been the subject of an extensive police investigation. However, these details have neither been confirmed nor denied by authorities at this point.

A police investigation is currently ongoing, and media updates will continue as the investigation unfolds.

"I don't get it, Dad. Why do they make death such a big deal? People die every day," Joelle asked as she scooped another mouthful of her favorite cereal into her mouth.

"Well, it's just something that they do to let the community know what is going on. And it's not a conventional way to die," I said, trying to sound as normal as possible.

"I think it's silly. It just makes everyone sad."

"Yeah, it definitely doesn't make anyone happy. But enough about that. Go grab your backpack, and let's get you to school!" I said, trying to change the mood of the conversation.

"But what if I don't want to go to school today? Can't we just stay home or go get ice-cream?"

"Joe, where is this coming from? I thought you loved school?"

"I do. I do. But I'm not feeling good today. I feel sick."

I went to feel her forehead with the back of my hand. She did, indeed, feel warmer than she should, as if she had a fever. "Oh, dear. You do feel a little warm. But I won't be able to take care of you today. Maybe I'll give your mom a call, and she can get someone over here to watch you."

"Daddy, no. I don't want you to leave. I want to stay home with you. You take care of me the best."

"Okay, okay. Let me call work, and then I'll call your mom and let her know that we are staying home today."

After only a few minutes of cartoons and a warm blanket, Joelle was out like a light. She fell asleep so peacefully and without complaint. I couldn't help but think about how blessed we were to have such a perfect daughter. I ended up not calling Rachel; instead, I texted her:

Joe is sick. Staying home with her.

I didn't get a text back, but she was probably in a session. Either a session or she was in her silent stage of tragedy. I decided to go to the office and grab my laptop so I could attempt to get some work done from home. Even though we were just starting a project, there was a lot that needed to be done. The planning stages are some of the most important, and they take a lot of time to create all the documents and project outlines. I had the time to take the entire day off without working, but I knew that it was something I would need to get done eventually. Besides, Joelle's cartoons didn't hold enough appeal to distract me from my tasks.

I left the cartoons running while Joe lay across the couch in a deep sleep while a yellow sponge was doing stupid things and giggling on the TV. It was good background noise so that Joe wouldn't wake up every time I started typing on my laptop. Every few minutes, in-between thoughts, I would glance over at Joe with her hair pulled up in a messy bun, just like her mom taught her. Everything about Joe reminded me of her mother. If anyone saw the two of them, they would know, without doubt, that Joe was Rachel's child, even if they didn't look biologically-related.

One thing that Joe learned from her mother was her love for me. She'd loved me since the day we brought her home. While she behaved like her mother, Joelle had always been a daddy's girl. There was no doubt in my mind that she would grow up to be just as successful as her mom.

~

Rachel and I knew we both wanted kids soon after we started dating. Rachel felt that she needed to get everything out 'in the open'. That was one of the reasons I fell so deeply in love with her; her brutal honesty and openness from the beginning. She laid everything out right after we started dating, from marriage, kids, and future plans, to even how she wanted her future house to look. We were still teenagers when we first started dating, since she was a freshman, and I was a sophomore.

Even all those years ago, she had her life mapped out, and everything fit like a puzzle. Everything except for her ability to produce a child. That put a pin in a lot of her plans and made her rethink everything. Nobody, including herself, could have guessed that she wouldn't be able to have kids.

One day, we were sitting in my dorm room, where we spent most of our time together, and she talked about how she wanted to have three kids before she finished her schooling. She had much longer to go than I did because she had her graduate program ahead of her. That gave us a lot of time to figure things out. However, it's unlikely she understood how hard it was going to be on us. After she graduated with her Bachelors, right before she went to grad school, was when we had the pregnancy ordeal. When she found out she couldn't have kids. Although it was bad timing for us career-wise, she wanted to have a child, and she was set on it. Like any good boyfriend, I supported her. That's when we applied to take in the next adoptable child. We had a stable income as I was working my first job from out of college as a team member for a project management team. Rachel was working part-time for a family friend while she was going to school.

Much like her family, her family's friends were also very wealthy. Her part-time employer was able to pay her a large salary and give her credibility that helped her in the future. We were living in an apartment that had two bathrooms and three bedrooms. On the surface, we were prepared to take on another child. But with Rachel still in school and working, and I just starting my career, we couldn't have been less prepared.

When Joelle joined us, Rachel took a semester off from her part-time job but continued her schooling. I stayed at my job and was lucky that they were tolerant of me taking time off to go to Joelle's appointments and watch her when nobody else could, which wasn't that often. As she started to grow up and learn her words, I was able to take more time off to spend with her. At times I would wonder if Rachel grew jealous of all the time Joe and I spent together. A part of me believed it was why we started going to the park as a family.

CHAPTER 8

Joelle felt better the day after her strange illness. I suspected that seeing the news about the murdered girl had unsettled her. We were still new to the area, and it might have scared her to think that this might be a bad neighborhood. Rachel and I agreed it was our job to make her feel safer, so we decided to spend the coming weekend with her doing fun things around the neighborhood.

It was a difficult decision because we had originally planned to visit Joelle's grandparents in Chicago that weekend. When we called to tell them, they had a lot to say, and it turned into an argument that I had to walk away from. I let Rachel handle it because they had a lot of opinions on the matter, and none of them were even worth listening to. With all of their money, they could have used some of it to buy tickets to visit us. It might have made Joelle feel safer. The truth was, even though they paid for everything, I didn't think they were happy that we moved.

After the call with her parents, Rachel didn't feel like hashing out the fact that someone had been found dead so close to our seemingly safe neighborhood. She simply said, "We can talk about it later. I'm too tired right now." I agreed, and we went to bed.

That morning, Rachel left before I had a chance to talk with her again. She sent me a text asking me to take Joelle to daycare because she had an early start at work. I simply texted her back.

Yes, my love.

Joelle was more than happy to wake up to see me. In one hand, I had my cup of tea, in the other hand, I had her donut. She liked the strawberry donuts from Dunkin' Donuts because of their 'pretty pink' color.

"Daddy?" she said when her eyes finally opened. She looked confused, but in a good way. It only took a few split seconds for a wide smile to shine across her face.

"Good morning, sunshine. I have your donut waiting whenever you're ready."

"Be out in a minute!" she yelled as I walked out of her room on my way back to the kitchen.

She came rushing out only minutes later in a pink shirt and blue jeans. She ran straight for the high kitchen chair, climbed to the top, and reached for her pink donut.

"Where did you get these, Dad?"

"Actually, dear, your mom got them for you last night after you fell asleep on the couch."

"I love my momma."

"Well, your mom loves you too. And so do I," I said while she shoved her face full of her donut. It seemed like record-breaking time. I'd never seen an adult, much less a child, eat a donut with such speed.

After she finished her donut, we gathered her princess backpack, she put on her bright pink Crocs and grabbed her lunch. We left from the kitchen into the mudroom and then into the garage. She jumped into her seat while I jumped into mine. Just like that, we left out the driveway and started our day. At no point did Joe mention the murder, the woman, or her feelings towards her safety. She looked like she felt perfectly fine. This was such a relief; I didn't want this to become a constant issue, especially not with us just moving here.

I dropped her off at her school and headed to work. I certainly wasn't in a rush, considering we still didn't have much work to do for a few weeks, so I decided to take the scenic route and get to know more about the area. I was rolling down the highway when there was a news clip on the radio that startled me. At that moment, all I could think was that I was glad that Joelle wasn't anywhere near the radio.

In breaking news, the body of the woman discovered on East Mercer Way just a few days ago has been positively identified as that of 25-year-old Kathren Arnoldson. Ms. Arnoldson *was reported missing on September 8th by her parents after she didn't return home from an appointment.*

An official autopsy has determined that cause of death was a drug overdose. However, it appears that this may have been administered under suspicious circumstances and police suspect foul play. The autopsy also indicated signs of severe dehydration and some recently broken bones, although these appear to have happened postmortem. There were no signs of struggle or sexual abuse. Police will release more information at a press conference later this week. Stay tuned for more updates on this ongoing investigation.

It was easy to understand how Joelle could be uneasy about something like this. Even I was left with an unpleasant sensation in the pit of my stomach after hearing the broadcast. Much like Joelle, I didn't understand why someone would want to do something like this.

~

I had never been the type of person to get upset over something that I had no control over. Truthfully, the fact that my wife was a psychologist had only strengthened that. Throughout college, I was the person she always tried her therapy on. Even though I never felt that I needed it, I was always the easiest for her to practice on. Through this, I learned a lot of good lessons, and sometimes I felt like I could almost be a psychologist myself.

One of the classes she had to take was about how psychologists cannot give themselves therapy. It's weird to think that someone is helping other people even when they cannot help themselves. It's even weirder knowing that when someone cannot help themselves, they can still be such help to others.

There were times when Rachel herself had to go to therapy after a crisis because she couldn't handle the pressure or the thoughts of the crisis. I never blamed her. I always thought she was strong for getting the help she needed, the help she deserved. I loved this about her.

That person being found killed outside her dorm room seemed to be the catalyst to convince her to seek out therapy the first time. She went to the school therapist, who didn't seem to help her as she wanted. But then she was able to talk to another therapist, one she chose, and she enjoyed that very much. It didn't take her long afterward to feel better, and she seemingly dismissed the entire ordeal.

She only needed a few therapy sessions for us to see her improving, even after the first session. After each one, she talked about it endlessly. However, she wouldn't discuss how the sessions went in terms of her own progress; she only talked about how inspiring it was that the person she went to was so helpful. She spoke a few times about the techniques the therapist used, and when she did, her face really lit up.

There was only one session where she discussed the details with me in-depth. She told me that she and the therapist had spoken about me because she was going to break up with me after one of our big fights.

However, after her session, she realized that she only wanted to break things off because of her father's opinion of me. This really helped me to understand the hatred her father had for me and how much her father's opinion could really impact our relationship.

Even after it seemed like she had recovered from seeing the body, she took a few more sessions. She told me that it was so she could see what it was like to be on the other side of the seat. I always believed this had been the reason she was such a successful therapist herself.

CHAPTER 9

We had a lot of things planned for the weekend, but the Seattle weather was not in a cooperative mood. It ended up raining all Friday, all of Saturday, and most of Sunday. Friday, we decided to order pizza and watch movies with Joelle and her friends, then took them all to the mall for some shopping on Saturday. After we dropped the girls off at their parents' houses, we went to the movie theater to watch a film Joelle had been dying to see.

Since Saturday was such a late night for us, Joelle and I slept in. Rachel never slept in, so she was up early in the morning for her run, except this morning, she had to wear a raincoat. Even rain didn't deter Rachel from her regular run. By the time I woke up, she was just getting back. She'd taken longer than usual and was strangely disheveled. Mud streaked her legs, and her hair was tangled with leaves.

"Long run today?" I asked as she started to take off her raincoat. I wanted her to tell me about where she'd been, without actually needing to ask.

"Yeah, I've just had a lot on my mind lately. I can't seem to shake the thoughts of this killing that happened down the street," she said, not looking up at me once.

"Hey, it's okay. It is a little too close to us. I don't blame you." I took a few steps towards her, and she lifted her head. Her eyes met mine, and I cupped her cheeks and gently kissed her on the lips. "Even I can see that this isn't something that we should take lightly. That woman seemed like such a nice person. Who would want to kill her?"

She didn't answer my question; she must've known it was a rhetorical one. We sat there for a few minutes holding each other. Over the past few days, she had been distant. I needed her in my arms just as much as she needed me in hers. I set aside my curiosity about the dirt and held her against me, smoothing her hair. "Perhaps it was a fall," I mused.

"I see it's only supposed to rain until about two in the afternoon today. We should take Joe to the park if it's not too wet. Or we could take her downtown and do some sightseeing," Rachel said. I knew that she really wanted to take her to the park the way we normally would because it would cement our sense of family. "Or we could explore the neighborhood, so she gets more accustomed to her new home."

"Yeah, I like that idea. We can see how it goes once we've had breakfast. We can ask Joelle what she wants to do. You know, we could always go to the aquarium or the museum. I think she might like one of those. But only if she doesn't want to go to the park, of course," I said, just to give her some more ideas because I doubt it would be dry enough to do anything outdoors.

"You already know we don't go to aquariums or zoos. That's just cruel. They keep those animals in cages and boxes all their lives when they should be in the wide-open wilderness, living their lives to the fullest. But instead, we keep them in confinement, where they get stared at all day by humans and trained to live a life that no wild animal should ever have to." She was so serious about this. I should have known not to bring up anything with animals in it. She had never agreed to take Joelle to a zoo or aquarium. I shared similar reservations, but for some reason, I just wasn't as passionate about the cause. I felt like a dick for even bringing up the proposition.

"I know, I'm sorry," I said with complete sincerity. "I was just throwing out activities that I saw when I Googled 'things to do in downtown Seattle'. I don't know. We can just see what she's up for. Maybe she's willing to get a little dirty in the muddy grass."

"Ha, yeah. Maybe."

Just then, Joelle came running to the kitchen where we were still standing. She gave me a huge hug that resulted in me picking her up and sandwiching her between Rachel and myself. We all started laughing and smiling at each other. It was a picture-perfect moment, one that I wanted to experience for the rest of my life.

Fifteen minutes later, Joelle and Rachel were sitting around the breakfast bar while I cooked up some eggs – over-easy, of course. Joelle picked bacon for the meat, which was a surprise because she really liked the sausage links. The bacon was cooking in the oven, the toast was in the toaster, and the strawberry jam just came out of the fridge.

Once the food was prepared, we all sat around the breakfast bar and stared out the windows as the rain fell. We were silent as we ate, but as soon as Joelle had eaten her fill, she started chattering about what she wanted to do with her day.

Rachel and I didn't even need to suggest activities for her. She had her own ideas, and apparently, she'd been thinking about them for a few days, just waiting for the rain to stop.

"First, I want to go to the park, and—" I cut her off right there.

"Joe, I think that it's going to be wet after the rain stops. I don't think we should be going to the park; we would all get too muddy. It wouldn't be as much fun as if we went on a sunny day. But, the choice is yours," I told her, not really giving her an actual choice.

"No, that's okay, we can go when it's sunny," she said, like it didn't affect her whatsoever. "I think that we should go down to the beach by the park, instead. The Catkin Point beach."

"You mean the Calkins Point Sand Beach?" Rachel said.

"Yes, Momma. It's close to home, and some of the kids at the school have been talking about it."

As usual, Rachel was the first to give an answer. "We can, but it'll be kind of wet out, and it's no longer summer, dear. It might be a little too chilly out at the water. Especially during fall."

"Yeah! Can we at least try it? If it's not nice enough out, we can go to number three!"

I chimed in, "What's number three?"

"Well, I want to go shopping at a used store," she mentioned with enthusiasm. "I want to get something *vintage*."

Rachel and I looked at each other and smiled. I laughed on the inside, and I'm sure that Rachel did too. We had always had money, but knowing that Joelle wanted to do some shopping at a thrift store amused me. I didn't even know she knew what that was.

Maybe now was the time for Rachel to tell Joelle that most of the clothes in this household were 'vintage'. For Rachel, it wasn't about the money; she cared about the sustainability of buying second-hand instead of new.

We were able to check out the beach Joelle wanted to go to. It was still a little wet, but as Joelle said, "Perfect for building sandcastles." We spent a few hours there, until four in the afternoon. After that, we were full of sand and needed a change of clothes. Since the park wasn't that far away from our house, we'd ridden bikes there. All of us had bikes with baskets in the front, great for carrying things like sandy towels and purses. We rode back to the house, showered, changed, ate a snack, and got in the car to head downtown. Just twenty minutes later, we had almost reached one of the parking garages in downtown Seattle.

Rachel knew where to go as she had visited a few of the shops before. When we first moved in, we left a lot of clothes in Chicago. Some of them were thrifted again, and the rest we left at Rachel's parents' house for when we would visit, allowing us to pack light. Luckily, they kept a guest suite there exclusively for us.

We spent what felt like hours in those shops, looking through clothes. I wasn't sure what the girls were looking for. I never understood how Rachel found such nice outfits in these seemingly messy racks. I sifted through a few but didn't find anything remotely close to what I would typically wear. How was she so good at shopping at these stores? I felt like they were purposely trying to hide the good items and only displaying the not so good.

They spent a lot more time going through the clothes and came out with a pile larger than I expected. When we got to the counter, the sales assistant told us they didn't use plastic bags. Rachel dug into her purse and extracted some folded up cloth bags that she used for our purchases.

It always surprised me how prepared Rachel was for everything. She would think about things so thoroughly and yet make it all seem so effortless. She turned around, bags in hand, and asked, "Ready, dear?"

"Yeah, right behind you." I followed Joelle and Rachel out the front door, and we walked outside.

"Can we go to another one, Mom?" Joelle asked, with the usual sparkle in her eyes.

"Of course, dear. But, if you want to get any more, you have to get rid of some of the things you have now," Rachel said.

"Why?" Joelle looked genuinely confused.

"Because you don't need so many clothes. It's time for you to get rid of some that you're outgrowing or that you don't want to wear anymore." Even that, Rachel said with such ease, as if she'd rehearsed it.

"Okay, Momma. How 'bout we get rid of some clothes and then go shopping for more?"

"I like that idea very much. It sounds good to me. We can get started on it right away when we get home."

It was already starting to get dark, as summer was ending and fall was beginning, and days were getting shorter. By the time we made the drive, the sun was already completely gone.

After we got home, Joelle called her grandparents and FaceTimed them for a while. It was the least her grandparents would settle for, since we hadn't visited them in Chicago. While they talked in the living room, I went into my office and sat down at my desk to check my emails.

"Hi, Timmy," Rachel said from the doorway. I looked up in mild alarm. I was too focused on my email to even notice she was standing there, but she startled me in just the right way.

I smiled as soon as I came to my senses and realized that it was her. "Hi, my love."

"Can I come in?"

"You're always welcome. Is Joelle going to be occupied for long?" I'd barely finished my sentence before Rachel closed and locked the office door.

"Yes." She walked closer to me, taking her shirt off on the way to my chair. "I was thinking maybe we could have a little chat." Her grin said it all; there wasn't going to be a chat – or any talking for that matter.

Before I knew it, we were getting hot and heavy. The desk was cleared off, making room for both of us to take our activities to the next level. But as soon as we started getting to the good part, we were interrupted by hard stomping that led up to the office door. Both of us were breathing hard.

"Mom!" Joelle screamed. "Grandma wants to talk to you before they go."

"Shit," Rachel said, running to put on her clothes. "Just a minute! I'll be right there."

Joelle started to tug on the door handle. "Mom! Can I come in?"

Just in time, Rachel and I both had our clothes back on, and she unlocked the door, letting Joelle know that she could come in. Joelle handed the phone to Rachel, and they both left the room, leaving me alone to my work again.

Rachel spent a good hour on the phone with her parents, which was a short chat compared to their usual phone calls. After she hung up, I was already getting ready for bed. She'd tucked Joelle in and came into the bedroom to join me in preparation for a good night's sleep. Usually, we would stay up a bit later, but my project required an early start, which meant that we couldn't finish what we'd begun earlier.

~

I'd never had anything against Rachel's parents. For some reason, her mom loved me, but her dad? Not so much. Whenever we'd visited them, they'd both been very nice to me. But Rachel had told me about her father's true feelings for me.

I'd come to the conclusion that I could never make him happy. I could go to the ends of the Earth for the damned man. Truthfully, I admired Rachel for being able to be honest with me. It's not easy to betray your own father to stay honest with your husband. Thank God she did, though. It meant I could stop attempting to please him.

Stewart, her father, had always thought I'd remain the foster kid I once was. The one who didn't appreciate anything, the one who got passed from house to house…and the one who was no good for his daughter. Even though Rachel had attempted to defend my honor, he didn't care to 'waste his time' talking about me, the foster kid.

During one of the first times I went to see her family for Sunday morning breakfast, I distinctly felt her father's hidden hatred for me. It wasn't anything that he said, per se, but he looked at me in a way that made me feel uncomfortable. It felt as if he wanted me to know that he was watching my every move. We were all talking at the breakfast table when Stewart had chimed into our talk about Rachel's future. This was nothing out of the ordinary; we were all extremely proud of her.

Rachel had mentioned that she was having a struggle with her classes. I was telling her that it would pass, and her next classes would be easier. Stewart quickly commented that struggle was something I knew far too well, as if to mock my tough upbringing. He was able to mask his rude comment by saying that it was because my major was so complex. He and I knew what he actually meant. It didn't take all that long for Rachel to tell me that he didn't care for me as her boyfriend.

CHAPTER 10

Since it was the beginning of a new phase in the project that my team and I were working on, Rachel took Joe to school in the morning because I had to get to the office early.

Work wasn't particularly exciting. I drank my morning tea first thing, had a briefing meeting with the team, and went over progress made during the weekend for those who had worked. As the project manager, I essentially made the rules. During a project, I let my team work whenever they wanted. As long as they got their tasks completed, it didn't matter when they did them. Usually, the team members were really good at getting their shit done, but once in a while, I had to buckle down on one or two of them.

I'd found that giving people more freedom made them more productive. When I was just out of college, I had a manager who did this with me, and I vowed I would run things the same way. If your team isn't happy, work always suffers.

I ordered in for lunch and decided to have a Mexican style meal. It wasn't my first choice, but it's what the majority of the team wanted. I didn't want to go through the hassle of ordering my own food when someone else was already going to do it. I had two steak tacos and two chicken. All loaded with sour cream, lettuce, tomatoes, and cheese.

I could have left when we got done with work for the day, but I decided to stay and chat with my team of software technicians instead. I was a little envious of the camaraderie they'd developed working together while I sat in my office and watched them from afar. Nobody complained about having the chance to spend the rest of the day hanging out. For me, the time was well-spent, gaining insight into my staff.

Midway through the conversation, my phone dinged. It would have been rude to interrupt the conversation, so I left it. After talking to them, I went back to my office and sat down. Forgetting that I'd heard my phone go off earlier, I was surprised to see a text from Rachel.

> **Pick up Joelle from school. I have an emergency session. I'll be home an hour or so late. See you soon.**

Normally, this would irritate someone, but I liked the fact that Rachel offered her clients emergency services. I had no idea if this was standard or not, but I'd always believed it should be. It showed how much compassion Rachel had for everyone. I'd never thought of myself as a good enough person to offer my time up like Rachel did, but I guess that was the difference between us.

I picked up Joelle, who was surprised to see me rising to the occasion and collecting her. Since it was Monday, and Rachel would probably come home from a long day, Joe and I would make dinner.

"How was school today?" The question every parent asks after a long weekday.

"Good." No further explanation. The ladies of the house both seemed to be having a trying day.

I pressed on. "Anything unusual happen today?"

"No, Dad. I'm just tired today. I didn't sleep very well." I was surprised she hadn't snuck into our bed the previous night. She normally did.

"I'm sorry, dear. You didn't come in with us last night. Did you?"

"No. I talked to one of my classmates the other day. Dave said that it's not cool to crawl into bed when I'm not sleeping good. So, I haven't come in since."

Few things irritate me, but this was certainly one. Sounded like Dave needed to stop talking to my impressionable daughter.

"You know, you don't always have to believe those boys. You can come into bed with us any night that you want. You're still not too old to stop being my little girl."

I could see her smile in the rearview mirror. After that, we didn't say a word the rest of the way home. That wasn't that long anyway; Joelle's school was so close to the house.

We got inside and hung up our jackets. Joelle went into her bedroom and I into mine. We both came out a few minutes later in our home clothes. Joelle hopped on a chair in the kitchen while I went in search of food. We usually had food ordered and shipped to us to make at home. Ingredients would be packaged so they just had to be prepared and cooked according to the directions. We'd get a package every week with a few days of the week in them. The rest of the time, we had to fend for ourselves. That night we were in luck.

"Do you want chicken fajita stir fry?" It looked easy enough with little effort.

"Yummm. My favorite!" I took that as a yes. I didn't have to ask Rachel. She wouldn't have ordered it if she didn't want it.

It only took about thirty minutes. Joelle set the table, and I got to the cooking and cutting. It was perfect timing. By the time I was getting done, Rachel had walked in the door. I checked the time; later than usual. Her session must have run over time. She went into the bedroom and did the same thing we did when we got home, got into her home clothes. She came out a few minutes later, giving me a kiss while I turned off the stove. She put together a quick salad to start our meal, and we all sat down.

We ate and talked, like usual. Joelle told her mom what she told me. Rachel gave nearly the same response, but it wasn't in the same tone. She said it in the sense that she shouldn't listen to others about what is and isn't 'cool'. I could tell that she didn't want Joelle to be sleeping in our bed anymore because she'd grown too big and took up too much of the bed. I would obviously disagree, but I let her have her parenting moment.

It was late by the time we cleaned up after dinner and ate ice-cream for dessert. We sat down on the couch to eat our ice-cream, and the next two hours went smoothly as we watched a movie. Joelle got to pick the movie, of course. Joelle was fast asleep before the credits rolled. I carried her to bed and returned to the couch with Rachel.

"How was your day at work? Did everything go okay?" I asked her, not prying, just curious about this patient.

"Yeah, we sorted everything out. They left feeling much better. It was just what they needed." Rachel always referred to her clients as they or them and never he or she. She felt that it was a breach of privacy between client and therapist. Also she never knew what they classified themselves as. In her field, it was better to be safe than sorry, especially when the sorry version could lose you clients.

"You couldn't fit them in during the normal workday? You must be having full days."

"Oh, yeah. I forgot to tell you," she said as if she didn't really forget to tell me. There was something lacking in her voice, her caring. "I've been having a lot of different clients. Most of them are from here. They're on edge about the murder."

That made sense. I hadn't even thought about how the killer out there could affect her business. She was good at what she did, so it didn't surprise me if her schedule was packed daily.

"Wow. That's good, right?" I asked, even though I already knew that it was.

"Yeah. I mean…" she paused for a second, "it's good, but I don't know that I want to be busy like this. I want to enjoy my time with Joelle. And of course, you." Just another reason why she was such a caring person.

"It's alright to think that. Have you stopped taking clients?" This was uncharted territory for me. I'd never seen her not want to help someone. What was I supposed to say to make her feel at ease?

"Yeah. I did today. I had to talk to the receptionist and tell her that she cannot take in any more people. I don't even have space for emergency calls anymore. I will have to stay late for every single one. I'm not sure that I want to continue the emergency calls. I don't even know if I want to continue as a therapist at all."

I was shocked. I had no idea how to feel. This wasn't like Rachel. "Honey, you have to keep doing this. It's your passion. You help people. It's what you do. You have to keep doing it." Was I saying the right thing? *'Should I be telling her to do what she wants?'* I wondered.

"You can't just tell me what I do and do not want to do. And you certainly can't choose what is or isn't good for me," she snapped. She was mad, I could tell. I just didn't understand why. She was the one who hadn't told me about her job being so demanding; she was the one who hadn't told me she didn't want to keep doing this.

"I'm not telling you what to do, Rachel. I'm telling you not to give up on the dream you spent your entire life working towards. How can you just wake up one day and decide that you don't want to be a therapist anymore?" I'd never known Rachel during a time when she didn't want to be a therapist. She'd wanted to help people since she was young, and she'd wanted to be a therapist since she was a teenager.

She started to walk away from me. Then she spun around and walked right up to me, pointing her finger in my face, saying angrily, but very quietly, "You don't get to make decisions for me. I haven't wanted to do this for a long time now; you've just never bothered to notice. Or ask. You know nothing about what I want." She didn't give me the chance to respond, not that I even knew what to say to her. She turned around and walked out. She went into the bathroom and closed the door lightly, but I could hear the 'click' of the door locking and the shower starting.

I went into the room, changing and getting ready for bed. Instead of crawling into the bed that Rachel and I shared, I went into the guest room. I figured I should let her simmer down and let her have her space. I didn't normally do that, but then again, I didn't normally make her so mad. I figured being in the doghouse meant keeping my distance.

~

Rachel and I had never been the type of couple to disagree or even argue. There were times when we both got angry or upset at each other, but it never reached the point of yelling or saying things we would later regret. When we were still living in Chicago, we regularly went to her parent's house for meals and let them spend time with Joelle. One of those times, while we were eating, Rachel's dad had asked if we knew where we were moving to yet.

Rachel looked shocked, as if she didn't know what he was talking about. I later found out that she knew all too well. Apparently, Rachel had already spoken to her parents about leaving the state. She didn't know where we were going to move, but it sounded like a sure thing to her and them. It bothered me that she'd never once brought it up with me.

During the dinner with her parents, I acted like I knew what was happening, like I was familiar with it. I didn't like looking weak to her parents or giving them any reason to think that I was not a good husband for their daughter. I waited until we were home that night, and Joelle was fast asleep.

"What was that? Today?" I asked calmly.

"What do you mean, dear?" Again, she acted like she had no idea what was going on.

"You know what I'm talking about. Moving? When did we decide this? When were you going to tell me that we'd decided to move to a completely different state?" She had made a decision for our family without consulting any of us.

"I never said it was set in stone. I just told my parents that I wanted to move away, get a fresh start," she said, in a sweet and caring voice, one that made it hard to stay mad. "I just don't feel like I like it here anymore. I need to get far away, and if that means leaving Mom and Dad, then that's what it means. But I don't want to leave without you. I just didn't know how to tell you. I was waiting for the right moment to bring it up."

"I understand, Rachel. But you never told me. You told them before you told me. I'm just supposed to get up and leave? Without any warning? Where are we going to go? When are we going to go? This isn't something you just think of in your head. It's something you should have talked to me about it." I raised my voice towards the end, but it was just ridiculous. I don't get how she could do something like that.

"I know. I know. I don't know what went through my head. I just didn't know how to tell you—"

I cut her off. "You didn't know how to tell me what? I'm your fucking husband. What do you mean you didn't know how to tell me? Shouldn't you be telling me everything? Because I tell you everything. Every. Single. Thing."

"Okay, I understand. I get that you're mad; I wasn't thinking."

"No, you really weren't."

"I just said that I know. But can you just hear me out? I…we don't belong here. We belong somewhere that we can build a family. Where we can live our lives in safety and comfort. I can't do that here. And wherever I go, it has to be with you and Joe." How did she do it? Just make something so frustrating sound so right? I needed to get away from her, away from her charm. I needed to give myself the space to get a clear head.

"Well, I need to think and process this. We can talk about it when I am ready, and no sooner. I deserve the same amount of time to think about this as you had. How long have you been thinking about moving?" I didn't know if I was going to like this answer.

"About a year." She said nothing else, but I was right. That's not what I wanted to hear.

I stepped away. Leaving that to be the last thing we said for a long time.

PART II

CHAPTER 11

Once again, I was waking up alone in the guest bedroom in time to crawl into our bed so Joe wouldn't notice that I hadn't been sleeping in the same room as her mom. As usual, I got there just as Joe woke up and ran up the stairs. Luckily, she hadn't been coming up in the middle of the night with nightmares.

It had been difficult for us to spend time together as a family, so usually, Rachel and I would spend time with Joelle individually. She would take her out to eat for dinner, telling Joelle that I was staying late at work, which was true. Then, when I'd get home, I'd take Joe to the park where we'd play until dark. I assumed this day would be just like the rest.

"I've got a few clients who requested late appointments today. I'll be going in at the regular time. But you have to pick up Joelle, feed her, and take her to the park. I'll be home whenever I get home," Rachel said to me after Joe went to get ready for school.

During the last week, I'd learned to stay out of Rachel's way, and under no circumstances, talk to her about her job or the future. I decided to let her cool down, for however long she needed. She had to figure out what she wanted, and she'd made it clear that she didn't want my opinion.

The workday went by in a breeze. I was happy to pick Joelle up and spend the rest of the night with her. Even if Rachel wasn't with us while we hung out, I still needed to be with Joelle every chance that I possibly could. I left work in time to arrive at Joelle's school at the exact time she was getting out. Since there was a pickup line, it took a few minutes for me to reach the front, but then Joe hopped right inside.

"Hi, Daddy," she said, being the usual cheerful Joe.

"Hi, dear. How was school today? Did you learn anything exciting?"

"No," she said quickly. Joe paused for a second, then asked, "Can we get pizza tonight?"

"Of course we can! I always love some good pineapple pizza." Obviously, I was joking.

"Ooh, I do too! How about extra pineapple!" She didn't think I was joking.

"I'm kidding, Joe. But we can get half extra pineapple and half no pineapple. That sounds like a good compromise."

"Okay. I like that."

We drove the rest of the way jamming out to her music on the radio. We were both smiling and cruising down the road, just the two of us. It felt good to spend this time with her, she was so happy, and that happiness rubbed off on everyone else.

You could tell she was still high on energy, especially after I let her have some soda. I wouldn't have to deal with her that night – that would be her mother's time. Whenever she got home from work.

While we waited, we went out to burn off some energy. Joelle had been enjoying the park closest to our house, so that's where we'd been going. Initially, we tried a new one every day, but eventually, she decided she didn't want to keep finding new spots. So, we stuck to her favorite.

I think Luther Burbank Park was her favorite because it was close enough to ride our bikes out there. It was good for me because I'd been cooped up in the office a lot. We made it all the way to the park while it was still relatively light out. We took the frisbee and the soccer ball, just in case she wanted options, but we both knew she wanted to play frisbee. We got to a spot that didn't have too many people and started tossing it around. I tried to tire her out the best I could. Even though Rachel and I weren't on speaking terms, I didn't want her to have too much trouble getting Joe to bed.

I got her to just the right point that she would crash as soon as she got home, hopefully. We got back on our bikes and went in the direction of home. It would be dark soon, and they usually controlled the parks after sundown, setting a time limit for visitors to leave.

We walked inside, and just as I expected, Joe went to her room to get ready for bed. As it turned out, giving her all that soda only caused her to want to use more energy. By the end of the day, she was worn out.

It took me a few minutes to realize that Rachel wasn't home yet, which was odd. She'd said she would be coming home late, but this was unusual for her. I decided to shoot her a text.

Where are you? I'm worried.

I waited a few minutes and then decided to tuck Joe in myself. I wasn't going to let her stay up and wait for her mom.

"Your mom had to work extra late. She said she wouldn't be home until after bedtime." I hated lying to her, but I had no option.

"But can I see her in the morning?" she asked, as if she was worried that she wasn't going to see her mother again.

"Aw, Joe. Of course, she'll be home when you wake up." With that, I tucked her in, gave her a kiss, and closed the door behind me.

As I walked out, I pulled my phone out. There was a message. *'What a surprise,'* I thought to myself.

Got carried away with a client. They needed extra help. On my way home. Don't wait up.

I wasn't sure whether to wait or just go to bed. It wasn't like we were sleeping in the same room together anyway. Also, this seemed very unlike her. She was paid by the session. Why was her session lasting so long? I had a lot of questions for her. *'Maybe I should stay up,'* I thought.

I sat on the couch, prepared to wait till she got home. I couldn't imagine her taking much longer now. It's well past dark, and no sensible therapist would be working so late. To my surprise, she walked in seconds after I sat down. Or so I thought…

As it turned out, I fell asleep almost immediately after sitting down. I checked my phone as she walked into the house from the garage. Midnight. It had been hours since she'd said she was on her way home. Where was she the whole time? What had she been doing?

"Where have you been? It's nearly tomorrow." I turned on my phone screen and showed her, "actually, it *is* tomorrow. What the hell, Rachel?"

"I know what time it is, which is why I said not to wait up for me," she said, walking through the house and upstairs to the bedroom. It was now becoming her personal room, while I was still in the guest bedroom.

"So, is this just how it's going to be from now on?" I gave her a second to answer, or at least justify her actions. When I didn't get one, I continued, "You coming home whenever you want, just doing whatever you want. While I'm stuck with the cleanup and the waiting up. What the hell are you actually doing? And why the hell am I not back in the bedroom yet?"

"Probably because you fucked up and said some stupid shit that you have no business saying. Especially when you don't know what I'm thinking." *I fucked up? Please.* She was exaggerating. But I let her have it because I was sick of sleeping in that bedroom.

"Okay, but I didn't know it would upset you. How am I supposed to know something that you don't tell me? This was the first I heard about you not being happy with your job. I didn't know you wanted to switch careers or that you're thinking about it." I walked up to her, which was the closest I'd been to her in a week. I grabbed her by the hand. "I'm sorry, okay? I didn't mean it."

"It's just that you don't get it. This has been my career, and I've wanted to be a therapist since I was a kid," she said, pulling her hands away and turning around. She braced her hands on the back of a dining room chair. "I don't know what to do, and I don't want your opinion to sway what I want to do. It's just something that I need to figure out on my own. And I didn't want to let you down by saying that."

Wow. How could I not see that? I should've known that this was hard for her. I paused for a second, trying to figure out how to respond. I had no idea what to say to her, especially now that she didn't sound angry. I didn't want to make her mad again. All I could do was hold my arms open. To my surprise, she came fast. We just stood there for what felt like forever, holding each other, spending all the hugs we've been banking up for the last week.

She lifted her head up and smiled at me. "I'm s—" she started.

"I know," I said, going in for a kiss. A long and much-needed kiss. Soon we were running our hands over each other's bodies. Searching every inch of each other, like we were unknown to each other. Which seemed true, lately.

In between our lips touching, she spoke one word. "Bedroom." We both took off immediately, leaving all the lights on in the rest of the house. Once we were inside, she closed the door, turned, and looked at me in a way that had become familiar. I grabbed her waist and pulled her close again.

The sex seemed to last longer than usual, but I'd never been one to complain in that department. Afterward, we washed off in the shower together.

It wasn't long before we were getting back into bed, freshly showered. I finally got to lie back in our bed, next to my wife. It was a blissful moment, and I enjoyed every second of it. I was enjoying it so much that I didn't even realize I'd fallen asleep until the morning alarm went off.

I reached over, expecting to find Rachel. She wasn't there. Finally, we were back to our usual routine. I lay there for a few minutes, just enjoying the moment. Soon enough, Joelle came running in and jumped into bed with me. Rachel came up with her cup of coffee in hand and joined in our morning conversation.

"Joe, who do you want to drop you off, and who do you want to pick you up tonight?" Rachel asked, catching me by surprise. We've never given Joe the option before.

"You mean, I get to choose? All by myself?" Joe was way too excited about this.

"S-sure." I looked over at Rachel to get confirmation because I wasn't really sure what to say.

"Yes, you can choose," Rachel confirmed.

Joe's eyes got extra wide. "Ooh, well... Mommy, you drop me off, and Daddy picks me up!" The judge had spoken, and that was the end of the trial.

"Okay, well, we'd better get going then! We don't want to be late," Rachel told Joe as Joe and I hopped out of the bed. She went running to get ready, and Rachel met me with a kiss. I was liking this.

"Good morning, love," I said to her between kisses.

"Good morning," she said, also between kisses. "What are your plans for the day? I'll be working the normal hours for a while. I shouldn't have to stay late again."

"That sounds great. Same here, we're still going strong with the project, and it's not going to be done anytime soon, but I'll be able to get off early enough to pick Joe up today." We were doing so well, so I had to drop the ball. "But I might not be able to pick her up all the time."

She handled it better than expected. "I know that, silly."

"Okay, well, go get ready, we don't want Joe to be late, and I don't want you to be late for work."

"You either." She kissed me, winked, and then smacked my ass on the way out of the bedroom. I appreciated all but the last.

As I was getting ready for my day, I realized that all my good work shirts weren't in the closet. I ventured to the laundry room, where I was sure to find some clean clothes that were left to dry. Sure enough, there was a stack of fresh laundry. However, I noticed that there was an abundance of dirty clothes in the basket. It was unusual for Rachel to leave dirty clothes like this out. A bucket beside the washer caught my attention. It was filled with water that smelled strongly of bleach, and a pair of Rachel's everyday work pants were soaking inside. The water was tinted pink. *Odd.* I picked up the bucket and went to ask her about it.

"Hey, Rachel. What happened to your pants?" I asked, with a level of confusion in my voice.

She giggled and responded, "Oh, those? They're my everyday pants. I painted the office I work in the other day. Just something about red that makes me happy. You know?"

"Oh, alright," I mumbled, satisfied with her answer.

Before I had a chance to turn around and head back to the laundry room, she gave me a quick kiss and said she was leaving. I returned the kiss and continued getting ready.

Later that day at work, I was sitting in my office, just finishing up with my take-out, when one of the team members, Kiana, walked in. "Don't you live on the island? What's going on over there?" she asked.

"What do you mean?" She didn't give me much context to work with.

"All those deaths…" She paused, then said, "More specifically, the killings."

"There's only been one, and that was weeks ago," I replied with a light chuckle to ease the seriousness of the subject.

"You didn't hear? There was another person found today." I didn't say anything; I was in shock. She continued, "They haven't released any details, but they did say it was a younger female found in a park by a ranger who was driving by early this morning. The report said that she was dumped sometime within the last 24 hours. It's crazy that it's the second one this year. I heard that area is supposed to be quiet compared to the area we work in."

"Wow. I don't even know what to say. I don't think we would've moved to the island knowing there was so much crime in the area. I thought we did our research well."

"That's the thing, they're saying this is strange because it's so rare on the island," she said, now sounding like a murder enthusiast.

"Really? That's just crazy. I'm sure there's a reason for this happening, and I hope they find the people responsible for these killings. I have a daughter who loves parks, for God's sake."

After I told her about my daughter, she toned down her excitement a notch, and the conversation became serious again.

"The likelihood of the murders being committed by different people would be slim. If it were my guess, I would think they are being done by the same person. But these are healthy, young women; not many other women would have the strength to kill them. I'm sure it's some creepy man." Towards the end, she started sounding like an enthusiast again.

"I don't even know what to say. I should probably call my wife and tell her."

"Sure, of course." She turned around and walked out. I picked up my phone to dial Rachel, but something stopped me from pressing the call button. I wasn't sure how she would react, and if she hadn't already heard, I wanted to give myself time to think about what to say before I broke the news. She didn't take the last death well. Now she might think there was a serial killer on the streets of our neighborhood. Anyhow, it was possible the body was found at a park on the opposite side of the island. There might not even be a need to get concerned; maybe it was a freak accident.

Maybe.

Instead, I decided to look into the murder myself. I did a search of the local Mercer Island online newspaper and found a newly updated article about it.

Another woman was found murdered today at the Aubrey Davis Park. Authorities are saying that the crime mimics the murder of Kathren Arnoldson. They have identified the body but will not release details until they have been in contact with immediate family.

Further details will be reported as the story unfolds.

After work, I went home and checked the website again. There was another update.

The body of Sofia Jones, a 26-year-old African American woman, has been uncovered at the Aubrey Davis Park, in the north-western part of Mercer Island. The discovery was made by a passerby, whose dog unearthed suspicious items, prompting the owner to contact the police. Official investigations located several black garbage bags in the area containing dismembered body parts. Disturbances to the soil around the site indicate that the body had been recently buried.

The results of the autopsy have not yet been released, but it has been confirmed that the body was decapitated.

CHAPTER 12

It had been two weeks since they'd found Sofia Jones in the park. If it hadn't been for the dog-walker, her body might never have been discovered. That part of the park was dense and filled with trees – visitors seldom ventured there.

She was smart, well-educated, and volunteered during any free time she had. She was highly thought of in her community and received mention for donating her eggs to a person she had met in passing while volunteering at a local homeless shelter.

From the sounds of it, this woman never did anything bad or unethical. She was friendly and definitely giving. It made no logical sense why someone would want to kill her. Police hadn't confirmed whether or not they thought this murder and the other one in the area were connected. But any person could tell that they were. Sofia was found dehydrated, with drugs in her system, and extremely bruised skin. They didn't say if she was decapitated before or after death, but my guess was that she was killed in the same way as the previous victim.

Rachel heard the bad news on her way home from work the same day that I found out. I was somewhat relieved that I wasn't the one who had to break that kind of news to her. She also didn't have an issue with telling Joe, which was a relief for me. I never liked giving her bad news.

After that, things had not been great. Rachel began staying late at work again, saying that she'd taken on even more clients since the murder, and things had been hectic. I thought she wasn't taking on any more clients, but I decided not to press further on the conversation. However, since she had been staying late, I'd had to pick Joe up every day from school. Since the woman was found buried at Joe's favorite park, I decided that we would no longer be going to any parks until the entire thing blew over. Maybe not even until the culprit was caught. We would just have to find other things to do as a family.

On Friday, I went to work a little late because I'd been going in extra early all week in order to leave early to pick up Joe. Since I knew I had to go to work the following day, I decided to leave before noon and surprise Rachel for lunch. After all that had been going on, I felt she deserved it.

Since it was a surprise, I didn't tell her about it, but I'd asked what she was taking for lunch, and she said that she would probably just get something to go. I called ahead to order take-out from a Chinese restaurant that neither of us had been to. It was just about time to go, and I gathered my stuff and left work. I picked up the food and headed on over to the building where Rachel worked. I'd only been to the building once before when she was still deciding if she wanted to rent it or not. Now, her sign was up, and I could see the plants inside the huge glass window. Her car was parked out front, so I knew she was in.

I sent her a text:

What are you up to?

I didn't want to seem obvious, just nosey.

I just finished up a session, about to head to lunch. You?

Now was my chance to go in. I didn't wait until someone walked out; I grabbed the food and headed inside.

"Hello, can I help you?" her receptionist asked.

"Yeah, I'm Rachel's husband. Can I see her? I brought her lunch," I said and held up the lunch for proof.

"I'm sorry, it doesn't look like she's in right now."

"What do you mean? Her car is parked out front, and she said she was here." *What. The. Fuck.* Where was my wife?

"Yeah, she finished up a session about an hour ago. She's been on lunch since. Her next appointment isn't for another two hours," she said while she checked the paper schedule on her desk.

"Oh."

"Sorry. Do you want me to tell her you dropped by?"

"No. No. That's fine. I'll just see her at home." I started to walk out, feeling humiliated. "Thanks," I said as I stepped out the door.

I got into my car and sat there. What the fuck was I supposed to think? Rachel didn't have any friends or family besides Joelle and me in this entire state. Yet, she'd lied to me. Her car was there, but she wasn't. *'She's fucking cheating on me,'* I thought. It all made sense. She'd been distant, 'staying at work late', and helping 'clients' late at night. Never in a million years did I ever expect that Rachel would cheat on me, but all the signs were pointing to it.

Anger started to boil up inside me, and all I could do was throw punches at my steering wheel. How could she? Why would she? With who? More importantly, how long? All these questions flowed into my head, and I couldn't find a single answer to any of them. All I knew was that she really fucked up. Was her anger a few weeks ago just her excuse to justify cheating?

How was I supposed to pick up Joe now and act like everything was okay? At what point did I confront Rachel? There were just too many questions, and I needed some time to think and cool down well before I went to collect Joe. I couldn't have the thoughts that were running through my head stay with me while I was near her. I might have exploded.

I had two hours to kill before I needed to fetch Joe. First, I went to one of the parks in Seattle, sat down, and ate my lunch by myself. Then I walked around for what felt like forever, just thinking and wrapping my head around things. It took me some time, but I came to the conclusion that there was no way my wife would cheat on me. Her reasons for lying to me had to be completely unrelated. After all, our sex life had been great lately. I didn't know where she would even find the energy to want to cheat. With that being said, I decided to talk to her when we got home. There was no need to hold this over her.

It was time for me to get to Joe's school. I was hoping that one of her friends would let her stay over, so I packed a small overnight bag and put it in the car. Even if she didn't end up going, it never hurt to have these essentials on hand for whenever Joe needed an unexpected change of clothes or a toothbrush. I hurried, getting there just a few minutes before she got out. I knew exactly what I was doing when I walked up to Joe's friend's parents and started talking to them.

"Hey, guys. It's been a long time since Joe has hung out with her friends. She's been talking about getting all of them together again. We should do it soon. What do you say?" I said, trying to guilt-trip them into taking her for the night. Out of three parents, one of them was bound to respond positively.

Juniper's dad was the first to speak up. I wasn't surprised. "You're right! Junie has been saying the same thing. She's desperate to get everyone back together. Say, maybe this weekend we can get them together? But I do have some weekend plans already, so I wouldn't be able to take them." Classic. The guy had tried to palm his kids off on us!

I took my chance before it got weird. "Yeah, now that you mention it, Rachel and I have a date night. We wouldn't be able to take them either. In fact, we were thinking of getting Joelle a sitter."

"Oh, don't be silly," Amy's mom pitched in. "It takes a village. Am I right? I'll take both Juniper and Joelle. Heck, I can even take Jenny if you want."

"That's awfully sweet of you. Are you sure? I wouldn't want to dump my child on your lap," Jenny's mom said, as if she wouldn't enjoy some time alone.

"Actually, that would be amazing. If you don't mind," Juniper's dad said. At least he was honest.

"No, I don't mind! I love seeing Amy have fun anyway. I'll just take them all home right now if you want. And then I can also drop them off in the morning." I was glad that my plan worked out. Rachel would have no excuse not to tell me the pure, honest truth.

"Thank you so much," was all I could say. I wasn't going to suck up to her, and I didn't want to talk to this bunch anymore. I wanted to get out before they started to pry. Luckily, the bell for school went off at just the right moment. "I'll go tell Joe that she'll be going with you. Just give me one minute." I headed towards the school.

Joe was one of the first to come out. She ran up to me and hugged me. "Daddy!"

"Hi, dear, I have some news for you. Amy's mom agreed to take all of you for a sleepover for the night! So, you'll be going home with her. I just came to give you a hug and a kiss."

She looked over at Amy, who was standing by Juniper and the other three parents. Jenny hadn't come out of school yet. "Yay!" she screamed. "Thank you, thank you, thank you!" She could barely contain herself, and she was too excited to stay next to me. She waved to me when she got over to the group. I waved back and got in my car.

Somehow, I felt a bit better knowing I wouldn't have to worry about Joe that night. I wished there was an easier way. A way that I could spend time with Joe and not worry about if Rachel was cheating on me. I sent Rachel a text:

> **When will you be home? We need to talk. It's serious.**

I pulled off and made my way home. It only took a few minutes to get a reply. I waited until I was home to check it. I hated people who would text and drive.

Yes, we do. I think there's something I need to tell you. I'll leave work shortly. Should be home in 1-2 hours.

Her receptionist probably told her that I'd stopped by, and now she wanted to confess. But it shouldn't take a couple of hours to get home. It took 30 minutes. Either she was not leaving work 'shortly', or she was leaving but had somewhere better to be. Or I was being paranoid. This time, I decided to chalk it up to paranoia. She deserved the benefit of the doubt.

I was surprised to see her home after an hour, almost on the dot. She walked into the house, dropped her stuff off on the kitchen counter, then headed to the bedroom and got into her after-work clothes. It was like she was in no rush to do anything in particular, just taking her time. Or maybe she was stalling…but I wouldn't fall for it.

"Where's Joelle? I thought you were picking her up from school?" she said, after looking around for a minute, undoubtedly trying to find her.

I paused for a minute, for dramatic effect. "Amy's mom took her and her friends; they're having a sleepover tonight. Isn't that just a great idea?" I folded my arms, waiting for an answer.

"Tim, take a seat. I think it's time we talk."

I went to sit on the couch, the small one, forcing her to have to sit away from me. "I couldn't agree more." She gave me a puzzled look.

She sat there for a minute, neither of us saying anything. I felt like I was at the edge of the seat, waiting for her to admit my suspicions. She put her hands over her face, and I could hear a small weeping sound. This was good. She knew she had done something wrong, and it was going to hurt her to admit it. It kind of hit me once I realized she was crying so hard, but she should be crying. What she did was wrong. She looked up at me, tears filling her eyes and running down her face.

"I—" she tried to get some words out, "I've been going to therapy every day. And I'm embarrassed to tell you." She dropped her head back into her hands and just stayed there till I spoke again.

Well, that was not what I was expecting. I had no words to say. All I knew was that my wife had needed me, and I'd been a complete jackass. I stood up and joined her on the other couch.

"It's okay," I repeated over and over while I held her as she kept crying.

We sat there for a while; she was slowly calming down and crying less. She could finally get some more words out. "I was scared to tell you. I haven't been to therapy since our time in college. I haven't been there since before Joelle came into our lives. I don't want her to see me weak like this. I don't want her to see her mom like this and think that I'm going to be some fragile person who cannot handle life outside of therapy. I don't want to be the person I've become," she just kept talking; speaking so fast I didn't even think I processed all of it.

"Is that why you don't want to be a therapist anymore? Because you think that you're weak?" I didn't fully understand what the problem was, but I was trying to be sensitive.

"Yes. How can I walk someone through their own problems when I have so many of my own? How can I be a therapist when I need a therapist? It just doesn't work like that. I can't be good at my job." She was so confident that she was doing the wrong thing.

"Hey. Remember in college? What they taught you in that one class you took?" I paused and waited for her to answer. She didn't, but she did shake her head – no, she didn't remember. "Just because you're in therapy doesn't mean you don't also have a talent for fixing people."

"But that doesn't mean that I should be trying to help people."

"Rachel, you are great at helping people. You are *meant* to help people. This is just temporary, soon you won't need a therapist, and you'll be able to go back to your old self."

"But what if I don't?"

"What would you tell your clients? That you just can't help them anymore? You have been helping them. You are not the problem; you are not a problem."

"Okay, you're right."

"I know I am. We will get through this," I said, knowing that I had to end the conversation and start a new one. "But you can't lie to me about things. I know you weren't at work when you said you were. I tried to bring you lunch. Your car was there, but you weren't. I even texted you, and you said you were there."

"I'm sorry. I didn't know you were coming. The therapist that I've been seeing is literally in the same strip as my office. She's been my competition, and she's very booked. When I need to see her, I usually take appointments from cancelations. They're usually around lunchtime, or she'll take me at night, after normal office hours. That's why I've been late, that's why I wasn't in the office for lunch. It has been every night." At least her therapist was right next to her; that was convenient. I felt so stupid for thinking that she was cheating on me.

"Rachel, what's going on that you need to see a therapist every day?"

"I don't know… I just have these bad feelings, and I don't know how to control them."

"What kind of feelings?"

"Depression, you know." She sounded remarkably nonchalant about having depressive thoughts.

"How long?"

"For a few weeks now, it's nothing serious. I just don't like the way that I think about things.

It's not healthy, and I don't like it."

"Okay. We can work this out. We can get this all together. Does this have anything to do with those women who got murdered?" It wouldn't hurt to ask.

She hesitated and thought about it for a minute. She replied by saying, "Yes. Truthfully it is."

That was all I needed to hear. I understood what she was going through. I understood her challenges. Even I had been getting worried about the killings that were happening. I couldn't begin to imagine what it would feel like to be a woman living on the island right then. The fear must be unreal.

We spent what remained of the night watching movies, having sex, and just enjoying each other's company. It seemed like the best way to go about the situation, especially knowing that we had the entire night to ourselves, which doesn't often happen when you have kids. All I knew was that I was damn happy that she wasn't cheating on me. But damn upset that she had been going through this pain by herself. Even more upsetting, I hadn't noticed that she needed me to be there for her.

CHAPTER 13

The weeks had gone by in a blur. It was nearly Christmas. Since it was our first Christmas in Washington, we decided to go back to Chicago for the holidays. It had been a few months since we'd moved, which was the longest time Joe had spent away from her grandparents.

The murders were still a hot topic in town, and the police continued to search for the person who committed these unthinkable acts. Rachel was still having harsh feelings towards the situation, but I had noticed some improvement. Her mood had been picking up, and she'd been talking a lot more about work again, just like she used to. She'd also been really good about letting me know when she was going to her appointments, and I'd even caught her on a few occasions writing in her poetry journal.

It was Thursday, and we decided to take off Friday to travel, so it felt like a Friday for all of us. Luckily, my company had a policy of giving time off around the holidays – unlike many others that booked overtime over that period. I'd grown to enjoy this job more than any other I'd had before.

Unlike me, Rachel had a lot of work to do. She was among the majority who had to press the edge of overtime during the holiday season. She was intent on going on this trip, though, so she had arranged to consult with clients via phone or video meetings. That way, she could work with patients while enjoying the trip, instead of staying home all vacation while her family spent time with relatives. The only downfall was that she would still have to be on-call and take appointments. But it was a much better option than not going at all.

After all the meetings we had before the holiday weekend, I finally got back to my desk for the day to notice a wrapped present. I had no idea who would have given me a gift.

"Hey, Jill, did you see who left this on my desk?" Jill looked up from typing just long enough to reply.

"Yeah, the Vice President dropped it off," she said with a smile before returning to her typing.

I decided it would be rude to open it in the office, so I sent a thank you email to the VP before walking out. Once I got to my car, I tore it open. The neatly formatted box underneath was small, thin, and long. I opened the top of it and was surprised to see a check. I could only assume this was my holiday bonus. Under the check, there was a letter.

Tim,

Thank you for deciding to join this company. It has been a pleasure working with you for the last few months. We have been watching you closely, and we have seen you flourish within our company. We know you will do great things, and we believe that you can do even greater things, given the chance. We hope that we can get you closer to the top soon, should your ambition stay the same. But for now, we offer you this annual bonus. The bonus is based on a complex algorithm consisting of date from your work history, company history, ethics, and determination. I'm sure you will not be disappointed. We certainly aren't.

Happy holidays and stay safe.
VP, Arnold Artme

My eyes widened. The amount was large enough to buy half of a brand-new car. It wasn't that I'd chosen the job for the paycheck. Rachel had always kept us well cared for in that department. I was drawn to the fact that the company appreciated my work and my dedication. The bonus was an acknowledgment of that. They were looking better and better every day.

I pulled out of the parking lot with a smile on my face. What could be better? It was Christmas time, we were going on a mini-vacation, and I would get to spend this time with my family. Even the traffic, the terrible holiday-city-traffic, couldn't take my mood down. I was a lucky man, and a lucky man I hoped to stay.

I rushed home, excited to tell Rachel about the bonus. I walked into the house, and everything was quiet. I took my shoes off and put my bags and jacket on the kitchen counter. I went to our bedroom but found nobody. I went to Joe's room... Nobody there either. I checked the living room again, still nobody. The only other place they could be was in the basement, but still, nobody was there.

I went upstairs and noticed that the sliding door was unlocked and cracked open. I got worried. Maybe someone had broken into the house. What if Joe and Rachel were inside the house when it happened? Where could they be? I ran to the sliding door, running onto the deck barefoot and into the snow that had piled up. I imagined the worst – having a murderer in the neighborhood was making me paranoid.

Instantly, I saw the footprints. There were two sets going down the stairs and a trail that led to the bottom of our yard, towards the water's edge. That's when I spotted two figures hiding behind a large wall made of snow.

The next instant, I heard "Fire!" and snowballs started flying towards me. I was taken aback.

"Got you!" I heard Rachel yell, followed by giggles from Joe.

Relief flooded me when I realized that they were just out having fun. I ran inside to throw on my jacket and my boots and went out the front door. My heart was still pounding from thinking the worst, but adrenalin mixed with excitement at the chance to play in the snow.

I was hoping I could sneakily hit them from the side, but I was sorely mistaken. They beat me to it and were ready to attack. One, two, three snowballs hit me. I went down to grab a pile of snow, balled it up, and threw it at Joe. Then I got a running start towards Rachel, tackling her.

"I won! I defeated the territory. Victory is mine!" It was a good game, but the two of them were no match for me. Seconds later, Joe pounced on top of Rachel and me.

We sat there giggling for a few minutes, then went inside to find something to snack on.

Since it frequently snows from Washington to Illinois during this time of the year, we had to watch the weather pretty closely, especially since the flight could be canceled at any time. The forecast showed some snow, but nowhere near bad enough to cancel the flight. I hated flying, especially the trip to Chicago airport, where somehow our flights were invariably canceled or delayed in either direction. Flying was stressful to me, so thankfully, Rachel would take control of our travel arrangements, generally booking First Class flights. I certainly had no objection to that.

In the morning, I looked out the window to see a noticeable amount of snow had fallen during the night. Since none of us had been back to Illinois since moving, we were all in high spirits. All of us were awake early and eager to get on the road. After eating breakfast, we decided to head out to the airport. Since it was still snowing, it's almost guaranteed that traffic would be terribly slow.

When we got to our gate, they were just calling the last of the people up to board. We were able to board pretty easily still. My favorite part of flying First Class was not having to clamber over anyone to get seated or be scrunched up beside strangers for hours.

The actual flight wasn't terrible, but I hated the taking off and the landing; those were the worst. The jarring on the way up and down made me nervous. Once in the air, I could just sit back and take a little nap or watch a movie and not be bothered the entire time. It was just like sitting on the couch at home.

The flight was about four and a half hours in total, which was tolerable. One spring break, Rachel and I flew to Paris, and that was a really long flight. The trip itself was well worth it, but the flights there and back were tough for anyone.

Once they announced landing, we all brought our seats up, turned off everything, and got ready. The landing was a little rougher than the take-off, but I maintained my composure.

As soon as we got off the flight, Rachel turned on her phone and called her dad. She told him that we'd landed, and he said he would be on his way. Luckily, they only lived a few miles away, so he would likely be here shortly after we got to the exit. We walked a little slower to give him some extra time and to stretch our legs. But once we reached the airport exit, he was waiting right out front.

"Hey, everyone, get on in. It's cold out here," Stewart said. There was no time for exchanging pleasantries, which I was perfectly fine with. Rachel went around the front and sat in the passenger seat while I threw down Joe's booster seat and sat her in it. I walked around to the other side and hopped in. *'Fuck, it's chilly out here,'* my inner voice muttered.

We'd started down the road and continued on the highway before anyone spoke. "So, how has winter been? Truthfully, Washington doesn't seem to be much different than here," Rachel asked her dad.

"It's been a pretty mild winter. Only a few snowfalls so far, which we're all happy about. Your mom and I have missed you," he said.

"Aw, Dad. We've all missed you too." Frankly, she was speaking for Joe and herself because I didn't miss the old fool.

We arrived at the family home after about twenty minutes, accounting for the winter traffic on a mid-morning Friday. We grabbed our luggage out of the car and headed into their large stately house. Rachel's mom was no doubt waiting for us to walk through the front door. I looked forward to seeing her again.

"Race you to the door," I said to Joe as I started picking up pace.

A smile lit her face, and in no time, she started running. I let her pass me by, allowing her to win, but just by an inch. Rachel's mom was right there to greet us a moment after Joe rang the doorbell. The front door swung open to a pleasantly smiling older lady. Nancy was a well-groomed mature woman, with impeccably styled, snow-white hair and bright red lipstick that had probably been on since she woke up. She'd topped off her usual elegant pantsuit with a cozy Christmas sweater.

"Joe!" she said as she reached down to give a welcoming hug to her granddaughter. She came up and looked at me. "Tim, looking as good as ever." Her arms were wide open, and I willingly returned the hug.

"You're looking great, too, Nancy," I said to her, being truthful.

Rachel and her dad trailed behind, having a chat as they walked up to the front door. "Mom!" Rachel said, then gave her mother a long embrace. "Oh, I've missed you and Dad so much."

"Us as well, my dear. Come inside, hurry, hurry. It's cold out there," Rachel's mom said, ushering us to come far enough inside to close the door. Once the door was closed, it only took a minute to adjust to the indoor lighting and temperature.

When we all got inside, the maid came and took all our bags, carrying them to our permanent bedroom on the second floor of this never-ending mansion. In the bedroom were all the clothes that we had left here, Rachel's old bed set, and a large number of pictures that made it feel more like home. Joe's room was right next to ours, but all her clothes stayed with ours.

"Can we go upstairs?" Joe had asked. Undoubtedly wanting to play with her toys.

Since the others were all talking, I responded to her happily, "Yeah, let's go, dear." The less time I had to spend with Rachel's dad, the better.

We made our way up the stairs, and I walked her to her room. It had been a while since we were last there, and she didn't quite remember where everything was. Once we reached the room, it was easy to tell that it was Joe's. There were storage trunks everywhere, each filled with toys. Joe went straight for one of the shelves and started to pull down some toys. The discovery of a tea set inspired a new game.

"Tea for you?" she asked, in a British voice.

I responded, "Yes, milady." I held the teacup up, waiting for her to pour me some air.

We played in her room for about two hours, but by then, it was about time for me to get ready to go to my foster parents' house. I was glad that Joe had distracted me this much because I was still nervous about what I might say to their new foster child. Nick was just about to graduate high school and was on the verge of choosing what he wanted to do with his future. I never had someone who was there to walk me through it, so I had to figure it all out on my own. I was hoping I could make a positive impact on this kid. I didn't want to see all of Angela and Louis' hard work go to waste.

Our old car was still parked in Rachel's parents' garage. It held many memories, and I was glad we'd decided to keep it there instead of getting rid of it. It had its moments, but overall, it was the first car that we purchased, before Joe was even in the picture.

I sat in the car, reminiscing about all the times Rachel and I had together, and then the good times we had shared once Joe came into our lives. I was half surprised when I turned the key and it started. Not only did it sputter a little, but it sounded quite different than our current electric family car. It took me a second or two to get used to it. I checked my phone one last time before pulling off to see my foster family.

The drive was typical for Chicago, and it was nice to have some time alone during the trip. Since I'd lived in Chicago my entire life, I knew the streets by heart. Especially the ones leading from Rachel's parents to my foster parents' house. I spent the time trying to think of the best thing to say to Nick, the new foster kid. It made me more nervous, the closer I got to the house. I wanted to make a lasting, positive impression on Nick, but I was afraid of messing up.

I'd never been in the position to be someone's role model before.

I pulled into their small driveway, parking in the last spot available. I assumed the other cars belonged to Louis, Angela, and maybe Nick. Before I even got out of the car, I saw Angela and Louis standing on the front deck, looking out towards me. A smile brightened my face; I missed seeing them. Behind them, I could see a figure, presumably Nick.

I got out of the car, walking faster to the front door. "Angela," I said, hugging my foster mom. Then, turning to Louis, I opened my arms wide. "Louis. I've missed you both so much."

"We've missed you too, son," Louis said to me while Angela stood there smiling. Since I used to live here, walking into the house was not awkward at all. I stepped inside and took off my shoes, remembering the rules that Angela put into place all those years ago.

"You must be Nicholas; it's nice to meet you," I said with a bright smile, extending my hand to shake his.

"Yeah, you too," he replied, ignoring my hand and turning to walk back to sit on the couch.

My face must've looked puzzled because Angela jumped in and responded, "He's a shy one. It took him a long time to talk to us. But hang on, honey, let me get those gifts you had sent here." She smiled and walked away.

"How are things going here? Any problems since I've been gone?" I directed my question to Louis, who was the only one standing nearby now.

He looked at me, saying, "We've definitely missed you, but things are going alright. A lot of people still ask about you, and you know what it's like. We love an excuse to brag about you." It felt good hearing him say that.

I meant to respond but didn't have time before Angela came rushing out, asking Louis if he moved the gifts from the study. He responded with a no, and they both turned to Nick.

"Nick, dear. Did you move the boxes that were in the office?" Angela asked, standing in front of him.

"Oh, were those yours?" he said, sounding arrogant.

"What did you do with them?" Angela pried.

"I sold them to get some extra cash. I mean, they were sitting in front of me. They were begging to go to a good family," Nick said with an insolent smile.

"I don't understand," Angela said, looking puzzled. "What do you mean?"

"Well, they've been lying here for months, and the allowance you've been giving me just isn't enough."

"You can't just take things that aren't yours!" Angela started to yell.

I was just as shocked as everyone else looked to be. I didn't know if I should step in or not. These were my gifts to my family. And this kid really was not my family. Part of me didn't want to interfere, but I was angry at having to find a new way to give my family their Christmas presents. The hand-crafted journal I had gotten for Rachel couldn't be repurchased and arrive in time for the big day, and Joe's new mini car was a limited edition. The more I thought about it, the angrier I became. The only rational thing I could do was leave.

From the living room, I could hear Louis chiming into the conversation. "None of those were yours to take. They were for someone else. They were valuable. What did you think you would earn out of this? Praise? Because you sure as hell didn't get anything good out of any—" I slammed the door.

I just started to drive as far as I could. Not in any particular direction, but I just kept going. I passed the highway and stuck to back streets. I ended up in the heart of downtown, during winter, and with snow starting to fall. I parked my car at the first open parking meter I found. I got out of the car and started to walk. I went all the way to Millennium Park, with the famous bean, and the ice-skating rink.

Since the winter days were shorter, the sun had already set, but the streetlights provided enough light to know where I was going. I sat on a bench and stared at the passersby for the longest time, just thinking.

First, I thought about how I was going to face my family once I got back. But that was the least of my concerns. I couldn't tell what I was more frustrated about, the fact that someone stole my family's Christmas gifts or that I would have to go back home to face Stewart empty-handed. He'd probably think that I just skipped on getting any presents for my family this year.

My phone started vibrating, and I could see that it was Angela and Louis. I was sure they were calling to apologize, but I didn't want to hear it right then. I let the call ring all the way through before I put it back into my pocket. I knew that it wasn't their fault, but they shouldn't have to apologize for the actions of a kid they'd taken in.

I continued to sit there, just letting the snow fall all over me.

After a while of sitting and pondering, the only gift that came to mind was a vacation. I could easily get away with planning a low maintenance trip that they would enjoy, and it would still look thoughtful. But at the same time, anyone can get anyone a plane ticket. I needed something better.

On the walk back to my car, I passed a local jewelry store. It couldn't hurt to stop in. They were pretty busy, considering the holiday was around the corner, and everyone was getting last-minute gifts.

"Looking for a gift for someone special?" the sales lady asked.

"Yeah, something like that." She must've caught on to my irritation because she didn't try to continue talking to me after that.

I waited for the man in front of me to leave the counter that held the necklaces and bracelets. It looked like they were about to close. The shop assistant rang the man's purchases up, and he left the store.

"Excuse me," I said, flagging the lady down. "Do you have anything that you could customize last minute?"

"Yes, we can customize anything. You're just going to pay more the closer it gets to the holiday," she said, which made sense.

"Okay. I need help finding something for my wife and my five-year-old daughter. The price doesn't matter. I just want it to look personal and nice." She understood what I was saying. I was practically throwing my wallet at the lady.

"How about you get a necklace for your wife? You can never go wrong with a classic necklace, with a single row of quarter carat benitoites. It's a rare stone, and not often a first choice. However, it has a beautiful blue hue, and it will grab people's attention. Then, for your daughter, get a diamond bracelet with her birthstone in the middle. We can also customize your daughter's bracelet to fit Pandora charms on it, so she can always add to it, even if it's not from our store." I was impressed. This lady had good taste.

"Yes, do that for my wife's necklace. But let's not make it a diamond bracelet for my daughter. I'm afraid she'll lose it. Could you just do a chain or something?" Jewelry wasn't my thing.

"Sure, wait here," she said, walking to the back and returning with a big book. We spent a good chunk of time going through different books and magazines from the store, trying to find the perfect combination. After picking everything out, I paid the down payment and left the store feeling better than when I'd walked in.

I decided to keep this to myself and never mention what Nick had done. After all, I'd needed a few second chances myself when I was his age. I wanted Rachel and Joe to form their own opinions about him when they got the opportunity to meet him. When or if that day ever came. I just needed to go back in a few days to pick everything up before Christmas. I was sure I could tell Rachel that I was going for a stroll, and she wouldn't think twice about it. I got into the car and started back to Rachel's parents' home. I was gone for a while, but they'd just think I was visiting with my foster family.

I pulled into the driveway, and most of the lights were out. Since it was dark, I could easily see the giant Christmas tree in the front window — one that the maids had probably put up. The tree took up most of the window, so I couldn't tell if everyone else was in the living room or not, but I would soon find out.

I sat there for a few minutes, in the same spot the car had been parked for many months. I was still trying to compose myself and decide how to approach the situation. Checking my phone again, I had three more missed calls. There were also a few texts and a news notification.

Missed call: Angela

Missed call: Angela

Missed call: Louis

Angela: I'm so so sorry. Please call me back. We didn't mean to upset you.

TOP STORY NEWS: Possible connection between two murdered women. New evidence could bring on additional leads.

I ignored the first four notifications and skipped to the news item. I opened the page up and started to read. Apparently, both of the women murdered on Mercer Island had donated their eggs to a local egg donor bank, Mercer Fertility Clinic. The article went on to say that the police of the area had thought the new suspect was someone who had access to medical charts, maybe even someone who worked for the clinic. They still thought the murderer was a male in his twenties or thirties. Someone strong enough to move the victims' bodies after killing them.

The article also mentioned that the egg donors were missing their donation cards from the Mercer

Fertility Clinic. Much like a debit card, they were designed to fit in a wallet. Female donors received a pink card with a white border, while sperm donors were given a similar card in blue. With the cards seemingly missing, I wouldn't be surprised if taking them was part of the killer's MO.

I was relieved that they were making headway on the case and that there had been no new murders during the holiday. Maybe even murderers took time off. I gave myself a few minutes to process the information and decided against telling Rachel about the article. If she wanted to stay updated on it, I was sure she would get the same notification as me. With that, I left the car and knocked on the front door of the house.

To my surprise, Joe was the first to open the door. I would've thought she would be either getting ready for bed or doing something with her grandparents. Rachel came up to the entrance next. She gave me a kiss and asked how it went. Lying, I said it was good and changed the subject to talk about what they were doing while I was gone.

Before going to bed that night, I remembered that Angela had called me a few times. I told myself I would call them in the morning and smooth things out between us.

The rest of the trip went by in a blur. We did a lot of the same stuff we'd been doing at our own house, just with the grandparents. I went to see Angela and Louis during the last few days of our trip. I admitted to overreacting and we were all able to move past it. I went to collect the jewelry the day before Christmas Eve and paid to have it wrapped. The smiles on their faces when they opened their gifts were priceless; I wished I'd recorded the moment. It would've been better had they received their original presents, but I put that disappointment behind me.

When we left to go back to Washington, our return home was well due. The house was cold and empty, since nobody had been staying there for the entire time we were gone. The mail had piled up, and Rachel sat sifting through it, sorting it out. Joe and I got together and did a little bit of tidying, especially in her bedroom. There was a mess of toys from her trying to decide what to take to Chicago, although she didn't need to take any in the first place.

CHAPTER 14

Being home felt good, and things had been going surprisingly well. I enjoyed seeing Rachel and Joe being content with their new jewelry. They both flaunted them everywhere, from around the house to just going to get groceries. I drew the line when it came to Joe wearing her bracelet while playing outside; the last thing I wanted was for those expensive pieces to go missing.

Even though the holidays had passed, I still hadn't spent the bonus I'd received from work. I wasn't sure what to spend it on. I wanted to get something for myself, but I didn't want to be selfish. I knew that there were things the family might like, but figured it couldn't hurt to window-shop.

Another weekend had arrived – in the past, that would have seen us hanging around the house, but things had changed. With Rachel's work schedule booked out, she'd decided to see her therapist over weekends. If she was working during the week and going to therapy on the weekends, she could separate herself from work and health. It was her idea, of course.

I would never complain, though. I got to spend my Saturday mornings with Joe. Her winter break was over, which she was pleased about. She talked nonstop about how much she missed her friends while she was away. I thought it would be a good idea to text all the parents to see if they wanted to bring the kids over for some fun outside, hot chocolate, and some winter movies. They all thought it was a great idea. Besides, I had to take them all eventually. I did pawn Joe off on the other parents a few weeks before, so I thought it only fair to return the favor now.

They all responded fast; some folks are happy to get rid of a kid for a while. I was confident that I'd planned a day that would make things a breeze. Hopefully, they'd play out in the snow, come in for some hot chocolate, and be too tired to watch a movie, so they'd all just fall asleep. While the kids were playing, I'd have time to figure out what I wanted to spend my large bonus check on.

The children started arriving in the early afternoon. It was sunny out and would have been warm if not for all the snow on the ground. The kids were all outside before their parents even left. The folks all lingered for a few minutes to catch up on gossip before carrying on with their day. It was never something that I enjoyed, but I'd grown used to standing there, nodding my head, and murmuring polite replies. Once the parents left, I made another cup of tea, grabbed my laptop, and sat at the table where I could see the children playing outside.

I logged on and first checked my emails. There weren't many new emails in either my work or my personal account, so I just responded to a few necessary ones and deleted the rest.

For a few minutes after that, I just sat there wondering where to begin my search. I had a decent amount of money. I could really buy anything that I wanted. I decided to go to our bank account to see *exactly* how much wiggle room I had.

To my surprise, the bank account was loaded. Our balance was staggering. Enough money to buy an island if we really wanted to. I could pretty much quit my job. I was in shock. I knew that Rachel was working, but I didn't realize she was bringing in that much money. I knew this couldn't all be from me.

I scrolled through to check the recent transactions. The list was endless, but the first few caught my eye:

SHELL Gas station$12.65

Verizon$206.55

Cash Withdrawal$12,000.00

Cash withdrawal $12,000? What the hell was that for? I knew that it wasn't necessarily my money, but I felt I should still know where all the cash was going. I texted Rachel immediately.

Rach, why was $12k taken out of our account a few days ago?

It didn't take long for her to text back. Before I even put my phone down, I had a response.

Just used it to take care of some bills.

How vague.

What bills? That seems like a lot.

Fast response again.

I take care of the finances for a reason. You don't have to worry about it. Just know that all the bills are paid.

'Should I let it go?' I wondered. To be fair, she did take care of all the household admin so that I didn't have to. But on the other hand, that was still a lot of money. I didn't know what kind of expenses cost that much, but perhaps I didn't want to know either. It wasn't as if there was an issue with money. If that had been the case, it would have been a different discussion. I texted her again, just letting her know the conversation wasn't over.

We can talk about it when you get home.

Then, I got back to my original plan to browse the internet for ideas on how to spend that bonus I was so proud of. Cars, high-tech toys, expensive watches – nothing I would ever buy. But I decided that if I was going to window-shop, I'd focus on the extravagant items.

Eventually, I moved on to boats. More specifically, yachts. It had always been my dream to have one. With the dock at the edge of our yard, the temptation was almost irresistible. But this was not the time, even though the extra cash felt like it was burning a hole in my pocket.

I continued to browse, and time slipped away from me. Before I knew it, the kids were coming inside because it was starting to get dark outside. I gave them hot chocolate to warm them up and turned on some Christmas movies. It wasn't long before Rachel came walking through the door.

Rachel wasn't alone.

In her arms, she held a furry dog. Not just any furry dog, a puppy. The puppy couldn't be more than two or three months old. The bundle of fur was all black with dark brown eyes and a blackish-blue tongue that stuck out of his mouth.

"A puppy?!" Joe yelled as Rachel took off her shoes, and the dog went running up to the kids. The kids welcomed the dog with open arms.

"Rachel. What the hell?" I said, probably with less surprise in my voice than I actually felt.

"Tim, don't swear in front of the kids."

"You brought a dog home, and you're worried about me swearing?"

She walked away and went into the bedroom. I stood there, not in a talking mood anymore. I stared at the way Joe played with the puppy. The smile on her face was priceless.

I must admit, the dog was cute. I couldn't hold a grudge against it, but I could feel some anger towards the person accountable for this decision. Rachel was about to get a piece of my mind.

I watched Joe and the other two kids play with the dog. He was fluffy, but the good kind of fluffy. I didn't know much about dogs, so I had no idea what breed he was. All I could say was that it looked like the type you would want curling up next to you on the couch. It also looked like the type of dog that you had to take to the groomers often.

"Daddy, what's his name?" Joe asked me.

"Well, dear. That's a very good question. You'll have to ask Mom that. But I'm not sure we're keeping him. I'll have to talk to your mother," I said, trying to be as honest with my daughter as possible.

"What do you mean? Of course, we're keeping him," Rachel chimed in from the background. How long had she been standing there? "You can name him whatever you want, Joelle." Bold move on her part.

I gave her a dirty look; this isn't the end of the conversation. To be honest, I was mad. Too mad. I thought it best to remove myself from the situation.

"I'm going to get some work done in my office," I said to Rachel. I walked away just in time.

"I think I want to name him Rufus!" I heard Joe say as I left the room.

"If that's what you want, Joelle," Rachel responded to her.

I headed to my study, closed the door, and locked it for good measure. I wanted nobody to bother me, especially not anyone who had recently brought home a puppy. I sat down at my desk, turned on my computer, and started researching again. It appeared that the dog was a Chow Chow. It looked like he would get a lot bigger and a lot fluffier. From what I read, these dogs did, in fact, require a lot of grooming.

Overall, my findings were what I expected. It would be a good dog if raised right, like all other dogs. The more I look into the breed, the less mad I became. I watched a few videos, read some articles, and by the end, I wasn't all that angry. But I wasn't not going to let Rachel off the hook. She was going to have to make up for this. My mind kept circling back to when she told everyone we were moving before discussing it with me.

Were we going to be in the same situation as last time? As I keep thinking, my trust in her began to diminish. How long had she been planning on bringing home a dog? Most places don't just let you make last-minute decisions to take a pup. I was also pretty sure that she got it from a shelter, which meant that she'd clearly thought about it. First, she had to apply, and some places even make you have a home visit.

My anger was starting to boil up inside of me. What the fuck was Rachel thinking? Making decisions, *especially* a decision like this, by herself. I thought we were a family; shouldn't we at least act like it?

Then my mind faded away from Rachel and focused on Joe. Was Joe even ready for something like this? A dog is a huge responsibility. Was I ready for this? When we'd discussed it in the past, we decided against getting a pet and just focus on Joe.

I heard the doorknob rattle.

'Please don't be anyone looking to talk,' I thought.

"Daddy, can I come in and show you Rufus?" Joe was at my office door.

"One minute, Peanut," I yelled back to her, making it seem like I'm in the middle of something crucial. But wasn't I? I felt like I was in the middle of a fucking crisis.

I stood there for a few seconds, in front of the door, with my hand on the lock. I needed to take a few breaths to prepare myself for what was on the other side of the door. Good or bad, I had to act appropriately.

The moment I pulled the door open, the dog scampered around me. The next thing I knew, it was trying to climb up my legs. I crouched down, placing my hand on the top of his head. I started to gently pet him, as if I were going to break him if I patted too hard. I ran my hands down his body in the same direction his hair laid, then started over again, repeating the same motions.

"Rufus, please be a good dog," I said, quietly enough that only Rufus and I would be able to hear.

I picked Rufus up and really got a good look at him. He was cute, I couldn't deny that. He was all black but had such pretty eyes, and his fur was even fluffier than I had thought, like touching a fleece blanket. He sure loved being petted, too. He was so happy as long as you had a hand on him. I stopped petting him for a second, and he dashed back to the girls sitting on the floor in the living room. Joelle and her friends loved the company of the new dog. They stopped playing with their dolls to focus on him, and I went back to my desk.

Ding, Dong. The doorbell rang. I wonder which parent this was.

I wasn't the one to answer the door, but I could hear the voice that responded to my wife. It sounded like Jenny's mom. A few seconds later, I heard another voice – Amy's mom. They must have carpooled here together. It sounded like my wife had a lot to chat about because they stood talking for a while.

"Joe!" Rachel yelled, "Jenny and Amy, it's time to go, your moms are here!"

I heard a series of groans and complaints, but within a few minutes, the girls were at the front door standing next to their still gossiping parents.

I continued to sit there. The last thing I wanted to do was get in the middle of the conversation, and I really didn't want to be talked to either. It was another ten minutes before I heard Amy's mom say, "Alright, we better get going now." It felt like anxiety hit me in the face. Once the kids were gone, Rachel would want to snuggle up next to me and watch a movie or something. That's the last thing I wanted. Luckily, Juniper's mom still hadn't arrived. Hopefully, they'd run late, and by that time, I could use the 'I'm tired' excuse and hop into bed.

Naturally, my plan didn't pan out, and Juniper's mom came shortly after the others had left. Leaving me home alone with my daughter and her mom. I tried to busy myself with Joe and let her stay up well past her bedtime. We sat there playing with toys, and I was even willing to play with the dolls. I really was avoiding Rachel, but in my opinion, I had good reason to.

At 10 o'clock, Rachel piped up, "Okay, I think it's time for bed. Don't you, Tim?" Normally, I would be the first to say yes, but today was a different story.

"Well, I think that everyone is just so excited and energetic that we have a dog now. It's only fair that we stay up for a bit and wear off some energy." I felt proud of my delaying tactic. I even allowed myself a sly smile.

"Fine, but I'm going to take Rufus outside."

"Okay!" Joe and I both said. She was so into the dolls we were playing with that she didn't even care that her mom was taking her dog for a walk without her.

We played until about 10:30, when Joe said that she was getting tired. Rachel still wasn't back, but I tucked Joe in and went to the bedroom to do the same. I walked in, noticing that Rachel had her pajamas laid at the foot of the bed. I moved them onto one of the chairs in our bedroom.

When I woke up in the morning, the pajamas were still there, and it seemed like everything was untouched. Thinking about it, I realized that I hadn't felt her crawl into bed that night. Perhaps she'd slept on the couch or in the spare bedroom because she could sense I was upset.

Since Rachel didn't sleep in bed with me, I didn't hear her come in after walking the dog. I got ready for my morning, knowing what waited for me on the other side of the bedroom door. I enjoyed the last little bit of peace I had before walking into a tornado.

I left the bedroom, and to my surprise, I heard no Rachel and no Joelle, not even a Rufus. I gave them the benefit of the doubt. Perhaps Joe was still sleeping. Maybe Rachel was on her early run, and she'd taken Rufus with. That made sense to me. So, I walked into the kitchen and started brewing my morning cup of tea; I chose Peppermint this time. Mug in hand, I stood by the window and stared out at the ocean. Watching the waves crash into giant chunks of ice that had built up along the edge of the water. Looking at the dock outside, that didn't have a boat on it. Surveying the moody sky reflecting against the angry water. It looked to me like a storm. The incoming thunderclouds seemed ominous, since I could imagine how big of a storm would be coming when my wife returned from her workout.

Except, she didn't come home. I wasn't terribly worried, but I knew that it was starting to get late, and Joe still wasn't up. I tiptoed towards her room, not wanting to wake her up if she was still asleep. The door was closed, and I inched it open, trying not to make noise. I cracked it just enough to see Joe, or should I say, lack thereof. Joe wasn't in her bed. I ran in a panic to the garage.

Nice. My wife took my daughter and the new dog out for the day and didn't say anything to me. If I was mad before, now I was livid.

I waited hours to see if they would come home, but when I didn't hear anything from Rachel, I grew nervous. I decided to put my pride aside and send her a text.

Where are you? And why didn't you say you were leaving?

Yeah, I sounded like a dick. But to be fair, she was a dick first by bringing home a dog without running it past me. I was surprised that she texted me back so fast.

Oh, you didn't look on the fridge?

The fridge? I walked over to the refrigerator, and sure enough, there was a poem she'd written for me. This wasn't like the normal loving ones. This one was... Harsh.

Tim,

I thought better of you,

But you're really acting like a dead limb.

You'd think you'd be happy that I brought home a dog,

After all, I did it for us,

Instead, you turned around and acted like a big hog.

Dick move, asshole.

I was pretty sure that the last little bit of that wasn't necessarily a part of the poem, but it was fair.

The poem wasn't elaborate, and it sounded like she rushed it, but I understood the angle she was coming from. I sent her a note:

> **Yeah, I did. Rachel, you brought home a dog and didn't even tell me. There is no way I wanted to sleep next to you or anywhere near you. Take a second and try to understand the position you put me in. We decided we weren't ready for a dog yet. But only a little bit later you come home with one. NOT EVEN TELLING ME. That's a little outrageous, you have to admit.**

I could've gone on and on about this, but I decided I'd better save that for when they arrived home. So, I sent another text before she replied.

> **We should probably talk about this when you get home.**

She replied fast. She must've been waiting for that response.

> **Sure. If we come home.**

This was how she always played it. The 'maybe I will, maybe I won't' trick. But I'd learned all her tricks; that's what marriage is all about. I didn't respond to her after that. Instead, I decided to go out. It was a weekend, and there were plenty of sports bars that I could hang out at. I didn't often get to go out and make friends at the bar, so I guess that made it a good day.

It was the winter season going into spring, so there were many different sports to watch. I got ready and headed out. There weren't many bars around us, actually. A quick google search only located one. I didn't want to go downtown because I wanted to be around people who fit my lifestyle more; it meant a better chance of making an actual friend.

We'd been in Washington for only a few months. We'd left our social circle behind, and we hadn't been anywhere to make new friends. Rachel and I hadn't been outside the house to do any socializing, and neither of us considered Joe's friends' parents as friends.

It only took a few minutes to get there, which meant it would be an easy drive home too. The bar was kind of quiet when I walked in, and they looked like they were just opening up. Servers were putting the silverware out and getting the bar set up. A couple of them greeted me, even though I doubted they were happy to see a customer this early in the morning. I was the only customer in the place, but I was sure another person would be coming in soon.

"What can I get you?" the bartender asked as I took my jacket off and hopped onto a barstool.

"Um, give me just a minute," I said, and she walked away and busied herself while I made my choice. I looked at the wide array of alcohol displayed in front of me. I never liked going to a new bar because they all have different types of drinks.

The bartender came back up to me, and I finally got a good look at her. She was tall, slender, and had long, dark hair. Her face was angular with high cheekbones, and her make-up accentuated her good features. "You know what you'd like yet?" She shot me a smile, and her teeth shone brightly beneath the dim bar lights.

"Yeah, I'll take a rum and coke to start." I glanced at her nametag and said, "Thanks, Matty."

"Yeah! Coming right up." She turned around and started to make the drink. She was probably relieved that I didn't order something time-consuming like a martini. She set the drink down in front of me and walked away.

I sat there, just stirring the cocktail stick around my glass. The TVs weren't on yet, so I was trying to look busy until there was something to occupy me. As if Matty could read my mind, she walked up to me, handing me the TV remote. "Choose whatever channel you'd like," she said to me. I gave her a small smile and grabbed the remote from her hand.

I turned on one of the sports channels. It was early yet, and there were a lot of pre-show programs. Every channel had the same theme, mostly a few men talking about the sports team and discussing what they thought would happen during the day's games. I figured football would be my best bet because the season was nearly over. My team wasn't in the playoffs anymore, but that was okay. I liked to watch them all. I sipped my drink and watched the pre-game shows.

It wasn't long before a group of men came in and sat at the other end of the bar. They were rowdy and not my style, so I kept to myself. They grabbed their drinks and headed to the dining area for some lunch. They were the only other occupants in the bar, so I could hear them ordering. My stomach started growling, demanding food. I looked around for Matty, but I didn't see her. I went back to watching my show, ignoring the loud men behind me. A few minutes later, Matty came walking past me.

"Excuse me, Matty, could I see a menu?" I asked.

"Yeah, definitely. Did you want another rum and coke?"

I didn't realize my drink was nearly gone. "Actually, can I get a whisky on the rocks instead?" I asked politely.

"Yeah. What's your name? I'll start a tab for you." "Tim," I told her, then continued to place an order for food, "And can I get a sampler basket of your appetizers?"

"Alright, Tim. Whisky on ice coming right up." She made the drink in front of me and said, "Here you go. Your food should be done shortly." She slid my glass across the bar.

She went to the computer, loaded my drink order to my tab, then disappeared again. Once more, I was the only person at the bar. Matty didn't come back until another person walked in, triggering the door chime.

"Hey there, Matty," the voice behind me called. I turned around to see a man who looked to be in his early 30s. Although I was sitting and couldn't gauge how tall he was, he seemed to be average height and was athletically built, wearing neatly pressed jeans and a button-down. His light brown hair wasn't particularly noteworthy, but as he got closer, I noticed intelligent brown eyes and a clean-shaven face. This might be someone I could have a conversation with.

"Hey!" she called. "The usual?" she asked him.

"You know it." By the time he had said that he was already at the bar. He chose a seat that was a few chairs away from me.

I watched as she made him a Jack Daniels, neat. I was impressed. I've never been able to drink warm liquor. She sat it down in front of him, smiling.

She turned to me, "Need another?"

"Um, yeah. Actually, I'll take the same as last time." She nodded and turned around to make the drink.

"Whisky drinker, huh?" the man asked me.

"Yeah, I haven't found a whisky I didn't like," I said with a chuckle.

"Me neither," he said. Then he stood up, sticking his hand out, saying, "Name's Cole Clemonte."

I grabbed his hand. "Tim. Tim Cardington. Nice to meet you."

"Likewise. New around here? I haven't seen you before, and I'm a regular," he said with a grin.

"Yeah, yeah. My family and I bought a house here and moved in this last summer. I haven't had a chance to hit the sports bars yet; today's the first time."

He watched me, listening, then nodded his head and said, "Yeah, I get that. This is the best sports bar you'll find in the area. I suppose you'll get to know everyone who comes here. Plus, it's far enough away from the mainland that none of the true city people venture out here."

"Wow. The reason I picked this place was that I didn't want to be around them anyway! Looks like I made the right choice," I said.

My food came, and I offered to share it with Cole. At first, he declined. After a while, he changed his mind and decided to grab a few of the appetizers. I was glad he did because I ordered way too many, to begin with.

For a while, we sat there talking. I found out that Cole had lived on the island all his life, and he met his wife in college. Cole swore that his wife, Stacy, was the most perfect person on the planet. She was the kind of woman who got involved in charity events, volunteered at the homeless shelters in Seattle, and even donated her eggs at the Mercer Fertility Clinic. They didn't have kids, which suited them, but Cole said that if they ever did, Stacy would be the first to volunteer to chaperone at school.

Cole worked in the medical field; he was the person who drew your blood, the phlebotomist. He mentioned that he only lived a few miles from the sports bar. He was about ten minutes away, the same as me, except he was in the opposite direction.

We talked for so long that we each had two more drinks, even though the football game had already ended. By then, I started to feel a little tipsy, and I figured it was time to get going.

I said goodbye to my new friend, then left with the promise to be back another day. I had such a good time that when I got to the car, I just sat there for a minute. I pulled my phone out of my pocket and checked it. I had a few missed calls and a few texts, all from Rachel asking where I was. I put my phone back down and drove home.

CHAPTER 15

As expected, Rachel had come home with Joe and Rufus. We each took a few days to think, and then came back together and discussed what had happened that weekend. Rachel blamed her questionable decision-making on the fact that her mental state hadn't been up to par. To a degree, I let that be the reason. However, she started talking as if everything was my fault because I wasn't 'willing to understand' what she was going through.

The conversation lasted a few hours, but by the end, we kissed and made up. I was no longer upset about the dog, and Rachel understood that she couldn't just make rash decisions without at least letting me know before she made them. That was when she told me she had one last present for the family. I pushed for answers, asking what she'd bought, but she wouldn't budge. Instead, she stayed quiet and told me I would have to wait and find out.

We woke up together on a Thursday in mid-February. After spending few days arguing about

Rufus, it was nice to finally be united again. Not to mention the crazy sex we were both still recovering from, from the previous night. Rachel normally would've been out for her morning workout, but she decided to take a cheat day and do a mini-workout during her lunchtime instead. She wanted to wake up with me, and I wanted to wake up with her. Joe came rushing into the bedroom like every other morning, but Rufus now followed her in. We all got up at the same time and started our day.

After settling in at the office, I headed straight to the breakroom to make a cup of tea. As I waited for my tea bag to steep, I checked my phone. I started by scrolling through the social media but stopped as I hit an article Rachel had shared.

MAN IN CUSTODY, POTENTIAL SUSPECT IN ISLAND MURDERS

I was surprised that she'd shared this, but I supposed it made her happy seeing someone finally getting the blame for these crimes. There hadn't been any new bodies found, but the article mentioned that if there were other victims, the snow would have covered them. The police thought they might find something once the snow began to melt, but the article said the man in custody wasn't talking yet. I was sure Rachel felt relieved. I hoped that if they had someone in custody, she could put it all behind her and recover from the issues she'd been having.

The rest of the day went by in a breeze; I was in such a good mood. Who knew that knowing a potential killer was behind bars could be such a mood lifter? I was actually excited to leave at the end of the day, seeing as how Rachel and I were on good terms again. I could finally return to the perfect household – to my loving wife, sweet daughter, and an adorable puppy. Things were almost back to the way they were supposed to be.

I drove home knowing that everyone would be home by the time I got there. I pulled into the driveway and opened the garage door. Just as I expected, Rachel's car was already inside. As soon as I pulled in and closed the garage door, I looked to my right and saw Joe standing at the door, holding Rufus in one arm, and waving with the other. A smile spread across my face. I rushed to grab all my belongings from the car so that I could go inside and hug my family.

I walked in the door with the dog jumping at my legs. Joe was talking about her day at school, and Rachel came up to give me a hug and a kiss. To some, this might sound like chaos, but to me, it felt like home. I'd spent a lot of time reflecting on where I was at in life, and I realized that I hadn't appreciated all my blessings before. I vowed that I was going to learn to enjoy the things I had because my life was damn good.

"Welcome home, honey," Rachel said after she kissed me.

"Mmmm, what's that smell?" I asked, knowing already what it was.

"Chicken Alfredo, just for you," Rachel replied.

She knew that was my weak spot, Chicken Alfredo. "What's the occasion?" I asked, sure there had to be an ulterior motive.

"No reason, I just love you, that's all," she said, raising her hands in a gesture of innocence.

I wasn't going to complain. Rachel rarely made the dish; it wasn't her favorite. The only time we generally had it is when I made it.

We all sat down to eat like a normal family. We sat at the dining room table where we could still watch the TV that was on in the living room. We were watching one of Joe's cartoon shows. It was hard for me to appreciate them because they're terrible compared to what Rachel and I grew up watching. There had been a few different occasions when I'd thought about getting Joe some copies of the cartoons we used to enjoy. Then I'd think about all the references she wouldn't understand, and it just became too complicated.

After dinner, I helped Rachel clean up the kitchen. She washed the dishes, I dried them and put them away, and Joe loaded up the dishwasher with the crockery that could go in there. We each grabbed a bowl from the cabinet, a spoon from the drawer, and our favorite ice-cream to end the night with dessert. Rachel told Joe she could only have a little because she had to go to bed, but we adults got to take as much as we wanted. I took full advantage of that. I piled my bowl up, almost to the top, leaving a little room for cherries and whipped cream. We took our bowls into the living room and turned on a movie that we knew none of us would finish watching.

In no time, Joe was fast asleep between Rachel and me. Rachel was ready to go to bed shortly after. I picked Joe up and carried her to her bed, tucking her in. Rachel followed me, giving her a kiss on the forehead. Then we both stood there. Rachel took my hand and rested her head on my shoulder. For just a few moments, we stayed and watched our daughter sleep peacefully. We walked into our bedroom together, and got ready for bed, succumbing to the temptation to extend those precious moments of intimacy. After, we lay naked in bed, and within a few minutes, I could hear Rachel breathing slightly louder, to signify that she was asleep.

The next morning was just as good as the night before. I woke up still happy, Rachel was still happy, and Joe was also still happy. This continued for a few days, which carried into a few months. Soon, it was the end of April. The weather started to warm up again, and everything was moving along as it should. Rufus was getting pretty big, much bigger than I thought he would.

As the police had predicted, another body was found after the snow melted. At first, they didn't know if it was a victim of the previous killer or another act of murder. If they did tack this onto the murderer in custody, it would make him a serial killer. Rachel didn't seem concerned about it. She believed that the man they'd apprehended was the murderer. I was not so sure. The suspect had been adamant that he didn't know anything, and he was either a hell of an actor, or he actually didn't know anything.

According to the report given by the local news station, Hannah Richards was only 22 years old when she was murdered. She was a native of the island and had lived on Mercer her entire life, but shortly before her death, she had planned to join a mission to build houses in third world countries. Like the others, the police couldn't find the donation card given to her by the Mercer Fertility Clinic, but they had found an appointment card from them in her wallet.

Like the previous victim, her remains were discovered dismembered, decapitated, and buried in garbage bags in a park. Battered, bruised, tossed out like trash – it seemed to be the killer's MO. It was more than I could bear to think about, especially since Hannah was said to have lived quite near our neighborhood. Not that it lessened the tragedy of her death. It just seemed so close to home. The police still hadn't released any details about what type of weapon was used, although they claimed it was a crucial part of the investigation.

Hannah's murder, along with those of the previous victim in the park and the woman discovered on the interstate, officially earned their murderer the label of 'serial killer'. However, Rachel seemed strangely unperturbed and had been increasingly excited about the surprise she had for us. I'd reached the point that I was starting to think it was something good. I'd stopped checking the bank account and was growing increasingly impatient. She said it would be ready any day.

One Saturday, I got up after a particularly stressful week. We'd just finished a project that ended up taking much longer than it was supposed to. It was the week after the project was completed, and there were a lot more errors than we'd anticipated. The project had to be amended before we could release it entirely. It was a relief that it was over now. It was the hardest assignment we'd had since I'd started with the company, but it wasn't anything out of my expertise.

Rachel told me that she wanted to take Joe out for a while to the mall, but she didn't want me to come with because she figured it'd be boring. Instead, she insisted that I go to the bar and spend some time with my now good friend, Cole. I texted Cole and told him that I would be at the bar for a few hours. He texted back almost immediately, saying that he planned to be there too. With that done, Rachel and Joe set out, and I got ready for the bar.

Once I arrived, I scanned the room. Cole still wasn't here.

"The usual?" the bartender asked. He was new, and I always forgot his name.

"Yeah. And grab Cole's drink too. He's on his way," I said, taking off my jacket and draping it over the chair that I'd be sitting in.

The bartender brought both the drinks, adding to my tab that I now paid weekly instead of daily. I sat there, sipping my drink. I assumed Cole would have arrived already. I called his cellphone a few times, but I got no answer. I started to think that he wasn't coming in; maybe he was sidetracked.

I ended up asking the bartender to add some ice to Cole's drink. I decided I'd just have his whisky, but on the rocks. I finished his drink faster than expected. I also shot him one more text, then waited thirty more minutes. It was nearly dark, and I was sure Rachel and Joe were already home, so I decided to head back.

I thanked the bartender and left, feeling a little disappointed that my only friend had flaked on me. The entire ride home, I kept trying to convince myself something important must have happened that he couldn't make it. Although he could at least have said something to me. I was just a short text away.

I pulled into the driveway and was surprised to see Cole's car parked outside. What was going on? Maybe he had come looking for me. He was blocking my path to the garage. I decided to pull up next to him and park in front of the garage, where Rachel would've put her car. I could hear Joe yelling in the backyard, so I followed the sounds. Her yells weren't of terror; they were of joy and happiness. I walked to the back, and it took me a few seconds to register what I was seeing.

Around the firepit sat Rachel, Joe, Cole, and his wife, Stacy.

"What's going on here?" I asked.

"Hey!" Cole said, dragging on the 'y' sound.

"Hi, honey," Rachel said, giving me a small smile.

"Daddy!" Joe said, running up to me. Rufus was barking in excitement and following Joe.

I repeated myself, "What's going on here?"

"We just gathered here, waiting for you to get home," Rachel said. The smile never left her face as she got out of her chair and started to walk towards me. She greeted me with a kiss and a sweet hug.

"What for?" I asked.

"Oh, it's for your surprise. I told you it would come soon." The smile was still on her face, but a little wider than before.

"Really?"

"Yes, let me get the lights."
"What do you mean, Rachel? We're outside; there are no lights out here."

"Just shut up! It's a part of the surprise," she said as she was walking away.

I walked over to Cole and Stacy. "How did you get wrapped into this?"

"Believe it or not, your wife got my number off your phone. She said she had a surprise to give you, and she wanted us to be a part of it," he said. For a split second, I let myself wonder how Rachel got his number from my phone and how long they'd been talking without me knowing.

I took a small breath and responded, "Interesting. When did she first talk to you? I've known there was a surprise for months now."

"Honestly, about two weeks ago. Sorry man, I didn't know how to keep you away for long enough, but not too long at the same time. I feel like a dick for leaving you at the bar by yourself," he said in a way that showed remorse.

I responded to match his energy, "Naw, man. It's perfectly fine. Don't worry about it! Seriously."

Before he had a chance to say anything, the lights turned on. They were super bright...almost blinding. Since the sun had already set, the lights were necessary to see clearly. Once the lights came on, it took a few seconds to adjust to the brightness. I had no idea we even had these in the backyard, but I assumed they were installed when the house was built because I would have noticed them otherwise.

When my eyes finally adjusted, I noticed the 'surprise' right away. A 66° ABOVE motor yacht. I'd been yearning for a boat like this forever. Not too big, but not too small. It had everything a family would need. It even had four bedrooms – specs I knew by heart.

I could hardly get the words out, "For me?"

"Surprise!" they all said.

"Wow. I don't even know what to say." I walked up to Rachel, grabbing her, and wrapping my arms around her. "Thank you so much. This is insane, Rachel!"

"You're welcome, my love. I told you I had a surprise."

"I know how much this thing costs…thank you. Thank you!"

Rachel let go of me, lightly smacking my arm. "What are you waiting for? Go check it out."

"Right, right. Let's go, everyone!" I said, being the first to run towards the vessel.

I rushed towards it; my feet hit the dock, and I stopped at the entrance. The door was open, waiting for me to enter from the side. I stared for a little bit, letting everyone else catch up to me. Then I took my first step onto my new yacht. I glanced back at everyone. They were all smiling.

"Hey, now you can take us out on the water instead of hanging out in that stuffy bar!" Cole chimed in.

Everyone, including me, laughed at that. Only seconds later, we were all spread out around the yacht, looking around at everything. Since it was dark now, I couldn't see out on the water, but the yacht itself was well lit. We spent the next hour sitting on board, checking out all the hidden cubbies and the beds. Joe insisted she'd get the master bed, but Rachel and I thought otherwise.

While everyone was talking around me, I took in the moment and made a mental note to remember it because it was perfection. My friends and family gathered around my yacht, laughing and chatting. What could be better?

CHAPTER 16

A few days later, we decided to take the boat out for a weekend. Rachel brought it up, and I thought it was a great idea. It would be the first time I got to spend time on my boat, and it would be with my family; I loved the idea. I told her that any time would work for me; whenever she was ready. To my surprise, she responded quickly, saying we should do it that weekend.

"Why this weekend? Isn't that a little soon to plan?" I asked her, knowing she liked it when things were organized in advance.

"Yeah, I think that it sounds great. It'll be a wonderful weekend. Plus, it's only Tuesday; there's plenty of time to plan."

"Okay, this weekend it is, then!" I responded, sounding a little more excited than I should have.

The rest of the week, we spent decorating and setting up the yacht in preparation for the excursion. Rachel even suggested that I invite Cole and Stacy. I thought that was a wonderful idea, and Cole said he could make it, but Stacy wouldn't be there because she didn't like to be out on open water.

Once it got to Friday, the day before leaving, Rachel broke the news that she would have to stay behind and work that weekend. I suggested we postpone the entire thing, but she insisted that we go rather than upset Joelle. I thought that was fair, and we decided that Joe, Cole, and I would go.

I picked Joe up from school that afternoon. I got there a few minutes early and decided to indulge in some school drama with Joe's friend's parents. Normally, I wouldn't do this, but I had to maintain the Cardington status at this school by participating in the shit-talking.

I got out of the vehicle and made my way over to the two parents huddled together and whispering.

"What's everyone up to today?" I asked, inserting myself into the conversation.

"We're just talking about that poor girl who was murdered," Amy's mom said.

"Yeah, it's terrible. Isn't it?" Juniper's mom added.

I replied, saying, "Yeah, wow. It really is."

"You know, my husband knows her dad. They play poker together every week," Juniper's mom stated.

Nobody said anything, but their curiosity was almost tangible.

"Well?" Amy's mom said, "Give us the deets."

"Okay, so here's what I know. Her family lives close by to all of us, right?" she said, then looked at me. "Well, actually, she lived almost right next to you, Tim. Just down the road from you."

"Really? Where?" I asked.

She gave me the address so I could see the house next time I drove home and then continued, "My husband told me everything that happened, and it's terrible, really."

"Just spill," Amy's mom said, sounding almost irritated.

"Well, she was found at another park. And my husband said that the police told the parents that the body was left in the open. The police think that the killer is getting either sloppy or more brazen. But the murder is almost the same. She was decapitated, just like the other two, and her body was shoved into plastic bags. She was cut into five pieces. Her legs cut off, and her arms. Gross, right?" she asked but didn't wait for us to answer before continuing, "And the worst part is that she was missing for an entire week before she was killed. A whole week. The killer was sick enough to keep her caged up for a whole week before killing her. What a pervert."

The information was a little more than I needed to know. I tried to tune out some of the conversation, but Amy's mom seemed so engrossed in the story that I didn't dare cut Juniper's mom off.

Juniper's mom started talking more, "The scary part? Her dad told my husband that she was complaining to them about someone walking around the house at odd times. Her parents never pressed about it since they lived in a good neighborhood, and they thought she was safe. She kept telling them that in the morning and sometimes at night, she would hear rustling in the bushes outside. They just ignored her. He told my husband it was the biggest regret of his life. It was probably the killer. I mean, think about it."

Luckily, the bell rang, and the kids started pouring out. I was feeling a little sick just thinking about the murder. Joe came out, saying good-bye to her friends, and we finally left. Once we got home, I lay on the couch for a while just thinking, while Joe played in her room. I was glad we'd planned the trip the next day. I could turn off my phone and not have to dwell upon murders.

Saturday morning, we said our goodbyes. Rachel shed a few tears; she hated being away from Joe for this long, but she convinced us that it was important we go. What we didn't realize at the time was that it was the worst decision we could've made, and nothing prepared us for the arrival back home.

The entire trip was casual and relaxing. We took some time fishing, and Joe spent a lot of time basking in the sun. It was a nice way to disconnect from society for a while, since there was very spotty cell reception. We were aiming to get back home Sunday, around mid-afternoon. I was glad that we didn't narrow the time down anymore because we made it back when the sun was getting ready to set.

We docked and anchored the boat, which was a two-man job. Looking into the backyard, I only saw one figure seated there, when both Rachel and Stacy said they'd be waiting. I was sure the other wasn't far behind. We gathered all our stuff and headed to solid ground. Once I reached the grass, I could tell that it was Rachel in the yard, but it looked as though she was crying.

When we approached her, she had tissues in her hand, and she was sobbing, with tears running down her face. I dropped my bags and instantly fell beside her to comfort her.

"What's wrong, my love?" I asked, kissing her forehead as a form of greeting.

"It—it's Stacy," she stammered.

"What do you mean? What happened to her?" Cole said, now tuning into the conversation with open ears.

"She—" Rachel continued, with a sob between each word. "She died."

Cole fell to his knees, reaching my level. His face was a mask of horror. I couldn't comprehend either.

A tear ran down his face, "You're joking, right? Tell me you're joking!" he begged Rachel.

"Cole, I'm so sorry." She walked over to him. By now, he was on the ground. Rachel crouched down and wrapped her arms around him.

"I— I don't understand. What happened?" he asked, even though he sounded like he didn't want to know.

"It was crazy," she began between sobs. "I just texted her, thinking that maybe we could do something since you were all gone. She said she would meet me here in a few hours. Well, the entire night passed by, and she never showed up. This morning, she hadn't responded to my texts or calls, so I drove to the house to see what happened to our plans. That's when I found her..." her voice broke. "She was dead. I called the cops immediately. They questioned me and told me that this was probably the serial killer."

The killer had struck again. I'd had my doubts for a while now, but I hadn't wanted to believe it. Yet, it seemed my suspicions were accurate. The man in police custody couldn't be the murderer.

At this point, I didn't know what to think. I was just as shocked as Cole was, and I felt terrible for the guy. This murderer was targeting women specifically. Even more specifically, women who had donated their eggs at the Mercer Fertility Clinic. I thought back when Cole and I first met, and he'd told me that Stacy was involved there.

"I'm sorry, Cole," was the only thing that I could muster.

Even Joe understood the gravity of the moment, and she sat there in the grass, staying silent. She'd never been in a situation like this before, but she understood what we were saying, and it left her speechless. Rachel was still holding onto Cole, and Cole was still weeping. I went over to them and crouched down, placing my hand on his shoulder, which was partially covered by Rachel's arms.

"Do you want to stay here?" I blurted, hardly thinking about it. I only figured it would be tough to go home and sleep in an empty bed…*their* empty bed.

"Would that be too much to ask?" he forced out, trying not to completely fall apart.

"Of course, friend. You're welcome to stay as long as you need to. Let's get inside before the mosquitoes eat us alive. I'll get some clean clothes for you, too," I said, helping him to his feet. He was a little weak, but I pulled his arm over my shoulder and helped him walk to the house.

Once we got up the stairs and onto the balcony, I took a quick glance behind me. The sun was almost done setting, right beyond my new yacht. I cast a longing look toward the serene image, and then returned to my grieving friend.

That night, after Cole finally got drunk enough to pass out, Rachel and I lay in bed.

"Can you tell me what happened?" I asked, breaking the silence.

"It was terrible, Tim. Truly gruesome," Rachel said. She went quiet, and for a moment, I was hesitant to push for details, then considered that she'd probably repeated the story for the police enough times to be a little desensitized.

"Go ahead. I'm ready," I urged her to continue.

"Well, when I first got there, everything seemed normal. We were supposed to meet up, so I didn't think anything of her not being outside and ready. But then I went to the front door and realized that it was open. I knocked a few times, but she didn't answer me or anything. I just went in." She paused.

"Thinking back on it, I don't think I should've done that." I nodded, silently agreeing.

"Anyway, I went inside and looked around. It was so still. I've never been inside their house before, but nothing looked off. It looked like ours, clean and homely. I kept calling for her. Eventually, I made my way outside, near the pool. That's when I saw the bags. Five big black trash bags. There was blood everywhere. I got scared. I didn't want to touch anything. I knew something terrible had happened. So, I called the police."

Rachel's face was wet with tears, and she couldn't talk about it anymore. I told her not to try. I didn't need to know more. We lay in bed, and I held her from behind. When I could feel she was asleep, I turned around and cried.

Over the next few days, I stood by my friend's side. I took some time off from work to help him to plan the funeral. Stacy's remains were so mutilated that Cole didn't want the body shown, so he opted for cremation. Understandably, he hadn't been himself lately. He'd been spending a little too much time at the bars, and I'd been with him, trying to make sure he was doing okay. After he got drunk beyond feeling anymore, and was ready to go back home, we'd stumble back to my house, and he'd fall asleep in the guest bedroom.

I tried multiple times to get more details about what exactly happened to Stacy. Rachel seemed to be the best source for that. The police left out many of the details that I got from Rachel, and it seemed that most of the news stations were only covering her murder in the same ways as the other murders.

There was only one mention of anything that differentiated Stacy's from the other murders. The police found a gem in her clothes, a rare one. It was only mentioned in one article that I saw. The gem sounded familiar, but I couldn't pinpoint where I remembered it from. Rachel wasn't ready to talk, so I decided to ask Cole his side of the story when he was ready to discuss it.

Since I'd been spending my time taking care of him, Rachel hadn't been home as much. In fact, I thought it was getting a little excessive. She'd been spending a lot of time at the 'office'. She'd leave at around six every morning and not come home until about eleven at night. Eventually, Cole got me drunk enough that I called her out on the noticeable bullshit.

After several days, I walked into our bedroom after saying goodnight to Cole. Joe was already asleep, tucked in by Crystal, the nanny who had recently joined our household. We had decided to get a nanny for a few weeks, so that I could focus on helping Cole while Rachel could concentrate on her practice and therapy. Crystal ended up being a huge help to us. Rachel and I had already agreed that we would continue to call her in whenever we needed her.

I sat on the edge of the bed, drunk and waiting for Rachel to arrive home. When she finally did, I noticed that she was dressed in a tan-colored jacket. She came into the room and took the jacket off in front of me. Underneath, she was wearing a black négligée and no underwear. She came towards me with that look in her eye that I knew all too well.

After having sex and getting back into bed, my eyes started to feel heavy. Before I dozed off, I had to tell her my thoughts. I knew I wouldn't consciously be able to say anything to her unless I was in my current state. Drunk.

"I think you're cheating on me," I said, and with that, I passed out. I don't remember anything after that for the rest of the night.

In the morning, I woke up with a killer headache. I sat in bed for a good fifteen minutes, replaying the night in my head. Trying to remember anything about what Rachel said in response to my bold statement. Like most mornings, Rachel was already out of bed. I lay back down. Cole wouldn't be awake for a few more hours. Eventually, I drifted back to sleep.

I wasn't sure how long I was out for, but I woke up startled. There was banging on the bedroom door. Then I heard the reason for it.

"Yo, Tim! Where the fuck is my morning Advil and orange juice?" Cole yelled with a little bit of laughter in his voice.

"Get the fuck in here, you dick," I yelled back.

He opened the door, and I was happy to see a smile on his face. Usually, I didn't get a smile, especially not this early in the morning. Speaking of morning, I glanced over at the clock; it read 11:46. Joe was probably at school and Rachel at work.

Cole and I sat there, chatting. It seemed like his spirits were doing much better.

"I think I want to head back home today. Can you come with me?" he asked. He hasn't been home since she died. He'd sent me on a few missions for clothes and such, but he hadn't been there personally.

"Of course, dude, you know I'll come with you," I said, but quickly added, "but after we get a beer. The bar's about to open, and that's the best cure for a hangover."

Cole laughed in agreement, and with that, we got ready for our day.

We stayed at the bar a little longer than expected, but we did grab some food, and it was light outside when we left, so we were still on the right track. Once we left the bar, it only took the usual ten minutes to get to Cole's house.

Once we pulled up, Cole asked if we could just sit here for a minute. The minute turned into about five, and we were both silent the entire time.

Cole broke the silence, "Now's as good as ever." With that, he unbuckled his seatbelt, opened the door, and clambered out of the car. I followed. He paused for another moment once we reached the front door, as if he was nervous about stepping inside. He entered the passcode to the front door entrance. There was a beep that let us know the door was unlocked, and he slowly pushed it open.

He stepped one foot inside, then the other. I stood behind him, waiting to see what move he made first. All of a sudden, it's like a switch flipped inside him, and he started walking around. He acted completely normal. Without worrying about what memories he might ignite, he made his way around the house. I stayed just a few feet behind him but still followed his every move.

"This isn't as bad as I thought it would be, especially not after the liquid courage." It was nice to see him joking like this.

"I'm sure the worst time is the first time," I replied, unsure of what to say to comfort him.

"Honestly, I had no idea what to expect during this. But I think you're right. I didn't need to get anything either. I just thought it was time to get past one of my many struggles since she died. You want to head out?" Cole said, unable to actually say her name.

With that, we left the house empty-handed. It was time for Cole to phase himself back into his everyday life, and he was on the right track. We decided to head back to my house and sit on the yacht. We drove back and went inside. When I got inside, I headed to the fridge to get some beers. That's when I noticed. There, on the refrigerator, a poem.

You think that I'm cheating

Tonight, you can rest assured,

I would never lie to you

Yes, I'm cheating,

I don't mean to leave you hurt,

It was never my intention to find someone new

I stood there, holding the poem in my hand. I was dumbstruck, thinking she was bold for pinning her feelings to the fridge like that. I didn't want to keep looking at it, and I sure as hell didn't want Cole to see it. I stood over the garbage can with the poem in my hand. I grabbed the lighter and set the paper on fire, dropping it into the can. I got my composure back together, grabbed the beers out of the fridge, popped the tops off, and then walked outside.

I met Cole in the backyard, near the dock. I had fishing poles in hand, and I had the beers; what an iconic duo we are. We started joking around and headed out to get on the yacht. At first, we didn't even fish. We just sat there and drank. After about two hours of just sitting there and drinking beers, we got our poles together and started fishing. We weren't fishing to keep or eat; we were just fishing to pass the time.

Before either of us realized how much time we'd spent on the yacht, I heard footsteps running in the grass. Joe. I glanced over to see her running up the dock, and she had her pink fishing pole as well. I got off the yacht to help her on board.

"Hi, Daddy," she said cheerfully.

"Hi, Peaches. How was school today?" I picked her up and sat her on my lap, forcing myself to put down the beer in my hand.

"It was good, kind of boring today. There's only a few more days left, and I can't wait for summer!" Joe had been talking about summer a lot lately. Ever since we got the yacht, she'd been wanting to go back out on the water for another weekend trip.

"Hang in there, my dear. Soon, you'll be out for the summer, and we can do anything you'd like."

"Yay, I can't wait. Can we do some fishing?" And with that, I set her up in the right spot while Cole stood up and cast his line into the water. I followed once I had Joe's line in the water. It was relaxing, and Joe was so content with fishing that she didn't talk because she was worried they would be scared away.

We all sat there in silence for a while, but eventually, Joe got hungry. We decided to head inside and ask Crystal to make some food for us. She'd grown accustomed to our irregular schedule and didn't mind adding some *ad hoc* cooking or cleaning to her list of duties. I was getting to like having the nanny around more and more.

Crystal suggested burgers, and we all decided it was a good idea. Cole and I thought they'd go perfectly with our beers. We hadn't eaten since earlier in the day, so just about anything sounded good to us at that point. Joe, Cole, and I sat and watched Crystal make the dinner. Honestly, I had barely talked to her before, but I had to admit, she was rather beautiful.

In her twenties, with long brown hair that had hints of purple at the ends, she was what I would consider to be average height for a woman. I wouldn't say that she was 'my type', but she was definitely someone you would notice if you were just passing her on the street. Even her voice sounded gentle, like she was meant to be around kids for a living. What I liked the most about her was that she treated Joe like an adult. Some of the nannies I'd met spoke to children with a slightly higher-pitched voice, which was annoying. Crystal believed that talking to them like babies made a child act more like a child. I really liked her approach to teaching Joe to be an outstanding little lady.

After the burgers were cooked, we all ate together. Rachel wasn't home yet, which was fine with me. I had no idea how to confront her at that point. Plus, it meant that I could really do whatever I wanted since she wasn't home to badger me. With that in mind, I decided to invite Cole to come to the bar with me. Naturally, he agreed. I gave Joe a hug and kiss goodnight before Crystal tucked her in, and we made our way out.

While we were there, I got a text.

When will you be home? I'm on my way now. We need to talk.

Rachel. Interesting. What could she possibly have to say to me that she couldn't put on a piece of paper and stick to the fridge? I decided to ignore the text; it wasn't important enough to me. She said what she said, and she had the time to put it on paper. She didn't get to make the rules anymore.

"So, I saw the letter on the fridge this morning. Want to talk about it? I figured you'd say something during the day," Cole said, looking at me sympathetically.

"No, I don't even know what to think about it yet," I said, then faced the bar, "Bartender? Can we get some shots over here?"

"Well, I think that you're a great guy. Just remember, it was Rachel who did wrong. There's nothing you could've done that would be equal to what she did," he said as if that made me feel any better.

"Yeah, I'm not beating myself up over it. She texted me saying we need to talk, but I have nothing to say to her at this point."

"You know what we should do?" he asked. Before I had a chance to respond, he answered the question himself, "We should find out who she's cheating on you with. I'm sure it won't be difficult; we'd just have to do a little snooping around."

It did sound like a good idea. "Alright, I'm in."

The rest of the night, we figured out our game-plan. We decided that I would go through her stuff to find the name of this man she was cheating with, or at least some details. In the meantime, I'd slowly be taking money out of our account and moving it to mine so that I could take Joe and Rufus and be able to afford to leave her. Cole said that he was more than happy to let us stay at his place since there was obviously room for us there. Of course, this was all decided over a few drinks.

We were laughing during the whole conversation, so I wasn't exactly sure how serious we both were. Although the idea sounded pretty good. I really wanted to know who this guy was that she'd been seeing. After all, that was the least I deserved.

"Last call," the bartender said.

"What the fuck? We've been here for that long? That's crazy. It feels like we just got here twenty minutes ago," I said, admittedly very drunk.

"Y-yeah. Let's get outta here," Cole said, slurring his words.

We staggered to the car and got inside it. Since it was my car, I got in the driver seat. Shortly after we got in and I started the car, the bartender came running outside. She demanded we roll our windows down, and I obliged.

"You cannot be driving home like this. I'll get you a cab." She made a fair point.

"No, no, no. It'll be fine. He's a good drunk driver. The best I know," Cole responded.

"She's right, Cole," I said, looking at Cole. Then, I turned my head to face the bartender. "Call my wife. She'll come get us." I handed her my phone, with Rachel's contact pulled up.

The bartender took my phone, called her, and told us she was on her way. That must've meant she was already home. I wasn't sure if that was a good or bad sign. Within a few minutes, Rachel pulled into the driveway. We both got in the backseat of her car, and the ride was completely silent; not even the radio was on. Once we reached the house, Cole and I managed to get inside. We said goodnight to each other and separated towards our own rooms.

Rachel followed me into the bedroom. She was already in her pajamas, so she was able to crawl right into bed. I stripped down to my boxers, crawled into bed, and tried my best to fall asleep. I could hear light snores coming from Rachel. I tried to lie there and drift to sleep, but my mind was racing too hard. I decided to get up and walk to the living room. I turned on the TV to one of those early morning infomercials. Apparently, that's what I needed because it didn't take long for me to nod off.

I woke up to Rufus jumping on me. That meant Rachel was back from her morning workout. Normally, Rufus slept in Joe's room, but every morning Rachel let him outside and took him with her so he could do his business. Sure enough, once I sat up, I could hear that Rachel was in the kitchen making breakfast.

I started to get up when I realized that there were muddy pawprints on the floor. Rufus must've been playing in the dirt. But it wasn't raining; in fact, it hadn't rained in a few days. Unless Rufus was digging a hole with Rachel this morning or playing by the water, there was no reason his paws would have been this dirty. Besides, Rachel's morning run was only around the blocks surrounding our house, where there was no loose earth.

I wasn't in the mood to talk about this, though. I decided to ignore it and get ready for my day. If Rachel wanted to clean up, she could be my guest. Instead, I decided to get up and start my day.

I looked at the living room wall to see what time the big clock said it was. It must be Saturday. Rachel seemed to be in no hurry, which meant that she didn't have a patient to get to. Or was it Sunday? Truthfully, all the days seemed the same lately.

"Are you ready to talk to me yet?" Rachel said, walking towards me with a cup of tea in hand. *'Ass-kisser,'* I thought.

"Ugh, nope. It's too early for this, and I don't really have anything to say to you," I replied.

"Tim, we can move past this."

"We? Or you? I'm sure you can find it in your heart to forgive yourself, but I can't. We have a family, and we have done so much. You literally threw everything away. For what? Sex?" I muttered, my voice tinted with bitterness.

"Not sex, we don't have sex. It's just emotional. He's helped me through this tough time. He's been my therapist in all this," she said, saying it as if she needed me to understand.

"Your *therapist*? You've got to be kidding me. You've been seeing him for months now? I thought you said your therapist was a female. Also, why didn't you come to me before you went to see someone else about this? I don't do enough for your feelings?" At this point, I felt hurt. To think that she went to someone else before she felt she could talk to me about her challenges.

"It's not like that, Tim. I didn't mean to develop feelings for him. It's something that is actually common. You see, when someone is there to help you work through emotional times, it's easy to grow attached to them. That's what happened. And that's it, I swear. We don't go on dates, and I don't see him unless I'm feeling agitated about the things going on near us," she said, trying to downplay the situation.

"So, you're cheating on me, but not physically. Just emotionally? And it wasn't intentional, but it's helped you through this tough time? What exactly is the 'tough time'?" I asked, just to be clear.

"Yes, and it's been since those killings started. I haven't been able to shake the anxiety, and it's really taking a toll on me." She got me, suddenly I felt bad for her.

"Alright, then end it. End this cheating spree, and over time I can forgive you," I said, putting my best deal on the table.

"No."

"*No?*" I repeated.

"No, I cannot leave this relationship. Not until I feel complete again." Complete? What the fuck!

"Rachel, I think this conversation is over." With that, I got up and went to take a shower.

After getting out of the shower, I heard sounds from the living room. The noise most likely indicated that everyone else was awake. I got dressed quickly, putting on a pair of jeans and an old T-shirt. I opened the door, leaving the bedroom, and got smacked with a strong aroma of bacon. I admittedly got a little too excited about this and speed-walked to the kitchen, where I found everyone else indulging in their food.

Everyone said, 'good morning', which sparked the morning conversations. We went around and asked what we were doing for the day. Rachel said she was staying home and doing some paperwork – which was no surprise to me. Joe wanted to go to the park, and Cole said he would be going back to his house and figuring some stuff out on his own. That just left me. I decided to take Joe to the park so that Crystal could do something else with her day.

After eating, Cole headed out pretty fast, as if he was in a rush. I assumed he wanted to get the day over with. Before he left, he mentioned that he might spend the night there, but he wasn't sure yet. He had to see how spending the day there would be. Plus, he had a lot of food in the fridge that would take a long time to clean out.

I waited for Joe to get ready so we could hit the park, which meant I had to sit there with my cheating wife. I was glad we sat in silence because I didn't want Joe to hear me curse out her mom. As usual, Joe took much longer than she should've and came out of her room with a beach bag full of things to keep herself entertained.

"Joe? You don't want to just play frisbee?" I asked her.

"No, I'm too old for that now. I want to do things by myself," she replied, which seemed like a valid answer. I grabbed the frisbee just in case, and we left for the park.

As we left, Joe decided she didn't want to go to the park we initially decided on, so we headed in the other direction, to another spot she'd grown to like. This choice was clearly not a good one. Once we reached the park, we saw multiple cop cars in the parking lot, accompanied by ambulances and the always-dreaded coroner. I tried to hurry out of there, but the number of vehicles made that hard.

"Woah!" Joe said from the backseat. "What's in that black bag?" she asked.

I decided to be honest with her. "It's probably a dead body, honey. Someone must've recently died here."

She didn't say a word. She was either too scared to talk, or she didn't know what to say.

"Can we just go home?" she asked anxiously after we got out of the parking lot.

"Yes, my dear. We can." I didn't think either of us felt like hanging out at the park after that. As we made our way home, we saw several news vans passing us, undoubtedly heading to the scene. I figured I could catch what happened later. I just had to turn on the news.

Sure enough, once we got home, Joe and Rufus went outside to play, and I turned on the TV. It was a Breaking News story, probably interrupting whatever show was on. Rachel walked into the door, knowing we were home.

"What happened?" she asked.

"I'm not sure, but I'm assuming it's another murder. It was at the park Joe wanted to go to."

"What?" she barked. "Joe saw it?"

"Not the murder, but the body in the bag and the cop cars, yeah." I'd be much more agitated if my daughter saw a murder happen. Also, I'd probably be at the station or the crime scene still.

"Tim, why would you let her see that? And why would you get so close to all of that? You could see it all half a mile away from the park. Unless, of course, you didn't go to the park you said you were going to." Classic Rachel, trying to put the blame back on me.

"Whatever, Rachel, I'm trying to see what happened," I told her, directing my attention back to the screen just in time for the story to begin. Luckily, Rachel didn't say a word.

Another killing, presumably by the same killer who's been stalking our streets. It looks to be another woman, which follows the pattern. The police are urging everyone to stay safe out there and stay aware of your surroundings. The police aren't sure who the killer is. The previous suspect was released from custody due to lack of evidence.

Although the police haven't given any more details, it's assumed that today's victim today was also decapitated and dismembered. Much like the other deaths, police are still unable to release any information about the type of weapon being used to kill these women. Stay tuned to this channel to receive the latest updates. Now, back to our regularly scheduled programming.

By the time the anchorwoman was done talking, Rachel had heard enough. She was already out of the room. However, she came back shortly after with her coat on. Under the coat, she was dressed like she was ready to go somewhere.

With one word, I knew where she was going. "Therapy," was all she said before heading out.

Shortly afterward, Joe came inside, asking where her mom was. I said she had to run some errands, and she would be home later. Joe, Rufus, and I curled up on the couch and watched a movie. Rufus was getting very large at this point, definitely too big to be the lapdog he thought he was.

Once Joe fell asleep, I got this crazy idea to see if I could find out who this 'therapist' guy was. I went into Rachel's office and started digging through papers. I had to work cautiously because I knew she'd be able to tell if I left things in a mess. I didn't learn much, but I did find a statement to her private bank account, which I didn't even know she had. It turned out that a large withdrawal from our account was used to fund her private account.

She needed the money for a reason, but the only information on this statement was the $12,000 deposit. I was a little irritated that I couldn't find anything else on the account. It had been a few months since she opened it. That made me wonder even more, what other withdrawals did she sneak around me?

I decided to call it quits on looking through papers because all I had to do was some research on our account to see how much she'd been transferring out. That would give me a better idea of the scale of money she'd been spending lately. I left the room looking just the way I found it and headed to the living room. But first, I stopped by my office to get a pen and paper to jot down all the fishy transactions I found.

Sitting on the couch, I opened up my banking app and started writing down the cash withdrawals.

$12,000—1/20

$12,000—2/20

$12,000—3/20

$12,000—4/20

It was always the same amount, on the same date every month. How did I not ever pay attention to this? I guess I never thought of looking into her financial transactions the entire time we were together. It only occurred to me to check the balance when I went into our bank account. I was never concerned about what was happening with our cashflow. I was only worried about us running out of money, like what had happened when I was a kid jumping through foster homes.

This made my concerns even more valid. It was time that I got my own account and moved some emergency funds. Even if Rachel found out about it, there was nothing she could do without telling me what she was doing with her bank account. Plus, with advances in technology, I could just open a bank account online. So, that's what I did. I opened a bank account with a bank where we didn't have our joint account. I learned that trick from Rachel.

I wrote myself a $50,000 check and deposited it into my new bank account. Assuming the funds got transferred, we'd still have a lot of money left in our account. It was my turn to take advantage of this situation. Luckily, I didn't need any additional approval from the bank to deposit the check in my new account with Mobile Deposit.

Afterward, I went to the couch to see if there was an update on the latest murder. I tuned in just in time to see them start the story.

SERIAL KILLER'S LATEST VICTIM

IDENTIFIED

The headline read across the bottom of the

screen.

"Police have confirmed that the latest victim of the Mercer Island Murderer has been identified as Carla Adams of Mercer Island. Carla, 31, was found dead at another local park. Carla was last seen nearly a week ago, according to her boyfriend, Fredrick Kassie. However, this wasn't unusual behavior for Carla because of her naturally busy lifestyle, say her parents. Carla was best known for her charity work in the community. She spent much of her time at local food banks, clocking in nearly 2,000 hours of volunteer time at one of the many shelters she visited regularly. The few people we were able to talk to about Carla all mentioned that she wanted to be in the police force. She recently concluded an internship with the local force and had taken several safety training programs offered at the local station. It has also been confirmed that Carla's donor card from the local fertility clinic is missing." The news anchor paused and then continued with the story.

"Police are saying this is the work of the serial killer who is wreaking havoc on the island. This is the fifth murder found with ties to the killer. The perpetrator of these heinous crimes remains at large, and police are urging everyone to stay safe. They are advising female residents to avoid going outdoors alone, and to stay home at night." The face of the victim flashed onto the screen, as well as images of the park where she was found. It was terrible to see that there was another victim, especially someone who seemed to have such a good heart.

"There will be a press release later this week. Stay tuned to our channel to watch live." The news anchor's expression switched from somber to casual as he

changed the subject with practiced ease. *"Now, Amanda, how's that weather looking for the week?"*

CHAPTER 17

It had been two months since I opened my own bank account; it was June. It has also been one full year since we packed up and moved to Washington. I didn't know so many things could go wrong within a year. Things had been spiraling downhill since the day we got here.

Rachel and I had been keeping our distance. As far as I was concerned, she didn't exist. She hadn't been willing to leave this guy, and in my opinion, she didn't think very highly of me. Since Cole had been back in his own house, I'd been sneaking over there whenever I got a chance. We'd also been spending probably too much time on the yacht. But to be fair, it was the middle of summer, and the heat wasn't being kind to me.

Work was a pleasant distraction that helped keep me away from Rachel. The only downfall to steering clear of Rachel was that sometimes it meant staying away from Joe and Rufus, who had been growing on me. I'd made it a point to take Joe and Rufus out on the yacht with me during the weekends. The last thing I wanted to do was push away my daughter while trying to avoid my wife.

I still had no idea who she'd been cheating on me with, but I'd been working up the courage to call the cellphone company and find out who Rachel has been contacting the most. Eventually, I took the plunge. I was still at work, but my lunch hour was coming up, so nobody would think twice about me being on the phone.

I went to the app to get the phone number for customer support, but I realized that I had no idea what the password was. Rachel handled the bills, so I had no need to remember the details. However, my name was on the phone account, and the statements were addressed to me, so I was pretty sure I'd have access to the information. It took far too long to get through the automated menu and even longer waiting on hold. After 32 minutes, a real person answered.

"Hello, I'm looking to get the phone records for one of the cellphones on my account," I told the operator.

"Hello, yes, I can help you with that. Can I get the last four digits of your social or your account number?" she asked. I rattled off my account number, and it took a second for her to pull up my account.

"And may I ask who uses this number?" she asked.

'*Shit,*' I thought. I felt like I had to lie. "It's my daughter's phone. She's young, and I just want to make sure she's talking to the right people."

"Alright, we understand that," she said. She paused for a moment and then said, "The best we can do is get you a list of the phone numbers she has been in contact with for the last month. Anything else, and we will have to take more precautions."

"Okay, that'll work. I really just need a list of the numbers she contacts the most and how often she contacts them."

"Alright, sir. I will send them to the email on file. Does that work for you?"

"Yes, that works. Thank you. Have a good day," I said, then hung up.

For the next ten minutes, I sat there hitting refresh on my email, waiting for that message to come through. After that, I started to get nervous. A part of me thought that maybe the email on file was Rachel's. I went to look at what email was on file, but then it dawned on me once again, I'd forgotten the password and couldn't get into the account, even if I wanted to. I went to reset that password when my computer dinged, letting me know that a new email had arrived in my inbox.

And there it was. The information I'd been waiting for. It must've taken longer to send because of how big the attachment ended up being. '*Holy shit,*' I thought. '*How many numbers are in this document?*' They must've included her phone activity for the entire year by accident. I was nervous to actually look at the document, so I decided to print it first before looking at it. That way, I could compare numbers to what I already knew and then go from there.

Fourteen pages printed. This had to be both texts and phone calls.

They were also in numerical order, so the top nine pages were filled with numbers that had less than the ten digits. I just assumed that these were the numbers that told you when you'd placed an order or if there was activity on your credit card. I skipped all of those. Then, I went to the numbers that were based in Chicago and crossed all those off. I was pretty sure she was not cheating on me with someone in Chicago.

After taking all those numbers out, I ended up with about 140 phone numbers. Fortunately, they included the number of times they'd communicated through text and calls. There was one number that really stuck out at me. Within the last month, she'd called it 47 times and sent 429 texts. Out of curiosity, I went to find my own number. Zero calls, and three texts for the entire month.

After the most frequently contacted number, the second most contacted wasn't even a fraction of that. The second highest came in with nine phone calls and no texts. That had to be something for work. Unless she contacted her new boyfriend by email, the top number had to be the guy.

I sat there, staring at the number. Should I call it? Should I throw it away and act as if I'd never seen it before? A chuckle escaped my lips for a second, till I realized I was laughing out loud. Of course, I was going to call it, and I would never throw it away. I'd need it for proof in the future, I was sure. But I couldn't phone it immediately. I put it in my top drawer, the one with a lock on it. I locked that sucker up and left it there, putting it out of my mind till I needed it again.

I finished the rest of my workday and headed home. I was excited to go home, not just because it was Friday, but also because I knew Rachel wouldn't be back till late. Her pattern had been kind of scattered, but it seemed linked to the murders. When there was a murder, she spent a lot of time with her 'therapist'. But, once the murder talk simmered down in the town, she chilled out with the 'sessions'.

Speaking of murders, the serial killer had killed a total of five people…five different women. Almost all the victims were in a state of severe dehydration before being decapitated, dismembered, and shoved into black garbage bags. It was like the killer kept them locked up long enough that they couldn't defend themselves. Then he killed them, cut them up, and tossed them out for the police to find. It was almost like a game. The worst part? They were all good women. He only killed sterling citizens.

The town held a vigil service for the fifth victim, Carla Adams, at the park she was found in. Rachel thought it would be a good idea to go and show support. Plus, she wanted to show a 'united front' in front of the rest of the community. We asked the nanny to watch Joe for the night so that she wouldn't have to tag along.

When we arrived, we each got a candle and one of those boats that floats into the water and disintegrates after a few hours. This was my first time attending a vigil, but I knew that they were doing things their own way for this one.

Several speakers shared a few words about Carla. We missed the first two, her parents. But the third person was the sheriff, who wanted to talk about the murder to raise awareness about the killer.

"Carla was young and had much of her life to live. Since she did internship work for the Police Station, she knew what to do to defend herself. The killer was just one step ahead of her, but that didn't mean she didn't put up a fight. Her defensive wounds proved that she wasn't willing to give up." He paused. "Carla had extensive training for situations like these, and that's why we were able to pull DNA from the killer off of her. She had scratched the killer, and there were skin cells left under her nails for us to test. We were able to run this DNA through the system; however, no match came up." He looked up from his note card, not needing to read what he said next. "This means that the killer hasn't had any previous convictions. The killer has never been arrested. This killer is smart. Too smart. I urge everyone to be more careful when they go out until we apprehend the perpetrator." He thanked the gathering and exited the makeshift stage.

A group of girls standing in front of us began to whisper among themselves.

"I heard she was found in the middle of the park. Not even buried," the first girl said.

The second girl looked astonished. "Really? That's crazy. Why wouldn't the killer bury her?"

"Well, my mom said that it's because someone probably saw him…the killer. She said that he was sloppy with this last murder and that this is the one that would get him caught," the first girl spoke again, grinning.

A third girl chimed in, "I also heard that the coroner said that she was killed just a day before she was dropped in the park. And she was severely dehydrated. She nearly died just from dehydration. That means the killer had her for days before killing her. Sick, huh?" She popped the gum in her mouth. "But do you know what I think is even worse? I heard that they found the body with one of the girl's legs falling out of the bag!"

"Eww!" the second girl said.

Rachel leaned in close, "Can we move somewhere else?"

"Yeah, let's get closer to the water," I said, pointing in the direction of the dam.

She led the way, and we moved away from the girls and their disturbing comments.

The cops had been on the news a lot, always giving their latest theory. Since the murders started out spaced apart but were getting more frequent, they thought the killer was getting less nervous. The killer truly believed that they would not be caught. Ballsy, some might say. I'd think just the opposite if I were a killer. But I wasn't a killer, and I didn't know shit about being one.

When we got home, I dismissed Crystal, and she went to do whatever a nanny does on a Friday night. Joe and I spent the remainder of the evening just hanging out. Rachel had said she had work to do and headed for her office. I heard the lock on the door click after she closed her office door. Cole stopped by, and we had a few beers by the fire where Joe fell fast asleep. Cole and I sat there just catching up. He didn't stay much longer after Joe fell asleep.

I carried Joe inside, and Rufus followed me. I put her in bed and tucked her in. Rufus curled up next to her bed and fell asleep quickly. I closed the door, but not completely. I left just enough room for Rufus to slip out if he needed to at all during the night.

I went to my bedroom and tucked myself in. It was late, and I was tired. It didn't take long before I fell fast asleep.

I was not the type to be startled awake, but this night was an exception. My sleep was disrupted by crashing outside the bedroom. Turning on the light,

I was surprised to see that it was four in the morning, and Rachel wasn't in bed. I grabbed the bat that I kept by my nightstand and quietly headed to the kitchen area, where all the noise seemed to be coming from.

The noises kept going; it sounded like someone was making a mess and stumbling around. I turned the corner to get a good view.

I lowered the bat.

A drunk Rachel was shuffling around the kitchen, looking for something to eat. She was singing to herself and making about as much noise as humanly possible in the wee hours of the morning.

I approached her. "Rachel?"

Apparently, I startled her because she loudly said, "Shit!" and jumped a little.

"Rachel," I repeated, "stop making so much noise. Joe and Rufus are sleeping, and I'll be pissed if you wake them up."

I looked at her, surprised to see bruised lacerations on her arm. The scratches were deep enough to bleed, but they seemed to be scabbed over. The light was too dim to tell what color the bruises were, but they seemed to be getting older.

"What's on your arm? How did you get those?" I asked.

"Rufus," she said bluntly. "The bastard jumped on me during our walk when he got excited. He scratched the shit out of me."

I'm not sure why I hadn't noticed them earlier. Probably not paying attention.

She put her finger up to her lip, signifying *shhh*. So, I did just that. I helped her make the rest of her salad – an odd choice for a drunk person, but this was Rachel. She sat down and only ate a quarter of it before she got up and put the bowl back in the fridge. She then walked off, making it into the bedroom. I assumed she fell asleep because I waited for about fifteen minutes and didn't hear any more noises.

I grabbed the blanket and headed for the couch. No way I was sleeping with her in that bed, drunk. For a moment, I sat there, then realized that I had a guest bedroom that was open since Cole had been gone. So once again, I got up and headed to the spare bedroom. It didn't take long till the sun rose, and I was awoken by the sunrise shining through the window. I'd forgotten how bright it got, otherwise, I would've closed the shades. I was a little irritated at being woken early on a weekend morning after a bad night's sleep.

I lay in bed, scrolling through random things on my phone. Once I felt I was ready to get up, I padded to the bedroom to get out of my PJs and into some real clothes. When I opened the bedroom door, I saw Rachel still in bed, which was extremely odd, but so was her coming home drunk at four in the morning.

When I walked in, she rustled around and opened her eyes. It was as if she was moving in slow motion. At that moment, a revelation hit me like a wave. I had no idea where it came from, but I knew what I had to say. I stood there, waiting for her to come fully to. She looked up at me.

"Good morning." A smile cracked her face.

I responded, "I want a divorce."

I turned around and walked out of the bedroom. I couldn't say where the words came from, but I knew in my heart it was the right thing to do. She couldn't have the best of both worlds, and she couldn't take me for a bitch who lay by her side until she was ready.

Rachel bolted out of the room after me. For someone who was undoubtedly hungover, she sure did put a skip to her step.

"W-what do you mean?" she stuttered.

"I'm pretty sure it means I want a divorce, Rachel," I said, knowing a silly question gets a silly response.

"I don't want a divorce. I love you, Timmy."

"How can you claim to love me and still cheat on me? Either we get a divorce, or you leave this other man." I was clearly done with whatever games she thought we were playing.

"Tim, I stopped. I stopped. I'm not seeing anyone else but you. I swear. Don't do this," she said with tears streaming down her face. I almost felt bad for her.

"I don't believe you," was all I could say.

"Let me prove it to you. But please don't divorce me. What about Joe?" she asked, in clear desperation.

"Prove it to me. You have one month. You will come home every day, on time. If I see you lying or not doing the right thing, a divorce will come." I knew it sounded harsh, but my sense of betrayal was overwhelming.

"Thank you, Tim."

"For what?"

"For giving me another chance," she said, grabbing my hand and kissing my cheek. "Now, I'm going to go get something for this headache."

She walked away from me, and I turned to the kitchen. If I was going to be up this early, I needed a cup of tea in my hand.

Since Rachel hadn't walked Rufus, I decided that I'd do that this morning. I went into Joe's bedroom and got him. Hooking up his leash and slipping on my tennis shoes, we walked out the front door. We spent probably thirty minutes roaming around in places I'd never explored. It occurred to me that I'd lived in the area for an entire year, and I hadn't even taken a stroll around the neighborhood. Rufus, on the other hand, seemed to know exactly where to go. He was excited to lead me on his daily route, more than excited.

He walked me to the end of the block, then continued further than that. He stopped, turning around near a house that caught my attention. It wasn't far from our home, and it looked similar to the rest of the houses on the block, but it still stood out in my mind. I pulled Rufus away and continued.

By the time Rufus had had enough, we were home. We walked in the front door, and he headed for his bed. That walk must have tired him out quite a bit. Joe was awake now, and she met Rufus at his bed to give him his morning belly rub.

"Good morning, Daddy," she said to me as she scratched his belly.

"Good morning, honey. How are you doing?" I asked her.

"I'm good. Crystal and I are going to town today."

"Alright, dear. Do you know what mommy is doing today?" The odds were slim, but maybe she knew.

"Yeah, she already left for work," Joe said. Rachel hadn't wanted her to know that she was in therapy, so she still believed her mom worked on weekends.

Joe took off towards her bedroom since Rufus was now fast asleep. I assumed she was going to get ready for shopping, but who knew. I was surprised Rachel had left so early.

A crazy thought popped into my head. I pulled out my cellphone and called Cole. He answered, half asleep, but he was fully awake when I got to the point of the call. I told him to get ready; we were going to see what Rachel was doing so early in the morning. In other words, we were going to spy on her.

I saw Joe leave with Crystal, and then I waited a little longer. I guess Cole really was asleep because it took him a decently long time to get over to my house. I was starting to get a bit worried that he'd forgotten about our plans. He got to the house and came inside while I was making some lunch. He arrived just in time to get a sandwich of his own. We sat down and ate, then got in his car and left.

I didn't want to take my car because I thought that Rachel would notice us. That was the last thing we wanted. I'd only been to her office a few times since we'd been on the island, but I still knew my way to and from the place. We got there in record time. Apparently, we got lucky with traffic. When we arrived, there weren't many cars in the parking lot. We parked a few rows down from the front of her office so we could watch people coming and going without them getting concerned.

We laid our seats back and started to watch. We saw one person leave shortly after we got there. Then, we saw another person go into the shop and come out an hour and five minutes later. Soon after they departed, Rachel and her receptionist left the building. The receptionist stood by Rachel's side, chatting to her while Rachel locked up the building. They looked to be done for the day.

I got this crazy idea to roll down the window in the hopes of hearing them. It was lightly raining, a slight drizzle, and some raindrops got into the vehicle, but I could make out their conversation anyway.

"No, I won't be coming back tonight. Tim and I are working things out," Rachel said. She'd been discussing her personal life with her receptionist. Odd.

"Oh, okay. That's fine. I'll see you here Monday, then? Or should I come in tomorrow, too?" her receptionist asked.

"No, take the weekend off. There's nothing for us to do anyways," Rachel said. There was a pause, but we were slouched down to avoid being seen, so I couldn't tell what they were doing.

"See you Monday, then," her receptionist responded.

Then we heard car doors open and close, followed by two engines being started. One pulled off, and the other followed a moment later. I decided to see where she was going, so I sent her a text.

> **I noticed you weren't home when I got back from the walk. I'm out to eat with Cole, but I'll be home shortly. When are you getting home?**

Seconds later, my phone dinged in response.

On my way home now. See you soon. XOXO.

The *XOXO* was something she used to do when we were dating, but she stopped before we got married. It felt comforting that she was starting this up again, but I wasn't sure how I felt about it. On the one hand, I should feel delighted that she was reverting back to the dating days. They were filled with sex, love, and respect. On the other hand, she was acting like this relationship was new, but she was the only one who had changed during all this. I was still regular old Tim.

Cole and I talked about the exchange, but since we didn't really see much, we decided to head home and call it a day. We stopped at the pizza place by the house on the way. We figured I'd better get home with some leftovers to make sure Rachel believed we had, indeed, gone for lunch. Plus, it was Joe's favorite, so I decided to get her some too. It sounded like a win-win situation.

Cole dropped me off and didn't want to stay, even after I begged for fifteen minutes straight. He said he had things to do at home. This didn't surprise me. Adjusting to Stacy's death had been a challenge in more ways than one. She was the one who had handled everything bill-related, and Cole was trying to manage everything on one income. I told him I would help him if he ever needed it, but he hadn't asked for help yet.

I walked inside, and all was quiet. Rachel must've been in her office, and Joe was still out with Crystal since I hadn't seen her car in the driveway. I decided to find out what Rachel was up to. I walked to the office and knocked on the door.

"Come in," she hollered.

I grabbed the knob, turned it, and pushed the door open. I saw Rachel, but she wasn't at her office desk. She was at her personal desk, the one with the typewriter on it.

"Hi, honey," she said. "I'm just doing some personal therapy. Did you just get home?"

It was nice to see her working through her issues by using her typewriter. Maybe she really was going to change and become a faithful wife again.

"Yeah, I just got home. Just seeing what you were up to. There's leftover pizza in the fridge if you want any. I also got Joe some," I told her, making sure she knew that I went out to get food.

"Okay, I might have some in a bit. I was thinking about making something to eat, but then I got so into writing that I completely forgot about it."

"That's okay. Just keeping working at it. I'm glad to see you using your typewriter," I said, walking towards her. I gave her a kiss on the forehead and left the room. I meant what I said. I was happy to see her at the typewriter.

I figured since nobody wanted to hang out, and I was left to entertain myself, I might as well get a jump on the workload for the next week. Who knew, maybe I'd even get enough done to take a few days off. I had no idea what I'd plan for a weekday, but I felt it was time for a change of routine. Maybe I could take Joe out to the museum or something.

If I'd had enough time, I would have taken the yacht out for a while, but it was already starting to get dark, so I'd have to bring it in just as soon as I took it out. I decided to see if I'd make it out the next day, although forecasts predicted heavy rain. The last thing I wanted to do was get caught on the boat during a storm.

After working for a few hours, Rachel came out of her office, and Joe came home. We all ate together, like a family again, plus one nanny. It was nice to be happy and not have to pretend. We all played together for a while, till it was time for bed. Then we sent Joe off to bed, and Crystal turned in too, while we stayed up. Sex was on the agenda – but something was different, not too different, but different enough for me to notice. Rachel had changed, and I wasn't sure it was for the better. Nonetheless, I enjoyed the intimacy, and I fell asleep satisfied next to my wife.

I woke up in a decently good mood. I was ready to start my day, and I decided to go in to work and get enough done to take the week off, or at least a few days.

I headed straight to my office and started up my computer. While that was warming up, I wandered to the cafeteria and got some hot tea to freshen up my motivation. By the time I got back, my computer was ready to get to work, and before I knew it, I'd plowed through a week's worth of tasks. When I looked at the clock again, it was 7pm – well past quitting time. On a typical day, I would have been home hours ago.

As I was packing up to leave, I got an urge to go into my top drawer and look at that paper I got from the phone company once more. Subconsciously, this paper has been weighing on my mind heavily. I stared at it longer than I cared to admit, and I decided to give that top number a call.

I worked up the courage to type the number in – but from my work phone, though. Whoever it was probably had caller ID, and I didn't want them to have an easy time finding out who I was. The call rang all the way through and went to voicemail. The voicemail was of little use, as it was just a generic message that said to call back or leave a message after the tone. I hung up. Sitting there, I was half relieved that nobody answered, but also half worried that maybe I was going crazy.

I was packed up and ready to head out when the phone rang. Usually, I let these calls go to the office voicemail. Today was different, though. Nobody should be phoning on a Sunday evening, especially not only a few minutes since I called that last number. I checked the caller ID and the numbers matched. I picked up the phone.

"Hello?" I asked, changing my voice and making it slightly deeper than normal.

"Hello?" the female voice repeated, "Did you just call me? Sorry I missed it; I was busy."

"Oh, oh… It's no problem. I was just calling to see if Tilda, my aunt, was there." I made that up on the spot, and for a second, I was proud of myself.

"Um…no? I think you have the wrong number," the voice on the other side said.

"Oh, okay. Sorry to bother you," I said a second before I hung up.

I stood there, thinking hard about the voice I heard. It was a woman's voice, and for some reason, I felt like I knew who it was, but I just couldn't put my finger on it. Then it clicked. I knew exactly who was on the other line, and I was shocked.

CHAPTER 18

I sat in the office parking lot in a complete state of confusion. It was hard to believe that Rachel was cheating on me with her receptionist, but I wouldn't put it past her. The facts were there, though. Rachel saw her assistant every day and spent a lot of time with her. Not to mention the number of times she'd contacted that number. It made sense that if she was cheating with someone, she'd be in touch with that person a lot.

A part of me couldn't believe it. I wanted to think that they just talked a lot because they worked together, but that wasn't how it looked. I couldn't think of a single reason why Rachel and the receptionist needed to be communicating that much about clients. But they could simply be friends. That could explain things. On the other hand, wouldn't they be hanging out if they were friends? I wasn't sure what to think about the situation.

I spent so much time sitting in my car at work, just in denial, that it grew late, and I was sure everyone else was getting ready for bed. After all, it was a Sunday night.

I got home, and, as I had suspected, everyone was fast asleep. I wasn't sure if I was even tired at that point. I figured I'd watch some TV, drink some peppermint tea, and try to calm my nerves. As I made my tea, my stomach started to cramp, and I rushed towards the bathroom.

I was in the bathroom for a good ten minutes, puking. I either had food poisoning, or I was really worked up over the situation. I guessed the latter. My emotions had never made me sick before; it was a weird feeling for me.

Before I knew it, Rachel was knocking on the door, asking if I was okay. Apparently, I'm a loud puker. I lied and told her I had food poisoning, and she went to get me something to calm my stomach. After setting it down outside the door, she went back to bed.

I woke the next morning with a cramp in my neck and a stiff back from sleeping on the hard bathroom floor. I didn't even remember falling asleep, but I was out the entire night. I got up off the floor, grateful that my stomach was feeling better. I got straight into the shower to rinse away the stench of vomit.

It was late enough in the morning to know that there was nobody home. Rachel was at work, and Joe and Crystal were probably out at a park or a playground. I was glad I took the day off; it was much-needed.

I spent the morning the way I would on a weekend, even though it was Monday. I made myself breakfast, sat on the patio, and watched the waves crash. I decided it would be a perfect day to go out on the yacht.

I'd never been on the yacht by myself, but everyone, including Cole, was busy. I grabbed the fishing poles, lunch, and a tea to go. It had rained the whole day before, but the forecast was sunny with rain in the late afternoon. If I was going to get out on the water, now would be the time.

I slipped her moorings, only to realize I didn't feel like fishing anymore. Instead, I just cruised around the waters for a few good hours. It was nice to be able to clear my head while there was nothing around me to distract me. I came to many conclusions.

The first was that, if anything, I should be pretty cool with the fact that my wife fancied another woman. That could be sexy. The second was that I had go through her things again, to see if I could get any more information on what she'd been doing. My first attempt hadn't been all that helpful, but who knew, maybe I'd get lucky if I had more time. The third and final thing was that I needed to find out more about Rachel's office rental from the property managers. I didn't know what I was expecting from that, but it seemed like a good idea. Perhaps he'd give me a key, and I could go set up some cameras to watch her on the inside.

I felt like a crazy person. Spying on my wife and trying to get proof of what she'd been up to. It seemed like my life was the storyline for a scary movie. And in every scary movie, the person looking for answers finds them in all the wrong places. But those were just movies, and there was nothing too terrible that I could uncover by snooping through all her shit. Plus, if it was overly important, she would've taken it to her office or locked it in a safe. If I found anything, it would be because she wanted me to find dirt on her, I told myself.

I forgot to bring the case of beer with me, but luckily, I kept the fridge stocked up on the yacht. I cracked open a beer, then another one, until, within just thirty minutes, I was three beers deep. At this point, I was feeling nice, and I decided to float my way around and just lie at the top of my yacht.

In my beer-fuzzy mind, I looked like one of those women in the movies, draped over the bow for hours trying to get a good tan. Except I was a male, clothed, and I wasn't looking for a tan. For a moment, I was happy again. I just lay there thinking about how far I'd come. From being that kid passed around foster homes, to marrying a *seemingly* perfect wife, then raising an actually perfect daughter. To top it all off, I was almost rich, living on a great island in a great house and spending time on my extremely expensive yacht. I was truly living the dream, from the outside looking in.

But I was on the inside looking inside, and it was not all it's cracked up to be. I understood why people say 'money doesn't bring happiness' because I was experiencing that firsthand. I went from not having any money to having lots of money…but I was not happy. I was happy before Rachel grew distant and found someone else to go to. But now? What did I even have left at this point?

By the time I got back from cruising around on the yacht, I was done feeling sorry for myself. I'd had my moment of weakness; it was time for me to get my shit together and fix all my problems. The best way to do that was to meet Cole at the bar and sit down for some drinks and tell him my game-plan. He really helped me through the process of snooping on wives. He even told me about how he once thought his late wife was cheating on him, so he went through all her stuff – only to learn that she was talking to his family about throwing a surprise party. He looked like a pretty big asshole in the end.

I was sure that Rachel wasn't throwing me any type of party, though. I felt like that was the very last thing she would do. Cole even agreed to help, but I told him that I didn't need it. All I needed was advice because I knew this had a fifty percent chance of going completely sideways. But good advice was what he gave. Cole said to get a rental car so that she wouldn't recognize me. I'd never even thought about that.

Luckily, it was easy to rent a car in a higher populated area. I simply went online and found one.

I picked out a red truck; she never would expect to see me in that. Cole also said that I could park the truck in his garage for some extra stealth. I was pretty pleased that I went to him for guidance because I never would've thought about doing half of it. I guess I was not cut out to be a spy.

We sat there just talking for a while, guzzling down beers like we did every time we were together. Then we parted, him going to his house and me going to mine. Rachel and Joe were both home and watching TV. I was surprised Joe wasn't in bed, but Rachel was being pretty lenient with her lately. I felt terrible that I was avoiding Rachel so much that it automatically meant I avoided Joe.

I decided to put my feelings aside for Joe's sake and suggested we all go out on the yacht that weekend. Everyone thought it would be a good idea, and Crystal was happy to hear she would be getting some time off. I figured I'd need a little vacation after following Rachel around all weekend.

We all sat and watched TV together for a little bit, and then we went to bed. Joe fell asleep on the couch, so I carried her to her bedroom and tucked her in. Rufus followed me and lay down right beside her bed. As I was tucking her in, her eyes opened briefly.

"I love you, Daddy," she said to me, and it made my heart feel warm.

"I love you too, Joe. Sleep tight—" I responded.

"Don't let the bed bugs bite," she said, finishing my phrase.

I left the room and went to our bedroom. Rachel was getting ready for bed, so I did as well. We shared the bathroom sink to brush and floss our teeth. Then I got into my PJs and lay in bed. Rachel had a whole nighttime routine that took much longer than mine. I was fast asleep before she even got out of the bathroom.

In the morning, I woke up and made it seem like I was getting ready for work. In my bag, I packed a pair of sweatpants and a sweatshirt so that I could change out of my work clothes. I left as usual, but instead of the office, I headed to Cole's so I could drop off my car and he could take me to collect my rental. We drove in silence; it was far too early for either of us to strike up a conversation.

He dropped me off right in front of the rental place and then sped away because he still had to get to work. I walked inside and approached the man at the counter, telling him I was there to pick up my rental. When he asked for payment, I gave him the debit card for my private account, not the one I shared with Rachel. Since Rachel still hadn't confronted me about it, I'd been quietly saving my own money to use when I needed it.

I figured this was the safest way to go about things so that Rachel would never find out. If it turned out Rachel wasn't doing anything shady, I hoped I'd never have to tell her about it, and the whole thing could be forgotten.

I signed the paperwork, and he went to collect my rental. He came through the front door after he parked it out front. He handed me the keys and explained the rules about renting. He gave me the return dates and said I had to bring the vehicle back with at least half a tank of fuel. I told him that would work, and I left.

My next stop was Rachel's place. She should've been at work for a while now.

I pulled into the parking lot, and it was a lot busier than it was the previous time when Cole was with me. There were a few cars out front in various places, but because there were so many different small stores, the parking lot filled up fast. I parked a few rows down from her office, in front of a shop that seemed vacant. I was close enough to see who walked in and out, but just far enough away that they wouldn't be able to tell I was watching them. At least, that's what I hoped.

Ten minutes into waiting, I saw a man walk into her office. It was 9:40 in the morning. At 10 am exactly, a female walked out. I assumed they got an hour each, and the man came early. Just as I had suspected, the man left at 11 am. But nobody came in after him. I thought she must have been at lunch, but then there was nobody who came any time after that man for the rest of the day.

I sat there till 5 pm and still nobody else came in. The way Rachel was talking, she had a ton of clients. How was it that on a Tuesday afternoon, she just didn't have any? She was using work as an excuse for why she was always gone, but it was obvious that was not what she had been doing while she was away.

It was 6 pm before she and the receptionist left. That really hit a nerve. They left together, and Rachel didn't need to stay past eleven this morning. Granted, I don't know what she did all day in there, but it sounded kind of fishy. Maybe, just maybe, she didn't have many clients that particular day. Perhaps she was spending the rest of the day on admin and getting ready for other clients throughout the week. I gave her the benefit of the doubt one last time.

They left just like last time, the receptionist waiting while Rachel locked the door, them talking, and then going to their own vehicles and pulling off. However, I had to say that it didn't look like they had a romantic relationship, aside from the connection that may just have been from them working together so closely.

Since they were both gone, there was no reason for me to stay. I left and headed for Cole's house so that I could get my car back. He wasn't home, but he gave me the passcode to open the garage. I switched the vehicles out and changed back into my work clothes. Before I knew it, I was on my way home to pretend to my wife and kid that I was working all day.

I spent the car ride home working on my acting skills. Thinking about my response for when they asked how work was. Also, I had to come up with an answer if Rachel asked why I got home so late. I figured I'd just tell her that I got held up, or I was helping another department. She didn't care to know that much about my field, so she'd believe just about anything.

I walked in with a little bit less energy than I actually had to make it seem like I had a long and stressful day. Half of me wasn't faking it. Staring at a door and waiting for people to walk through it all day can be a strain on the eyes. I greeted everyone, along with Crystal, who was making mac n' cheese for dinner. I was impressed to see that it wasn't boxed. I was always a sucker for a homecooked meal.

We all sat down and ate, Crystal included.

During dinner, Rachel's phone rang a few times, but she just looked at the incoming call and let it ring through. There was only one person I could think of who would be calling her like that.

"Are you going to get that?" I asked after the third time she denied the call.

"No, it's just Grandma; I'll call her back later," she said – as if I were going to believe her. She called her mother 'Grandma' for Joe's sake, so she wouldn't get confused.

"I want to talk to Grandma," Joe chimed in.

"Maybe later," Rachel said to her. "Finish eating."

With that, we were quiet again as we ate. I told Crystal that I could watch Joe for the rest of the night and that she could take the evening off. It wasn't a big gesture as there were only a few hours left in the day, but I wanted to spend the time with Joe.

As I expected, Rachel headed to her office when she got done eating. I knew she wasn't calling Grandma because she would've done that out in the open if that were true. But I didn't care at that point. That night wasn't about Rachel; it was about hanging out with Joe. And that's just what I did.

I spent the rest of the night doing whatever Joe wanted. At first, she wanted to play with Rufus and show me all the tricks she had been teaching him. It only made me think about how much I'd been missing out on.

After we played with Rufus, we went to her room and played with her toys. She had really gotten into dolls, and she had far too many to even remember their names. Every time she brought in a doll, she gave it a new name. I liked that she had an imagination, though. She never used the same name more than once, and she'd created a lot of funky, unusual ones. To be honest, I didn't even think I could spell them all out, and fortunately, she didn't ask me to.

While we were playing, Rufus lay in his bed in Joe's room. There was a bed that stayed in her room and another that was in the living room. He basically followed Joe around anywhere she went. He was pretty good at making a bed out of just about anything. To a degree, I loved Rufus because of how protective he was of Joe. I knew that he would do just about anything for her and would always be by her side, even when I wasn't. The other part of me loved him because of how good of a dog he just naturally was. I gave Rachel credit because she couldn't have picked a better dog.

After a while, Joe told me that she was getting tired, so I tucked her in for another night.

When I went to the living room, Rachel was watching TV. She must've known we were playing and let me have my own time with Joe. That was one thing I respected about Rachel. She often paid attention to what I needed, even when things were bad between us.

"What are you watching?" I asked her.

"Nothing really. I turned the TV on a while ago and never bothered to change the channel. Did you want to watch something?" she asked.

"Um, yeah. Let's catch a movie together. Is that alright?" I asked her.

"Yeah, come sit with me, love."

I went and sat next to her. We lay there together and watched the whole movie. There were times when I could feel Rachel starting to doze off, but then I would give her a little nudge, and she'd be right back up again. It was those small things that I really enjoyed about us. I just wished that I could forget about everything else she'd done.

When the movie was over, we went to bed.

I woke up to my alarm the next morning. I pretended to get ready for work, knowing I wasn't actually going. A part of me felt bad for spying on her while acting like a good husband. Then I thought about what she'd been doing to me and decided my actions were completely justified.

My day played out just like the day before. I got the rental, sat outside her little shop, watched, and waited. I did this for three whole days. Frankly, I was disappointed with what I found; it wasn't helpful at all. There were very few clients who came in over that period, not nearly enough to keep the place open. Yet, she stayed there till the same time every day, and then went home. She acted like she had full shifts and came home right afterward. I don't get how, or even why, she would stay there that late. To add whipped cream and a cherry to the deception sundae, her receptionist stayed there the entire time as well. What were they doing?

I had to go into the office on Friday because I had some weekend work to do. I figured while I was there, if I got any free time, I could call the landlord of her office and see if I could get a key or information on what she might be doing there.

Sure enough, I did have plenty of time to get done with my work and call the landlord. I just had to find the phone number for the property, which wasn't very hard. I did a simple internet search of the area and found the empty shops close to hers. I thought it safe to assume that the same person who owned her shop owned the rest of them. I found the number on the website and called it.

It rang a few times before a gentleman answered it, stating the name of the company.

"Hi, yes. I'm calling to see if you can give me information on a place that my wife rents out," I asked, being honest.

"Um, I've never been asked that one before. But I'm guessing the answer would be no," he responded.

"Well, my name is also on the lease for it, so technically it's also mine, right? And I should be able to get an extra set of keys, correct?" I asked.

"Can I ask why you'd need them if your wife has the keys? Can't you just ask her?" he asked.

I told him my problem, with how I didn't trust her, and she'd been lying and keeping things from me. I said I was just trying to get to the bottom of the problem. He understood, then told me a story about a time when he and his wife were having a fall-out. It seemed like the guy really understood where I was coming from. But, we could've avoided the storytime.

"What's your wife's name? Or I guess your name, if you're also on the lease," he asked.

"Timothy Cardington," I said.

"Ah, yes. Your wife is Rachel, right?" he asked. Which he could have known by just looking at the leasing work.

"That's correct," I said, feeling a little irritated that this was so complicated.

"Well, let me take a little look here," he said, and the phone went quiet for a few minutes; the only thing I was able to hear were papers rustling around. I didn't say anything, I was waiting for him.

After about five minutes, his voice came back onto the phone. "Well, I found some interesting things." He gave no indication of what those 'interesting things' were. It sounded like he was trying to build suspense for some stupid reason, but I wasn't having it.

"And what would that be?" I pressed on.

"It seems that she actually has two places rented. I'm not sure if I can exactly say this to you since you're only on one of them. But it looks like she rents two, right next to each other," he said, with a little excitement in his voice.

"How is she paying for both of them?" I asked. "Because she pays for the one under my name out of our joint account." "Well, it looks like she pays both of them out of the same account. She uses one check to cover both of them each month. You never noticed that the bills were twice the agreed-upon amount?" he asked me, as if I was in charge of the finances.

"Um, no. I guess I haven't," I said, then thought about what I could do. I blurted out the solution, "Could I get the keys for them?"

"Well, I could probably give you a key to the one that your name is also on, but I'll have to charge you for an extra key. The other place, I can't. You're not even authorized to know about it in the first place. I'll get you that key and not tell your wife, if you don't tell anyone about me giving you that information. Do we have a deal?"

"We sure do. Can you mail it to my buddy's house? I don't want her to find out, ever," I said.

"Yes, that'll work."

I gave him Cole's address and my credit card number to pay for the key. He said it would take a few days to make a new one and get it in the mail, but I should have it within a week or so. I told him that was fine, and I hung the phone up.

I called Cole afterward and told him what I'd found. We had a decently long conversation about it, he was as shocked as I was, but he understood the need for me to find out what was going on. It was now clear that she was definitely hiding something, otherwise, she would've said something.

Just like the guy said over the phone, the keys came within a few days. Cole texted me as soon as he got the mail the next weekend. I went to get them from Cole's house, and we decided to grab a beer and talk about my game-plan.

"I think I'm just going to go in one night and see what kind of information I can dig up," I told Cole.

"But aren't you worried that you'll come across some confidential information? Aren't there laws about that or something? Tim, you could get into some serious trouble. Especially if you don't know what you're walking into," Cole stated, making fair points, but seeming nervous about it.

"You're right. But I'm not going to be looking through her client files. I'm just going to see if I can find some information on this other building. Hopefully, she has something out in the open on her desk," I said, really hoping that she did.

"So, when will you do it?" he asked me.

"I'm not sure yet. It will have to be when she's not there. Or that receptionist. But it seems like they're usually both there or neither one is there. I'll just have to play it smart," I told him.

"Did you want me to go with you to be your lookout?"

"I'm sure I'll be fine, but I wouldn't mind you coming just for some moral support."

"That's okay, man. I'll just stay back and watch you figure it out," he said with a chuckle, obviously joking.

With that, we finished up the beers we were working on and headed home.

I didn't sleep well all that night because my mind was just racing. I was wondering what could be in the other room. It could be something crazy, or it could just be a storage space. But then wouldn't she just get a storage unit? I had no idea what she could be doing with that second space; it literally could be anything.

I spent a few days watching Rachel's pattern. She worked her regular shift most weekdays, but then she liked to go in on some weekends. She'd changed her routine after I asked her for a divorce. She had been home a lot more. The only thing I didn't know was her receptionist's schedule. I couldn't take off work to watch them, but I was sure I could just play it by ear. Besides, while I was watching them, the receptionist had always left at the same time as Rachel.

I spent a long time working up the courage to go over there. I decided that I would go on a weekday, specifically a Friday evening. When I knew that Rachel was home with Joe. If her receptionist wasn't there, I'd go inside and check things out.

The next Friday came and went. I was too nervous to head over there. I decided I would go on the Friday after. However, the following Friday, I did the same thing. Over the next few weeks, I tried to find it inside me to snoop on my wife. Then, I had my last chance. It was the Friday before Joe started school again for fall.

I had planned to go out with Cole, and Rachel knew that. I had the perfect cover already. I just had to get Cole on board. I called him, telling him that I still wanted to go get drinks, but not until we'd checked out her building. He got excited and said he would meet me there once he got out of work. He was working overtime too, but I arrived before him and waited in the parking lot.

As I had expected, nobody was in the building; neither Rachel nor the receptionist.

After about 45 minutes, Cole came rolling into the parking lot. He jumped out of the vehicle and came up to mine. I unlocked the doors, and he hopped into the passenger side.

"So, what's the plan, Stan?" he said, cornily.

"We're just going to go right in and get down to business. Look for anything, read everything. There might be something important somewhere in there that they leave out in the open," I said, seriously.

"Okay, let's roll."

We got out, I locked my car doors, and we headed for the front of the building. I got to the office door, pushed the key inside, and twisted it. I heard a click, and we were opening the door.

A small alarm started going off, letting us know that we had to put in a security code, or the police would automatically be called to the scene.

"Shit," I said.

"You don't know the code, do you?" he asked.

"Shh," I said, "I'll just take a few guesses."

I concentrated. I started with Rachel's birthday. Wrong. Then I tried Joe's. Wrong. Finally, I tried my birthday on some whim. Wrong.

I started to panic, thinking of important dates or codes. The alarm was still going off, making me nervous. I knew we only had a limited amount of time before the police were called. Then it practically slapped me in the face. Our wedding anniversary.

The alarm stopped. We both took a moment to calm our racing hearts.

"Dude, that was close as shit," Cole said to me.

"Tell me about it. I'm just glad we got in. I was worried we would have to break some shit," I said, only half-joking.

Cole chuckled. "Alright, where do we start then?"

"You hit the reception desk; I'll head to her office," I told him as I was walking to Rachel's office.

There was a room obviously designated for consulting with clients, and it was clean and minimalistic. Then, there was a small room used for her office and paperwork. I walked towards it, and when I opened the door, my eyes shot straight to the walls. They were indeed a deep red, a shade that matched the color of blood once it hits air. Which meant, at least, that Rachel wasn't lying about the red-soaked clothes I'd found.

The next thing I noticed was the un-Rachel-like mess her entire office was in. Her desk had papers strewn across the surface. She had multiple bookshelves filled with notebooks, books, and other miscellaneous things. I headed towards her desk and went to the drawers. I tried all three of them; all were locked except for the one that held random things like erasers, pens, pencils, and sticky notes. There was nothing useful in there.

Expecting the filing cabinets to be locked, I tried them anyway. Sure enough, they were locked, all of them. I went back to sift through the clutter on her desk.

She had everything from personal to work-related documents spread there. I saw bank statements from our joint account, the bills she was working on paying, and the bill that said she had two places rented here. I took a picture of the last document.

I moved to her work documents. I didn't understand what most of them were for, but I read them anyway. I saw some lists of medciations she'd apparently been researching for clients, but I took pictures to look up later. I then moved onto the bookshelves. I skipped over all the books that she had about therapy and went straight for the notebooks. I grabbed the first one to the left and cracked it open. It was her daily journal.

I put that back, but only because it was an old one. Then I went to the one, all the way on the right of the shelf, and opened it. This one wasn't filled with journal entries. Instead, it had her poetry. I read a few; some were about love and others about pain. I put it down after getting a little teary-eyed. I kept searching for a more recent journal. Finally, I found it. When I opened it, the first entry was recently written. I flipped in a few pages further and found the entry from that day.

I didn't have the time to read them all, so I took pictures of about 50 different entries. I had to go to the journal before that one to get them, but I did it anyway. I felt bad for going back to read Rachel's personal thoughts, but again, she had these sitting out. That was not my fault. Well, not *entirely*.

I went through everything I could and found what amounted to nearly nothing. I called it quits and headed to see what Cole had found.

When I walked out and saw Cole, he was sitting at the receptionist's desk.

"Sarah," he said, pointing at her nameplate on her desk.

I never realized that I didn't know her name, but it didn't make a difference.

"Interesting. What else did you find?" I asked him.

"Oh, not much. Just a bunch of scheduling things. You know she doesn't have that many clients, right? She only has like ten in total. I thought she was successful?" he said, trying to bash her. Honestly, it didn't affect me. I thought the same thing.

"Anything else?" I asked.

"Oh, yeah," he said as a big grin formed over his face. He raised his hand, and there was a key gripped between his thumb and pointer finger.

"What's that for?"

He didn't say anything. He just used his other hand to point. Telling me that it was the key to the place next to us, her other rental. A grin the same size as his was plastered across my face now.

"Let's go check it out, Cole," I said, rubbing my hands together, signifying something mischievous.

Cole practically hopped out of his seat, and we rushed, like little kids, out the door to the office next to us. I couldn't see anything through the windows since there was a curtain that covered them. But I let Cole do the honors of unlocking the door this time.

He opened the door, we stepped inside, and I flicked the light switch.

"Wow!" he said.

"Yeah, this wasn't worth the hype, for sure," I said, starting to walk around.

The room was seemingly empty. Besides the curtains, there was no furniture. There wasn't even a carpet. It looked like the place was under renovation or something because it was nearly empty, not even soap in the bathroom to wash your hands with. We checked out both of the other rooms in the place, and still nothing. In any of them.

We were slightly disappointed with what we found…or didn't. We locked the door and went back to the office. Once inside, we agreed that we'd explored everything we needed to for the day. We locked up shop, activating the alarm again, and left.

We regrouped at the bar near our house and talked about how disappointing our mission was. We chatted over a few drinks, then went our separate ways, telling each other we would get back together soon.

I made it home, and I greeted everyone like I was just out with Cole, even though it was so much more than that. Joe was playing with Rufus, and Rachel was watching TV. I sat down on the couch, and Joe and Rufus came rushing towards me, ready to play.

I got on the floor and played with both of them. They soon got tired, and we snuggled up with Rachel till they both fell asleep. Rachel and I just had an ordinary conversation about work and what we each had planned for the weekend. I told her that I had to go into the office during the weekend. Secretly, I was just going to go over all the pictures I took of the stuff I found while Cole and I were out 'getting drinks'.

She told me that she didn't have anything planned, and she asked if she could take Joe out on the yacht that weekend.

"Sure…I mean, to be fair, Rachel. You were the one who got it for me. You can take it out whenever you want. Plus, Joe really likes fishing out there. I think you might have a good time," I told her.

"Okay, thank you. I'll have to see what the weather will be looking like for the next two days and see when it will be the best," Rachel told me, sounding excited.

"Who knows, maybe Sunday will be better, and I can come out with you two. Plus, it's the last chance we have before she will have to do homework during the weekends. And it'll get too cold to take the yacht out soon; we'll have to put it away for winter," I told her.

I did want to go with them if they went Sunday and I really could have gone on Saturday too, but I'd already told her that I'd be busy. It would look suspicious if I didn't follow through with my plans.

"Let's go to bed, huh?" I suggested.

She agreed with a single nod. I put Joe to bed while Rachel headed to our bedroom. I made sure to keep my phone in my pocket, just in case she felt the urge to go through it, specifically my photos. After all, she did once get Cole's contact information from the device. She was good at being sneaky. I couldn't take any chances. After tucking Joe in, I headed up. Rachel came out of the bathroom almost as soon as I closed the bedroom door.

My jaw dropped when I saw her wearing red lace lingerie. The top was the length of a T-shirt, and it fell just above her butt cheeks, which were hugged by a pair of lace panties. I hadn't seen her in anything like this in what seemed like forever. She was also wearing the benitoite necklace that I got her for

Christmas. It glistened beneath the indoor lights, distracting me for a brief second before I returned my eyes to her body.

I stood there, debating how to approach this situation. While I was thinking it through in my head, she walked over and made the decision for me. She planted the first kiss on my cheek, then she migrated to my lips. We started passionately making out, and then she pressed me back till I was right against the bed. With force, she shoved me onto the bed, my legs still hanging off. She practically ripped off my pants and climbed on top.

After I came, she cleaned up. Without a word, she climbed into bed, but this time, wearing more comfortable clothing. She curled up next to me and fell asleep. I lay there, thinking about that necklace I had got her. Something about it was bothering me, and I decided to get up and take a look at it. On closer examination, I noticed that there was a gem missing. My mind buzzed with questions I couldn't ask while she slept. I took it, placing it in my nightstand, saving it until she asked about it later. That way, I could ask her about it too.

CHAPTER 19

It was Saturday, and my only plans for the day were to go through the pictures and see if I could get any information from them. I had to admit, I was becoming quite the detective. Although I was excited, I was also nervous about finding answers.

When I woke up, I was overly excited to head out. I told her that I was going into the office, even though that was a lie. I packed up my bag, including my laptop to use during my research. I decided to head to a coffee shop and get some tea.

I went to one that I'd never been to before, it was closer to the city, but it turned out to be well worth the trip. They had all the types of tea I liked. It was actually difficult to choose which one I wanted. I love a good coffee shop with a tea variety. I ended up getting a strawberry rhubarb-flavored herbal tea.

I sat down at a corner table with just two seats. They were kind of busy, and I didn't want to be taking up chairs that could be useful to other people. I sat down and watched the people rush around for a few minutes. My tea would take a while to cool down anyway, so it was fine that I took my time.

I grabbed my charger and plugged in my phone. I'd turned off my phone the previous night so that there was less chance for Rachel to see what I'd been up to. I didn't think she would have tried to go through it but, I didn't want to take any chances. My phone had only twenty-three percent charge, so I figured a charger wouldn't hurt. Luckily, I picked a spot by a wall that had a charging port.

I went to my pictures and started with the one I'd taken of all the medications she'd been looking into. I googled every single one of them and even searched for correct doses, just in case my wife was a secret drug dealer or some big kingpin. Everything seemed to be normal, so there was really nothing to worry about there.

I slid to the next picture, which started the journal entries. She seemed to write fairly short journals, and they were surprisingly vague. I guessed they were just for her to vent and get all her feelings out there.

I sat and read every single one of them. Most were about her feelings of guilt. For what? I was not exactly sure yet. A lot of them were also about how well she and I were doing, and our relationship. I was happy to see that she did actually value us. Yet she never referred to the person she was cheating on me with. In all of the pages, she didn't once mention anything about a lover. She only wrote about guilt…but so much guilt for cheating? Also, she would have been with the guy, or girl, when she was writing all these things. She never mentioned breaking it off or even anything about the relationship.

I felt confused about the answers I got rather than satisfied. I left the coffee shop, no closer to the truth than when I walked in.

Rachel had texted me, letting me know that she'd decided to take Joe and Rufus out on the yacht. I taught her only once how to sail it, so she said she wouldn't go far. Besides, I was sure she wanted to get a tan more than she wanted to catch fish, and it was the perfect day for sunbathing.

I called Cole up, asking if he wanted to hang out. Unsurprisingly, he was free. I suggested a bar; he countered with a bar and grill because he was hungry. I told him where I was, and we found a place in between us. He was also out bumming around, so he was closer to me than if he'd been at home.

I started driving, and it only took me about ten minutes to get to the place we'd agreed upon. Neither of us was familiar with the joint, so it would be a nice change of pace. I walked in, getting us a table. I was surprised by how busy everything was today, even for a Saturday.

Cole was right behind me and arrived before I even got my drink order. Luckily, I'd ordered for both of us.

"Hey, Tim. How's it going today?" he asked me.

"Hey. Yeah, things are going fine. Although I read all the pages I took pictures of, and I'm just so confused about everything," I told him, getting straight to the point of this gathering.

We discussed everything that happened. He didn't know what to think after I told him all I'd uncovered.

"The only thing I can guess is that the thing she's feeling bad about is the cheating, and that's why she never mentions it. Maybe she feels so terrible that she can't even tell her journal that she cheated on you. Man, that's fucked up. But maybe that's it, and she's just trying to forgive herself," he said, sounding slightly sympathetic about her feelings.

"But still. Even if she cheated, don't you think that there's a little more to it, from the way she's talking? I don't know. I just feel like that's not what she's sorry for. I even went all the way back to when she was actually cheating, and she never once mentioned it. Isn't that just a little off to you?" I vented to him.

"Yeah, yeah. You're right. It does sound a little bit wacky. Maybe you should go back? I'm sure she'll have different things on her desk another day. It might be helpful," he said, giving his advice.

"Good idea, I'll do that."

We continued our conversation, but it took a completely different direction. Cole mentioned that he was thinking about asking a girl from his job on a date. At first, I was shocked to hear that he was even thinking about going out with someone. But as he kept talking about her, I could tell that he was ready to move on, and I was more than happy for him.

He told me all about her. It started as just a work friendship, but after Stacy died, it turned into a flirtationship. He wasn't sure how she felt about him, but he said it seemed mutual. She was there for him after the death of his wife and then just never left the picture. She sounded really nice from the way he talked about her.

I told him that I was happy that he was ready to move on. He sounded relieved that I gave him my approval. I got the impression that he needed someone's approval so he wouldn't feel like he was betraying his late wife.

When the waiter came back, we ordered a full course meal and began eating as soon as they brought out the appetizers. Since being in Washington, I'd been more into seafood than ever before, so naturally, I got seafood for my main dish. Cole ordered some fancy bar steak that honestly didn't sound good to me at all.

After eating, we moseyed our way over to the bar, where we had a few more drinks. It was only about five in the evening. Still, I figured I should go spend some time with my family, especially before Joe went back to school and summer came to an end. I told Cole he was welcome to come over, but he said he was going to go see that girl he liked and ask her out on a date. I told him to let me know how it went.

I made my way home and was happy to see the family hanging out in the backyard. I walked out there, and everyone was excited to see me, especially Rufus. They had a little campfire going, and they were just about to roast some hotdogs and s'mores. It seemed I arrived at the perfect time.

We enjoyed the night and let it get dark outside. The bugs were terrible, but Joe and Rachel were having too good a time to call it quits just yet. Rufus was passed out but woke up as soon as we brought out the food. He lay at Joe's feet until she roasted a hot dog and gave it to him, then he went back to bed. We all sat there laughing and having a good time until Joe said that she was tired and ready for bed.

We let the fire go out then headed inside. Joe had a few bug bites, so we put on some ointment to help with the itching. Then, we applied it on ourselves because we were bitten up as well. We tucked Joe in, then both Rachel and I headed to bed ourselves. While I was in the bathroom washing up, I heard some clinking noises in the bedroom. I went to investigate and found Rachel lying on the bed, eating a bowl of ice-cream.

"Save any for me?" I asked her.

She produced a faint smile and reached around herself, pulling another bowl out from her side. She shook it, letting me know that I could take it. It was thoughtful of her to get me a bowl of ice-cream without me even having to ask for it. If I didn't feel like she was hiding something sinister, I'd say she was the perfect wife.

We ate in bed, talking about small, random things. We reminisced about how sad Rachel was when Joe went to her first day of school in the area. It seemed like that was a lifetime ago, when it was only a year before. We talked about how different things were then.

The conversation was good. It made me a little sad thinking about how simple our lives used to be, knowing they weren't anymore. We lost track of time, just talking to each other. We hadn't spoken like this in a while, and it was nice to see the sun peeking up while we were still chatting and joking around. We went to bed, knowing we would be woken by a wide-eyed, bushy-tailed little girl and her dog in just a few hours.

It was Sunday, the day before Joe started school again. She had all her things packed and ready to go for her first day. Rachel liked to get a running start on the back-to-school shopping, so Joe had all her things packed for some time now.

None of us had anything planned for the day, and the nanny's position came to an end that weekend. We said goodbye to her, and then we spent the rest of the day playing with Joe, and just enjoying the still-summer weather. We played up until it was just about bedtime for Joe, then we had some ice-cream and called it a night.

Before bed, Rachel went to help Joe pick out her outfit, as she usually did. It was a mother-daughter bonding experience that I was glad not to be part of. I couldn't tell the difference between what was in style and what my great-grandma would wear. They very well could be the same thing, for all I knew.

Rachel came back to tell me that Joe wanted to wear a pink-and-white striped dress with a pair of white tennis shoes. I nodded in agreement, saying it was a good choice. But again, I didn't know shit about fashion.

In the morning, I woke up early enough to see Joe off to school. We'd agreed that we would both drop her off every first day of the school year. This year, Rachel didn't cry. She seemed excited to see her off.

Like the previous year, we took the entire day off to make sure that we were emotionally ready to see her off for yet another year. We decided to get a nice lunch at a place downtown. Most of the schools in the area started today, so it shouldn't be overly busy at any restaurant. Especially with the adults still needing to go to work.

After dropping off Joe, we went back home to get ready for lunch.

"Have you seen my necklace?" Rachel asked me vaguely, but I assumed it was the one I had in my nightstand.

I went to the drawer and pulled it out. "You mean this one?"

"Yeah, why do you have it?" she asked, looking curious.

I let her take it from my hand before continuing, "Why are there stones missing from it?"

"Oh," she said nervously, "I meant to tell you about it. But I felt bad. I have no idea what happened; they just seemed to fall out of their settings. I felt guilty that I didn't notice it when it happened." There was that word again, *guilty*. "I didn't see it till a week or two ago. I promise I will replace them. After all, it's my fault that they were lost."
"But, I thought you just said it was an accident? If it's an accident, then there's nothing for us to worry about. We can just take it to the shop the next time we're in Chicago," I told her, grabbing her hand, comforting her.

We were able to get seated right away at a small table set for two. We sat across from each other, and she ordered a glass of wine.

"And for you, sir?" the waiter asked.

"Actually, make it a bottle and bring me a glass too," I said, reaching across the table for Rachel's hands.

"You've got it," the waiter said and then walked away to retrieve it.

"I can't believe you're going to have wine. You never have wine with me," she said, with the biggest smile spreading across her face.

"Yeah, I know. But I thought we could do something special today," I said, which surprised her in a good way.

Truthfully, I was just hoping she'd get a little drunk and spill some details about that other office or whatever she was using it for. Somehow, I doubted it, though.

We discussed a few things, mostly about how well we thought Joe was going to do that year. It was a little bit of a brag, but she really was a smart kid, and we knew she was going to excel in her classes.

We got our food, ate it, and then sat there and finished the bottle of wine. I had one glass the entire time. I used the excuse that I was driving, and we couldn't just bring an opened bottle of wine home with us. So, we sat there while Rachel finished it.

After lunch, we walked around town. We'd never been to this area, and everything looked so pretty as summer made way for fall. It was still early enough to be hot outside, so Rachel was wearing flowing linen pants and a tank top, almost like what she would wear to bed. I wore a golf shirt and khaki shorts, one of my go-to outfits.

We walked until our feet hurt, then we got back to the car and went to a park that overlooked the ocean. We grabbed a blanket I always kept in the trunk and lay on the grass. Rachel and I rested there, entwined and in silence, for what seemed like hours. Casually watching the puffy clouds flow past us.

We only left because it was time to fetch Joe. We got there only a few minutes before she was let out of school. The downside to getting there on time was that we were last in the long line of cars. We would be waiting a while to get out of there, especially if parents got out to chat. Rachel and I complained about this often, but never to others.

It took us 45 minutes to get out of the school's parking lot. We didn't leave our car once, but apparently, everyone else under the sun did. We weren't too upset about it, though, since it was the first day back. It would get better after this.

We picked Joe up and then went home. The previous year, we'd gone out to eat, but this time Joe said she missed Rufus, and she wanted to spend time with all of us.

When we got home, we sat down in the living room and talked about Joe's first day back at school. She said it was good, but one of her three regular friends didn't want to hang out with them anymore. She said that Amy had found another group to hang out with, and she didn't seem interested in being Joe's friend.

"Oh, honey, that's her loss. At least you have the other two still," Rachel said, trying to make her feel better about the shitty situation.

We talked for the rest of the night. Rachel and Joe made dinner while I sat at the breakfast bar in the kitchen and commented from the sidelines. Rufus lay at my feet the entire time; he wasn't interested in getting into the kitchen. After dinner, we put on a movie, and when that finished, we headed to bed.

I offered to take Joe to school in the morning, meaning that Rachel would have to pick her up. Luckily, she agreed to this. I was glad she did. It meant that she would have to leave work and stay home with her until I got home. This was all apart of my plan to sneak back into her office.

The day went by in a hurry. Rachel texted me, letting me know that she was going to fetch Joe, but she admitted that she forgot to leave on time, and was running a little behind. I was sure she told me this in case there was an issue with school calling to find out if someone was going to pick her up. I finished my work for the rest of the day and made my way to her office building.

It was a Tuesday, but even for that, the parking lot was almost empty. I thought about turning around and going home because of how quiet it was. I was worried I might get caught. But then again, I'd already made it that far, so I figured I might as well go through with it. I wouldn't need too much time; I was going straight for her desk to find something new. I was sure the rest of the office was virtually the same.

I went to the door, unlocking it and typing in the alarm code to disarm it, just as before. I didn't want to waste any time, especially because I didn't have Cole as my

lookout man. I went directly to Rachel's office, glancing around to see if anything had noticeably changed.

It had only been a few days since I'd been there last, but that should have been enough time for her to rearrange her desk and put out some new material.

Sure enough, there was a lot more on her desk than there was during the weekend. I soon realized that it was the same paperwork, plus some new items. The thing that stood out the most to me was a thick envelope, opened, but addressed to me. The address was for our old Chicago home. I'd never seen this before. Attached, by a paperclip, was a typed-out poem.

I don't know how to tell him,

my dearest husband, Tim

My entire heart, full of guilt

But I'm worried that he might leave if he found out

What if he left me and this home we built

I opened it up, shocked by what I found. It was a letter, along with some pictures and information to reach the senders. The senders? They were my biological siblings. I haven't heard from either of them since we were separated in foster care.

A tear left my eye. I had never expected to hear from them again. I barely even remembered their names at times, much less what they looked like. I stared at the pictures before I read the letter. There were five pictures. One of them was of us when we were younger, another of my sister, one of my brother, both of them around our mother, and the last one was of them beside our father's grave.

A few more tears came streaming down my face. I stared at the pictures then hastened to open and read the letter.

Brother,

I know we haven't spoken in years. I hope you still remember us. It's Margret and Nate here. We were recently reconnected, and we were wondering if you would like to reconnect with us as well. There have been so many changes in our lives, and we think it's time to catch up. I hope you read this and get excited to hear from us, and we hope you haven't forgotten about us. We miss you every day. Please reach out and let us know that you're okay and well. We would also like to know what you've been up to with your life.

We miss you, dearly.

With love,

Margret & Nate

After all these years, they'd reached out to me; they wanted to know me. My heart was full of pain and love, all at once. My heart also started to feel anger building up. The date of the letter was just weeks before Rachel decided we should move. She knew this entire time that they were trying to get in contact with me. Instead of telling me, she hid the letters and told everyone we were moving. It had been over a year since they sent the letter, which meant it had been over a year that they hadn't gotten a response back.

I took photos of everything, then put it back. I made sure I took a few pictures of their phone number, too, in case one turned out blurry or they somehow get deleted. Then I left, locking the building back up and heading for home. On the ride there, I found myself driving slower than usual, just trying to let the memories of us as kids flow back through my mind.

I'd honestly never thought this day would come. I'd been sure they were gone forever. I'd tried so hard to suppress the memories, and now I had to let them back in. The good. The bad. The ugly. It was an emotional car ride. I even sat a few blocks away from the house for a while to regain my composure. With all the tears and laughter in the car, I needed a few minutes before I went inside and had to pretend everything was okay.

I spent the night pretending I was perfectly fine, which I'd become pretty good at it. Although, I kept sneaking glances at my phone to look at the pictures my family took without me. Thinking about it now, I wondered how much I'd missed out on and if there was any way for me to be able to catch up. I told myself I would call them the next day, and I did.

I sat there, the phone ringing. There was only one contact number, so I had no idea who I would get on the other end of the line.

"Hello?" a male voice said, answering the phone.

"H-hello," I stuttered in disbelief that someone picked up so quickly.

"Hi, yes. How can I help you?" the man asked.

"Oh, right," I said, forgetting the person didn't know who I was. "Is Nate or Margret there?"

"Hold on," the voice said. In the background, I could hear the man yelling for Margret to come to the phone. Then, I heard footsteps and someone picking up the phone.

"Margret here. What can I do for you?" she asked in a way that seemed almost inhumanly calm.

"Margret, it's Timmy. Your brother," I told her.

"Timmy? Is it really you? We thought you'd never call," she said, suddenly sounding a little emotional.

Her response triggered something in me, making me emotional too. I told her everything that happened and explained that I would've contacted her earlier had I known she sent a message. She understood the situation and told me to come over soon. I had to tell her I no longer lived in Chicago, but I would love to see her.

It all happened so fast. I didn't know what I was saying until I hung up.

I agreed to travel to Chicago to see them the following week. What was I going to tell my wife? What was I going to tell Joe? All of a sudden, she had an aunt and uncle. Was I supposed to keep them away from each other? There were so many questions up in the air from this conversation.

Also, was this the secret that Rachel was keeping from me? I couldn't believe she would actually be worried about me finding out my family wanted to contact me. There was plenty of me to share; it was not like I would have left Rachel after finding out my family still thought about me. At least not back then…

CHAPTER 20

I told Rachel and Joe that I had a business meeting. I explained to Rachel that one of the projects we worked on was giving trouble, and we had to go to the client to redo the entire project. I said I should only be gone one week, but it might be longer. It really was a good thing she didn't question me further. She might have found out that our company didn't do anything like this. Ever.

I had a hard time leaving them, as I figured. But this was the opportunity of a lifetime, and I would've been silly not to take it. Even if I did find out some things that I didn't want to about my long-lost family, at least I would know. This would either be the start of something new and beautiful, or it would be the end of a chapter in my life. I guessed I'd find out over the next week.

I had made plans to leave for an entire week, but I waited to book my return flight. Since I told Rachel this was a business trip, I used my personal account to fund it.

I spent the majority of what remained of the week spending time with Joe, sending emails to my brother and sister, and preparing for the trip.

Joe was pretty upset to see me going out of town for so long. I promised I would make it up to her. I was leaving Sunday afternoon, so I had plenty of time to spend with her. I picked her up every night that week, even if I took her to school in the morning. I didn't do anything but hang out with her until she fell asleep. We even took the yacht out a few times, which she enjoyed every time.

Rachel and I also agreed that it might be a good idea to hire a nanny again while I was gone so that the tasks weren't too hard on Rachel. I actually suggested this so that Rachel wouldn't ask too many questions about my trip.

As Sunday approached, my anxiety began to build about meeting my siblings again. I had no idea what kind of people they were or if they'd inherited any of our parents' shitty traits. I also decided to do some research on the rest of the family. What I found wasn't all that surprising. Our mom had checked into a mental facility to seek help a few years before, and she chose to stay there. Our dad...well, that was a different story. Apparently, he never wanted to leave the drug addict lifestyle, and it caught up with him. He died a few years back from an overdose.

Sunday came, and my family was at the airport, dropping me off. There were a few tears from Rachel and a boatload from Joe. Neither of them really wanted me to go, but they knew that I had to. I got onto the plane and received a text from the number I saved for Margret.

We will be there to pick you up from the airport. Safe travels, Timmy.

With that, I boarded the plane, turned off my phone, and got a few hours of quality airplane sleep. I awoke with the flight attendant letting us know that our plane was descending and would be landing within the next couple of minutes. I was asleep long enough to miss the free snacks and drinks, but I really didn't mind.

When our flight landed, I took out my phone and turned it on. I know that they say to wait until the plane isn't moving, but who honestly follows that rule? Certainly not me. I let it load and get signal, then a few messages came through. One was from Rachel, asking me to text her when I landed. I shot her a text right away. Then, I got a message from Margret, saying that she and Nate had arrived at the airport and were waiting for me to come out. I replied, saying that the plane had landed, and I just needed to grab my bags, and then I'd be on my way.

It took longer than it should've to park the plane and let us out. I rushed to my baggage gate, but it took forever for them to get our bags out. I was probably just being impatient, but everything seemed to be taking longer than normal. I finally got mine and headed for the parking lot.

There were a lot of cars out there, so I called Margret, and we talked through the area so that I could find their vehicle. I told her to stand outside of it and flag me down if she saw me. But to be fair, I'd never sent her a picture of myself, so while I knew what they looked like, they didn't have any clue as to what I would look like.

She gave me a description of the vehicle she was in, and I was able to find her before she saw me. Both she and Nate were outside the car. I approached them with arms wide open.

"How was the flight?" Nate asked me.

"Honestly? I slept through the entire thing. So, good, I guess," I said, being as honest as possible.

"Are you hungry?" Margret asked.

"Actually, I am, a little," I responded.

"Well, let's go get something to eat, then. I know the perfect place," Margret said. We all went to the car, and I threw my bags in the trunk.

"Do you want shotgun?" Nate asked, but I could tell he didn't want to give the seat up.

"Nah, that's fine. I'll take the backseat," I told him.

I never imagined myself debating with my brother about who would get the front seat of the car.

I guess I never imagined a lot of things that were about to happen that week.

We spent the car ride discussing the menu of the little restaurant we were going to. Turned out, Margret lived downtown. Naturally, that meant the place she wanted to go to for dinner was also downtown.

When we got our food, I found out that Nate didn't live downtown, but he much preferred the suburban life anyway. In fact, he didn't live that far away from the first home I'd shared with Rachel. Nate said that he'd been living there for a while, and we'd probably crossed paths at some point when I lived in the area.

We talked all the way until it was closing time. We talked about how their lives had been and how ours were currently going. We all decided to save the heavy stuff for the next day. Then I would be meeting the kids and Margret's husband.

Margret dropped me off at my hotel, and I fell asleep quickly. I woke up to the alarm I set. Then, I called Rachel while I was pretending to get ready for work. This was the best way for me to convince her that I was on a business trip. I doubted she suspected a single thing.

We were going to get food and spend some time out on the water. They hadn't closed the lakes yet, so Margret still had her boat parked out on the water. There was a different feel to the Chicago waters versus the Mercer Island waters. The difference was noticeable, but I liked the change. It had been over a year since I'd been out on these waters.

Once we were far away from the shore, we didn't have an issue with starting a conversation. The first thing we talked about was our mother and father. Apparently, Mom checked herself into a rehab center when Dad overdosed on drugs. It was sort of a wake-up call for her. She'd been sober for nearly ten years. About two years ago, Nate looked her up and reached out to her. She agreed to let him see her, and they'd been meeting up almost every week since. After that, Nate tried looking for both of us. He was able to contact the system and easily get a response to where Margret was. But my foster parents didn't respond immediately to the request.

Nate was able to get in contact with Margret, and they worked on finding me. Then the request was answered, and my foster family gave them my contact information. That's when they sent me the letter. I had explained to them that I didn't get it until the day before I called them. They understood but didn't have a high regard for Rachel because of it. I guess we had mutual feelings towards her at that point.

The rest of the day, we just spent enjoying each other's company and catching up on things we'd missed. We even spent a little bit of time trying to reminisce about the good times, but Margret wasn't old enough at the time to remember much. The conversation was more between Nate and me, but Margret was just as happy to listen.

The following day, I took a taxi to meet all of them. It was Nate, Margret, her husband, and her two kids. Nate said he had a girlfriend, but they weren't serious enough yet to be meeting the family, and he didn't have any kids.

Everyone in the family seemed to be really great and got along together. Margret and Nate talked like they never were apart from each other, and it was good for me to find out all this new information about my long-lost family.

Nate had tried to set up an appointment with Mom, so we could all meet her, but she declined it. She said she wasn't stable enough to see all of us again. I could understand that, although it did hurt a little, knowing she was alive but not being able to see her, let alone talk to her.

At the end of the trip, I was sad to be leaving them. At the same time, I was happy to finally be going home to see Joe again. Seeing how Margret was with her two kids made me want another, but I didn't see us going through the adoption process again. I was fine with just giving all my attention to Joe and making her feel extra special.

I got home after an entire week of being in Chicago. Luckily, Rachel still believed that I was working the whole time, which was a good thing for me. I thought about confronting her about why she had done it, but a part of me couldn't bring myself to ask her. I wasn't even sure if this was the only thing she was hiding from me. If she could hide something like my family, I could only imagine what else she was capable of. I didn't like thinking about it, but I had to stop myself from asking her and blowing my cover. At least, until I knew the entire situation.

Especially when it came to that other unit she was renting. I didn't understand what need she would have for it; it just didn't make sense. Even more peculiar was that there was nothing in it when Cole and I went there. She'd had it for over a year, and it didn't seem like she'd even used it.

I got home on Sunday night, just in time to eat dinner. When I arrived home, Rachel was just paying Crystal and sending her on her way. I was glad I missed it because I never enjoyed that part; it made me feel weird for some reason. Rachel was extra excited to see me, which was surprising, to say the least.

When I walked inside, Joe was there, ready to play. Apparently, she'd been waiting for me all day because Rachel forgot to mention that I wasn't going to get home until later that night. I felt terrible that I made her wait, but I had to remind myself that it wasn't my fault Rachel didn't tell her.

Everything about our Sunday night was normal, almost repetitive. Except, Rachel and I had sex. It was definitely a surprise, and I always accepted these types of surprises. It was nice to see Rachel happy to see me home again. It made me feel like she was really putting in an effort to mend our broken relationship.

Although she was making an effort, and that was duly noted, I still couldn't shake the feeling that something was going on. I decided I would go back to her office to see if I could uncover anything else. Then I'd check out that other office and see if anything had changed there.

If she was redesigning it, there was a purpose for it. Whatever that purpose was, I needed to know. I had no idea when I'd be going back, but I decided that this time, I wanted Cole to be by my side. Not only did I like having him to talk to about all this, I liked having him to be a lookout for me. It was nerve-wracking being both the look-out and the snooper. Plus, this time, I'd have two places to investigate, so I would need the backup.

The next day, I called Cole up. I told him that I had some things to tell him since I hadn't seen him since I got back from the trip and I hadn't updated him about my family while I was there. I also told him I wanted to plan the next visit to Rachel's office. I needed to find out if he was up for coming along. We decided to meet at the bar to plan and talk the next night.

It felt like the day was dragging by, along with the next. I was looking forward to grabbing some drinks with Cole again.

Finally, it was time for me to leave work, pick up Joe, and then go to the bar with Cole.

Over the week following my return, I'd been dropping off and picking up Joe. I figured that it would be helpful to Rachel if I took over the school run since she did the same for me all of the previous week. Since I told her that I had plans with Cole, she said she would get home early as well, to give me enough time to spend with him, which was sweet of her.

That night, Rachel came home when she said she would, and I left just in time to get to the bar at the same time as Cole. We walked in, and both ordered a whisky, mine on the rocks, and his neat. Cole suggested we get a table because he was starving. I agreed, and we sat at our usual booth. He ordered a sandwich, and I got a basket of French Fries.

The conversation started with small-talk, then it moved onto the juicy things. Cole was on the edge of his seat, listening to me talk about my week away visiting family. He stayed on the edge of his seat when I told him I wanted him to come back with me to Rachel's office.

At first, he sounded a little bit hesitant, but he was easy to convince. Especially after I told him that she was still hiding something. We planned to do it the next week because Cole was busy until then. I told him that would work with me too because more would have changed in that time, and Rachel might get further with her plans for the extra room.

We spent the rest of the evening catching up and drinking. At the end of the night, I confirmed the details one more time.

"So, Friday night, just like last time. You'll meet me at her place, and we will go into both rooms again. Right?" I asked him, summing up the plans.

"Yeah, I just hope we don't get caught. Y'know?" he responded.

"I know. It'll be fine, Cole," I said. And with that, I went home to my wife, kid, and dog.

CHAPTER 21

The week leading up to Friday night was so uneventful it seemed to drag by. Cole had been trying to get out of our plans ever since the day after we made them. He felt uneasy for some reason, but every time he expressed his nervousness, I reassured him. He understood how much I needed this. I kept telling him that if I was destined to get caught, I would've been already.

This time was different. When I pulled into the parking lot, Cole was already there. He had scoped the place out and seen that there was nobody inside either of the buildings. There were noticeably more cars in the parking lot, but that was to be expected. A few stores down, there was a boutique that had a massive sale going on. End of season, or something. However, the lots directly in front of the Rachel's two places were empty.

We moseyed over to the door, opening it and entering the code smoothly. I went straight for the office, and Cole went to grab the key again. The office seemed basically the same. There were new papers on the desk, but nothing important, and I breezed through them.

Cole joined me in the office to tell me he'd found the key. Since there was nothing new in the office, we went to check out the other place. There were still curtains covering the windows, so no-one could see in from the outside. I let Cole open the place up, and we walked inside. Cole reached for the lights and flipped them on.

The room was completely furnished. There was carpet, new paint on the walls, even furniture that made it look like a decent little office. This was definitely a significant change compared to the previous time we were there. I was impressed but also suspicious.

"Why do you think she redid everything?" Cole asked.

"Truthfully? I have no idea. Maybe she just wanted to change the way it looks," I responded.

"No offense, but this doesn't really look like her style, Tim." After he spoke, I took a look around.

"You know, you're right. It really doesn't. I didn't think about it until you mentioned it," I responded. The floors were carpeted a deep red, with light brown walls. It really wasn't Rachel's style, and the budget carpet gave it away. Even the furniture looked cheap, which was never her style. The entire place looked more like a showroom than a business space. It's almost as if she were staging it for some reason.

"You know what you should do?" Cole asked me with a devilish twinkle in his eyes.

"What?"

"You should call the landlord and see what she told them she was renovating it for. They might be able to give you a reason. I'm pretty sure that she would need to either notify or get approval for the changes in the place," Cole said to me, which actually didn't sound unlikely.

"You're right. I'll do that first thing Monday morning," I responded.

"You ready to head out then? Since we have nothing else to be doing here," Cole said. I was sure he was just eager to leave.

"Yeah, yeah. Let's get out of here," I said.

With that, we locked up and headed out. While in the parking lot, Cole told me that he and his new lady were going out of town for the weekend. But he assured me that we would be getting together for drinks as soon as he got back again. I agreed and made my way home.

During the early part of my ride home, I thought about all the things going on in life. I was thinking about my job, Joe, Rachel, and even Rufus. There were so many things happening, and I realized that I'd spent far too long worrying about what Rachel was hiding. I was letting so many things just pass me by. I told myself that I would work more on being a family man rather than a snooping family man. But first I had to find out what the office was for.

Towards the end of the drive, I thought about how obsessed I had become with this. I wasn't sure why I felt like I needed to know her secrets. It just seemed like she was hiding something terrible from me. Until I found out what that was, I didn't think I could just 'give up' on my search. But at the same time, I needed to spend more time with my family.

I decided to make a choice based on what I found after calling the landlord of her office. If I learned nothing of importance, I would stop digging into her secrets. At some point, I had to give it a rest. But, if I did find something, I would continue my search.

When I got home, it was dark out, but just barely. I walked inside, and the entire house smelled of homecooked food. The aroma got me thinking pasta, and when I saw Rachel cooking in the kitchen, I knew what she was making. Chicken Alfredo, once again. She would make it all from scratch, sauce too. She was working so hard on dinner that she didn't even notice me coming in.

I walked in and snuck up behind her, hugging her and kissing her neck. I could sense the smile stretching across her face, and then I felt her turning to face me.

"Well, hello, handsome, welcome home." She greeted me with another kiss.

"Hello, my beautiful wife. What inspired this dish tonight?" I asked.

"Just thought I'd do something nice," she said promptly.

A nice gesture, indeed. I went to find Joe and Rufus, who were guaranteed to be somewhere together. And sure enough, I found them playing 'teatime' in Joe's room. Rufus didn't look amused. I turned around quickly so she wouldn't spot me and ask me to take Rufus' place.

I rejoined Rachel in the kitchen and sat at the breakfast bar to watch her finish cooking. I wasn't going to offer my assistance; it looked like she had it handled. She was about halfway through, from the looks of it. We sat there just talking about our day, week, and finally, our plans for the weekend. We hadn't really been communicating well lately, so I decided that I would initiate the conversation. It seemed like she really enjoyed it.

Rachel tasked me with getting Joe ready for dinner. By the time I convinced her to stop playing teatime, Rachel was finished with dinner and had it on the dining room table, ready to eat. I took my usual seat, then Joe, and finally, Rachel.

It was mostly quiet while we ate, but Joe did talk about her day and week, just like Rachel and I did earlier. For the most part, she did all the talking while we just smiled, nodded our heads, and listened to her. Most of Joe's days were the same. But then again, so were Rachel and mine.

We spent Friday night watching a movie and just enjoying each other's company. We discussed things to do for the weekend since none of us had any plans. We decided to spend our time outside, whenever the weather let us.

It wouldn't be long until the ground would be covered in snow, and it would be too cold to be doing outdoor things. We convinced Joe to go to the park, although she only agreed to go to one on the mainland. We also had to bribe her with ice-cream and pizza. But we told her that we could have a picnic and eat at the park. Then, she wanted to go shopping again.

We weren't sure what the weather would be like. Our phones said there was a twenty percent chance of rain on Saturday but an eighty percent chance on Sunday. We made plans for the park activities on Saturday and then shopping on Sunday.

I was actually looking forward to a family-filled weekend. I lay in bed, thinking about the last time we'd all spent the weekend together. It had really been too long.

"What are you thinking about?" Rachel asked.

"Just about the things that we've been missing out on. Or, I guess things *I've* been missing out on," I said, with a small amount of regret in my words.

"It has been a while, but we're going to have a great weekend. Together. All of us. It'll be a good thing," she said, knowing just the words that would make me feel better about the situation.

"You're right," I told her. Then, I opened my arms and said, "Come here."

She crawled into the bed, lying under the cover but still in my arms. We lay there for a few minutes until I heard her breathing change. She was asleep, and I was at peace. I fell asleep with her still in my arms.

When I woke up, she was gone, as usual. I got up, made myself tea, and waited for her to return.

The rest of the weekend went as planned, almost. It ended up raining Saturday morning, so we went shopping then, but we were able to go to the park on Sunday for a few hours. It did rain Sunday, but not until the late afternoon. We were home for a while before the rain hit.

The entire weekend was great. It went so well for me that I didn't even think about calling the landlord of Rachel's office until I was at work on Monday. I actually spent a few good minutes debating whether or not I even wanted to call. Did I actually want to know what she was doing with that extra space? But then again, would it hurt if I did?

So, I picked up the phone and called the guy again.

"Hello?" He picked up after the first ring.

I told him who I was, and he remembered.

"Oh, yeah. Tim. Yes. Yes. The one who was having those problems in his marriage. Did things get any better with that?" he asked, sounding a little too pushy. I ignored the question and moved on with why I had called.

"Yeah, I have a few questions for you. And also, thanks again for getting that key for me. It was helpful, to say the least," I told him.

"No problem, man. What's the question?"

"I was wondering what she classified the other building as? If you could tell me, I would appreciate it," I said to him.

"The other one? Um, yeah. Let me take a look at the paperwork. Sometimes they put it down, but it's optional," he said.

Both of us went quiet for a second, then he spoke up again. "Looks like storage. She put down storage."

"Interesting," I paused, then continued, "I found a key to it and went inside twice. The first time, it was completely torn apart. Then the second time, it was all put together. Did she get approval for renovations?"

"Well, we don't need approval. As long as the place looks the same when we get it back, that's all we really care about. There's a fine if it's not returned in the same quality or better than what we gave it in. But hold on," he said abruptly. The line went silent for a second, as if he put me on hold.

"Alright," I said, even though I was probably talking to myself at that point.

No response. I sat there, waiting for him to come back on the phone. He might've taken another call, I thought. I just decided to put the call on speaker, so I could get work done while I waited for him to return.

About three minutes passed, then I heard his voice on the other end of the line. "Yeah, sorry about that. I just saw something interesting, and I had to find out the full details before I told you."

"And what was that?" I apparently had to ask, since he stopped talking after saying that.

"It looks like your wife isn't keeping that place anymore. She had a three-month contract. It looks like she called a few weeks ago to say that she isn't going to be renewing it. Her last day in it is in a couple of days, at the end of September."

"That sure is interesting. I guess that answers the rest of my questions," I said, not sure of what else I could say. I was delighted to hear this but confused. Why didn't she need it anymore? What was it before? A thousand thoughts ran through my head within a matter of seconds.

"Yeah, congrats, bud. Sounds like whatever she was hiding from you isn't in the picture anymore. Anything else I can do?"

"No, no. That's it. Thanks for being a big help. I hope this is the last time we'll have to cross paths," I told him, in the politest way possible.

He laughed at that. "True, I hope the same. Goodbye, Tim, have a good day."

I hung up the phone, and I couldn't help but smile. It seemed like that chapter of my life was closed. I didn't have anything left to worry about. I still wanted to ask her about it, and maybe someday I would, but it was over with. She was no longer hiding things from me, and this was the best form of proof I thought I'd get.

Maybe things could go back to normal now.

CHAPTER 22

October came round, and things had been going pleasantly. I'd been working on forgiving Rachel for hiding so much from me. It had been tough because I knew there was a lot she hadn't told me and probably never would. I knew I just had to accept that and cut my losses. But that was much easier said than done.

Besides my own personal feelings, things had been going well in the household. Rachel and I had been getting better at communicating again, and we'd been spending a lot more time with Joe. Rachel and I were even having a little more sex than usual, and I was always a fan of that.

Cole and I hadn't been hanging out as much; he'd been spending a lot of time with his new girlfriend. I could respect that, though. It was tough watching him work through the death of his wife. I was just glad to see him happy with someone. Luckily, we had been able to go out for drinks at least once a week, and this was one of those days. It was a Tuesday, which meant I couldn't get completely sloshed, but that didn't mean I couldn't enjoy my night out.

I left work and texted Rachel to let her know that I was leaving and remind her that I was going out with Cole.

> **Don't forget I'm out with Cole tonight. Heading there now, just leaving work. I love you.**

She responded within the same minute.

> **Didn't forget! I hope you have a good night out. Joe and I are going to get pizza. See you at home. I love you too.**

She'd probably put it in a calendar and added a reminder.

I drove straight to the bar we normally met at after work, and of course, he was there before me. He worked on the island, so his commute was about a quarter of the time of mine. The perks of that were that my drink was always there waiting for me.

"Hey, how's it going?" I asked him.

"Things are going good. I think I might propose to her. You know?" he said, turning the conversation serious very quickly.

"Already? You've only been together for a few months," I asked, just to make sure that it was something he'd actually thought about.

"Yeah, you know. Stacy died so quickly, and it just shows that you can die at any moment. There's no point in waiting. I know that I want to marry this girl. It wouldn't make sense for me to wait. Plus, I'm about seventy percent sure she'll say yes," he said, with conviction.

"Okay, if that's what you really want to do. I'd say go for it."

We sat there, and each took a sip of our drink. Since we were at the bar, there was a TV nearly directly in front of us. The TV program had ended, and the channel's daily news came on. Since we weren't talking at the time, it was easy to tune in.

The news station started by giving their introduction, followed by the topics of discussion for the day. This caught my attention. There was going to be coverage of the serial killer story, but it wasn't going to be discussed until halfway through. They always do that to make people watch the rest of the news to reach the interesting part.

"Do you want to stay to watch what they have to say about the murders?" Cole asked.

"Um, yeah. I will," I told him, but after thinking about it more, I said, "But you can leave if you want. I know this might be a sensitive subject for you."

"Yeah, I think I'll head out. See you next week, though. I'll let you know how it goes with the proposal." We shook hands, and he headed out. I asked for another drink.

I waited there, scrolling through my social media while the news played in the background. Finally, the previous story came to an end, and it was time for the breaking story. I listened as the news anchor started to talk about the murders.

A few weeks ago, the suspect in custody was released due to the lack of evidence. Further questions were raised when a murder occurred while the suspect was in custody. However, there has been new light shed on the Mercer Island Murderer, who has been linked to five separate murders.

The police have just released a statement, citing multiple anonymous sources claiming to have witnessed events on the days of each of the murders. Today, we have the Sheriff here to explain the situation.

Then, they switched the camera to Sheriff Danson. He was in his office at the station.

Yes, thank you, Sharon. We've been receiving multiple anonymous calls that are helping us with a new lead. We're finally ready to share these latest updates. From the first one, a few days ago, a caller stated that they saw the latest victim with a male. It was dark, so it was hard to see clearly, but the caller described him as being of average height, wearing a hooded jacket with the hood up. The second call was about the first victim. The caller informed us that they saw a man with the first victim the day before she went missing. The caller stated they were a friend of the victim. They didn't come forward initially because they'd suspected the man was a romantic connection but later realized that he may have been the killer. They described him as having light brown hair, and he was, again, of average height.

With this news coming to light, we are able to take a different approach to the murders. We urge anyone who has possibly seen the victim with a male matching this description to call us. Even if you don't have additional information about the suspect, any sightings of strangers with the victims before they were taken will be very helpful. I want to tell everyone to stay safe. It's clear that the Mercer Island Murderer targets women who have a connection to the local donor clinic, Mercer Fertility. However, we advise all residents to stay alert, regardless of whether they've had dealings with the clinic or not.

Thank you for having me, Sharon; stay safe out there. And remember, we are working hard at solving this. We will take any information we can get to speed up the process.

Sharon, the news anchor, came back on to introduce the weather for the next couple of days. That's where I lost interest. I paid my tab and went home.

When I got in, Rachel and Joe had already settled down and put away the pizza. Rachel knew that I wouldn't be back in time for dinner, so she made a plate that I just had to put in the microwave. She even got a pizza without pineapple, just for me.

Rachel and Joe were sitting on the couch, watching an animated movie when I came in through the door. Rufus came running straight for me, while Joe stayed sitting down. Rachel slowly rose and walked towards me. It seemed safe to say that someone else was a bit more excited to see me. Rufus started licking my face and jumping up at me, but I didn't mind because I was crouched down to his level. Once Rachel got to me, I stood up, dried my drool-covered face, and went in to give her a kiss. She returned the favor and kissed me back.

I looked past Rachel to find Joe. She was still sitting on the couch, absorbed by the movie. I focused my attention back on Rachel and gave her a big hug and a kiss. Rufus sat at our feet, ready for more attention. We exchanged our usual greetings, and she went to warm up my dinner.

"Well, hello," I yelled in Joe's direction.

I finally saw a head pop up from the couch. Joe had a huge smile lighting her face.

"Daddy!" she yelled back. "I didn't know you were home already!"

Joe got off the couch and started running towards me. I crouched down and swooped her up into my arms when she got close enough. She was at my level and almost strangled me with her tight hug. I let out a little cough.

"You're squeezing a little too tight, dear," I told her when I was nearly out of breath.

She giggled. "Oops, I was just so excited to see you! I missed you today."

Then she proceeded to tell me all about her day. There was a new girl in school. She and Joe really hit it off, and she was already asking for a playdate. Being the good father I was, I told her yes. Until I learned that her mother had told her no. Then, I had to change my answer. At least until we met the parents and made sure they weren't crazy people. We couldn't be too careful with the Mercer Island Murderer out there still.

By the time I finished eating, it was time for Joe to shower, and Rachel went to help her with that. I knew that Joe would go to bed right after her shower, so I told her that I would be in the bedroom whenever she was ready.

I went to our room and turned on the TV there. I was tired, but I wanted to stay up until Rachel got back. I felt like I just needed to talk to her and make sure that she was okay, especially with the murder stuff that had just come to light. Plus, they'd finally put a name to the murderer, which I was sure wouldn't sit well with Rachel.

I was dozing off when I heard her come into the bedroom.

"Hey, my love. How was shower time?" I mumbled, trying to drag myself from sleep.

"It was good. I think next time, I'm going to have her shower all by herself. She seems like a big girl now. Plus, she complained the whole time I was in there," she said, then sighed. "I can't believe she's so grown up already. It's almost scary how time has flown past."

"Yeah, it is. I still remember the day we brought her home. It's been a crazy ride these last few years, but I'm happy it all happened," I told her sincerely.

"Me too," she said. "Hey, did you watch the news by chance?"

"Yeah, I did. You?"

"No, but I saw an article from the news page that talked about how they'd labeled the murderer the *Mercer Island Murderer.* Seems a little over the top for me. Almost like they're trying to keep the killer alive in the media," she said, which actually sounded pretty accurate.

"Yeah, I meant to ask you about that. How are you feeling? You know, since they labeled the guy and they made the announcements from the anonymous callers," I asked.

"Anonymous callers?"

"Oh, you didn't hear? There were a few callers who mentioned seeing a man with the first and last victims just before they were kidnapped and killed. I thought you heard that," I told her, hating that I was the one to break the news to her.

"No, I didn't hear that. I only heard about them naming him. Wow," she said as she rubbed her head. Then she sat down and put her head in her hands.

I moved over to her, rubbing her back and pulling her into one of those long, drawn-out hugs. Finally, she pulled away but kept her gaze on me.

"I don't know how to feel about this," she said. "I thought that they would never be able to catch the guy. I'm glad to see someone saw it and that it'll get taken care of faster now that people might start coming forward. Did they say what this guy looked like? I'll have to keep a lookout when I go places now."

"Yeah, I think all they said was that he was a male, of average height, and he had light brown hair. But that's all that's been reported," I told her, remembering what the sheriff had said.

"Okay, that's not very helpful. I feel like that's half of the men here. But I guess I'll just steer clear of any guy with brown hair then."

She looked at me, then giggled. "I guess I don't have to worry about you being the murderer."

She tousled my blond hair and laughed some more. I let out a small laugh as well, just to reassure her. I didn't really find that funny, but I was glad to see her able to joke about something that she'd had issues with for the past year.

Rachel fell asleep, but I lay there thinking. Thinking about everything, from Joe's day at school, to Rachel and my falling out. It still bothered me that we even got into that situation of distrust and lies, but to think back on it, it didn't start until these murders did. I pulled out my phone, looking at the calendar. Then, I went to google, looking for the dates of the killings. It lined up.

Everything that happened between us occurred when these killings began. We were happy until then, and all the lies that she told were condensed down to the times the media found out about each crime. I never realized how much this affected Rachel. She'd been scared and acting out because these murders weren't sitting right with her.

Even when she needed me the most, I continuously snuck into her office and dug through all her papers. That's not what a good husband does. And while all this was happening, I didn't spend enough time with my child either. That's not how a good father should behave.

Suddenly, things came crashing down. I was a terrible person. For starters, I wasn't there when my wife needed me. To the point that she resorted to cheating on me, possibly even with another woman. Then, I wasn't there for my daughter because I was so busy going behind my wife's back that I didn't pay attention to how big my little girl had gotten. I let all the wrong things distract me, and now I was left with nothing to show for it.

My wife had an extra unit that she claimed was used for storage. So what? And she admitted to cheating… Sure, it broke my heart, but she was working on fixing that. I'd gained nothing from spending so much time worrying about what she was doing behind my back or in the past.

I lay in bed, letting these thoughts run through my head. After all, I did deserve every single one of them. I had too much pride to admit that I shed a few tears that night. I lay there until the sun came up the next morning. Even though I had work, I felt so terrible that I had to call in sick, which fortunately wasn't a big deal.

I was awake long enough to see Rachel get up, but I pretended to be asleep so she wouldn't ask any questions that I wasn't willing to answer. Once I knew that she was out of the house, I got out of bed. I had to move fast.

My plan was to make breakfast for everyone before Joe got up, and Rachel was back from her walk. So, I got started. I started by making some pancake batter. We hadn't had pancakes in months, and I thought it would be a sweet treat. While the pancakes were cooking on the griddle, I got out the bacon. I layered the bacon on a cooking sheet and put it in the oven to cook. Then, I got out the eggs.

The eggs are the tricky part. Joe would only eat scrambled eggs, while I usually liked mine over easy. Rachel didn't care how her eggs were; she liked them every way. But today, scrambled eggs sounded better. It was all cooked within twenty minutes.

I went to wake Joe since the food would be cold if she wasn't up soon. Plus, I wanted to eat as soon as Rachel was back to make sure there was enough time for Rachel to get to work and Joe to get to school. Although it was Rachel's turn to take Joe to school, taking the day off meant that I could focus on her.

Joe was pleasantly surprised to see me waking her up. I helped her pick out an outfit that consisted of pink and white leggings and a matching pink top, finished off by a pair of white tennis shoes.

It took only a few minutes to put the entire outfit together. When it was done, we moseyed over to the kitchen, where Rachel was already standing.

She must've just walked in. She already had her shoes off but was taking off her windbreaker.

"What is all this?" she asked.

Joe ran up to hug Rufus, and then she took a seat.

"I just wanted to do something nice. I took the day off today and figured I would make us a quality breakfast," I told Rachel.

"Oh! I didn't know you were taking the day off. What made you decide to do that?" she pressed.

"I just feel like I've been missing a lot. I wanted to make sure that I was there for the important things, including making breakfast and taking Joe to school," I said, giving her the short version.

"Okay, well, good. Then I suppose I can leave a little later than I had planned," Rachel said while we took a seat.

Joe sat between us because she loved the middle seat. But I secretly believed it was because she loved sitting in between Rachel and me so we wouldn't kiss in front of her. We still found a way to kiss.

Rachel ate like she was still in a hurry. To be fair, she did want to take a shower before she left for work. We usually didn't eat sit-down breakfasts during the week, so it was understandable that she needed to get a move on. I told her I would clean up so she could take her shower. She kissed Joe on the head, me on the lips, and rushed towards the bathroom.

"Will you be dropping me off and picking me up?" Joe asked.

"I sure will. Are you excited?" I returned.

"Yes! Can we go to the park and get food? Then for dessert, we can get ice-cream!" she said excitingly.

"Of course. Anything you'd like."

"Can we skip school, then?"

"Nice try, but no. Your mom would not be happy with me if I let you stay home from school," I said to Joe, just as Rachel was getting out of the bedroom.

"What would I be unhappy about?" she asked, smiling and strolling towards us with her hair still wrapped in a towel.

"Oh, nothing!" Joe said to her and giggled.

Rachel just smiled and started packing lunches.

Lunches! I'd been sitting there the entire time, laughing with Joe when I could've been making lunches for everyone. But Rachel seemed more than happy to do it, so I let the thought escape.

Just as I had promised, I took Joe to school. Before I walked her to class, I reminded her that I would pick her up and we would be doing things together that evening. I gave her a hug and a kiss.

When I got back to the car, I saw my phone had a notification from Rachel.

> **Thank you for taking her to school and making breakfast. I don't know what has gotten into you, but I love it. I love you, Timmy Cardington.**

I smiled, mostly because I didn't often get these kinds of texts. But I also smiled because I enjoyed being there for them that morning. It was one of the better mornings we'd all had, mainly because it was simple and easygoing. Just our little family enjoying each other's company.

I responded:

> **I'm glad you enjoyed it. It was a nice change of pace. Hoping to make it last. I love you, Rachel Cardington.**

I wasn't expecting a response; that's not usually Rachel's thing. So, I put my phone down, put the car in drive, and went home.

I wasn't sure what I was going to do while everyone else was occupied that day, but I figured I could find something useful to do. We had people to mow the lawn and do the housework, so there wasn't much that I could do, except make dinner.

Although I was never a great chef, I could be persuaded to make a pretty decent meal. I opted to skip the spaghetti and go for something a little more classy. I decided to make spinach and ricotta ravioli with a delectable tomato cream sauce. I turned the TV on for some background sounds while I cooked.

I was preparing to start cooking, gathering all the utensils I would need when I realized something was missing. There was an empty space in the knife block, where we kept all our good knives displayed on the kitchen counter. It seemed odd that the knife was missing when all the dishes had been cleaned.

I chalked it up to Rachel taking the knife to work with her to eat lunch one day and just never bringing it back home. I made a mental note to ask her about it later in the evening if I remembered. For now, it was time to get cooking.

It took a long time to make, and a lot of time on google. However, I wanted to make sure everyone got a rounded meal for dinner – one that wasn't from a restaurant. I tested it to make sure it tasted good, then it went into the fridge to wait for dinner that night.

I knew I'd told Joe that we could get pizza, and we still could. Since Rachel wouldn't be home for a few hours after we got home, Joe would have plenty of time to digest her food and be hungry again. After all, she was a growing girl.

I found some things to do around the house, then spent even more time rearranging my office. Since it was fall, I decided to do some fall cleaning. It took me a good three hours to get done with the office.

By the time I was finished, it was time to get ready and go get Joe. I decided to change my clothes because moving all those shelves was a workout in itself. I put on my usual polo shirt and khaki shorts since it was still nice enough outside.

I was about to turn the TV off when I noticed the BREAKING NEWS UPDATE banner slapped across the bottom of the screen. I grabbed the remote, and instead of switching it off, I turned the volume up.

Today, we are back with the Sheriff Danson of the Mercer Island Police Department, who has more details about the murders. Police recently reported receiving calls from several anonymous sources saying they'd seen the victims with a man who might have something to do with the murders. The Sheriff is here to give us an update on the progress.

The camera switched over to the Sheriff's office.

Thank you again. As everyone knows, there is still a murderer at large. After yesterday's announcement, we have received an overwhelming number of callers looking to either help or give details about what they've seen during the days leading up to the victims' deaths.

Here's what we've gathered from a few different sources. For starters, the new suspect is a male, white, with short, light brown hair. He is of average height for a male and seems to blend in well. We are unsure of his eye color. He has been confirmed to be seen with every victim. He is most likely armed and or dangerous. Please be on the lookout for someone matching this description. Even if you're unsure of someone with these characteristics, please don't hesitate to call us immediately.

Since they have been seen with every victim, we are assuming—

I turned off the TV. The rest of it was just repeating things to drill the details into the citizens' minds. For a breaking news story it wasn't much of an update. They probably thought people would be more inclined to listen to a breaking news story rather than tuning into the news daily.

I went to pick Joe up from school and texted Rachel when I collected her to confirm that I was indeed picking her up. We went to get the pizza that I had ordered ahead of time and headed for the park. We hadn't been to the park much since the incident, but Joe seemed quite happy to go again. I was even able to take her to that same one. We conquered her fear of that park and ate our pizza on the blanket, in the grass.

I brought a bottle of the sparkling grape juice that looks like a bottle of champagne to make her even more excited. I ate a lot faster than she did, so by the time I was done, she was just finishing her first slice.

This could have had something to do with the fact that she talked a lot while eating. But, I sat there and watched her eat and tell the story about everything she did that day.

After Joe got done eating, we played outside with the frisbee I kept in the car. When Joe was tired out, we left to get her ice-cream and headed home. By the time we arrived, Rachel was just about to pull in herself.

Although I'd hoped she'd be hungry again in time for dinner, Joe confessed that she wasn't yet. I told her that was fine and she could have some whenever she got hungry again. I, on the other hand, was more than hungry. I'd tried not to eat a lot of pizza, and I'd skipped the ice-cream so that I would be hungry when Rachel got home.

I still warmed up all the food because I assumed Joe would want some once she realized that we were all eating again. Rachel walked inside while I was working on warming up the food.

"Smells delicious in here," she said as she walked over to Joe to give her a hug and say hello.

"Mommy!" Joe said excitedly. Joe wrapped her arms around Rachel's neck and gave her a big, sweet hug.

"Hi, honey. How was school today?" Rachel asked Joe.

"It was okay," Joe paused. "But I had lots of fun with Daddy today. I wish you were there."

"Next time, my dear, I will be," Rachel said while she walked over to me to see what I was up to.

I told her what I'd made, and she was pleasantly surprised. She probably thought I wasn't capable of making anything as fancy as spinach and ricotta ravioli. She also assured me that it tasted *so* good. But I wasn't sure I agreed with her. It wasn't terrible, but it also wasn't as good as I was hoping it would be.

"Wow. Wow, I really like this. You might have to make this more often," she said, with a mouth full of food.

"Yeah, it's alright," I said, a little disappointed.

"So, there's something I'd like to ask you," Rachel blurted out.

"What's that?"

"This Halloween, Joe has a few days off from school. I was thinking we should go back to Chicago for a few days," she said with her sweet voice.

I pulled up my calendar on my phone to check if I'd be free. "I've got a new project that'll be starting then. I won't be able to make it. But I'm sure that you two could go by yourselves. I think Joe would like that."

"Are you sure? I wouldn't want to go if you wanted to go with and couldn't," she said sympathetically.

"Yes, love, I'm sure," I said, putting my hand atop hers and squeezing it lightly. The downside to this was that I'd finally decided to do more with the family, and now I was missing out on a family trip.

I would just have to make up for it when they got back.

That night, I had a weird dream. The dream started with Cole, Rachel, and I sitting around the yacht. Something made me notice Cole's clothes. In my dream state, I was certain that his clothes matched those worn by the suspect mentioned in the news. He startled me, but then he did the unthinkable. He pushed me into the water and grabbed Rachel. I kept telling myself to get up, to go save her, but I was frozen in the water. I watched him as he shot her in the head, point-blank. Blood ran down her face as she collapsed onto the floor of the yacht while my ears were still ringing from the gunshot. Afterward, he turned around and stared at me while I lay there in the water, still unable to move.

Then, my perspective changed, and I was above the scene. Rachel was on the ground while Cole cut her up. He started with her arms and then moved to her legs. Blood was everywhere. If I'd been awake, I would have been sick.

That's when I woke up. I was panting, and my eyes were filled with tears. I looked over and saw Rachel lying by my side, and I got up, relief flooding me. I walked to the bathroom and splashed cold water on my face. Then I forced myself back into bed and lay there thinking.

I eventually dozed off again, telling myself it was all just a dream.

...Right?

CHAPTER 23

Over the next day, I couldn't shake the memory of that dream. For some reason, it just seemed real...too real. Cole had been asking to meet for drinks, but something kept stopping me. He couldn't possibly be a killer, but my imagination kept grasping at signs.

I guess the dream was a subconscious message to look closely at the clues. And the more closely I looked, the more it seemed to make perfect sense.

Cole worked in the medical industry. That could give him access to the medical records of the victims. The police description was vague, but if I thought about it, it could be him. Average height and build, light brown hair... Then again, a lot of others looked the same. And I was sure hundreds of men in the medical industry had light brown hair. It could just be a coincidence.

Then, there was the undeniable fact that Cole did have an alibi the entire day that his wife was murdered. He was with me. On a yacht. He couldn't possibly have killed her. Unless he was the brains behind the operation and he wasn't alone.

But even that was stretching it. After all, Cole used a gun in my dream. The police never released any details about the murder weapon. There was no way for me to even know that a gun was used, right? It could have been strangulation for all I knew.

Still, an uneasy feeling was tearing me apart from the inside.

Perhaps I should just ask him about it. Well, not directly ask if he was the Mercer Island Murderer, but ask him how he felt about it. Or, I could just call the police and see what they said. An anonymous tip felt less dangerous than facing a possible serial killer.

I called the police department and shared my fears. They thanked me and told me that they would look into it. I was pretty sure nothing would come of it, but I knew I wouldn't rest if I didn't do something.

A few hours later, I got a text from Cole.

You'll never guess what just happened.

I played dumb.

What?

He responded.

The police just questioned me AGAIN. About the murders. Can we get a drink?

I decided to ring him up. The phone only rang once before he picked up.

"Hey, you calling to get some drinks? I could use one," Cole said as soon as he answered.

"Yeah, how are you feeling about the whole thing?" I asked, trying to gauge his feelings and interpret his response.

"I'm blown away. Why would I even be considered a suspect? It's honestly absurd," Cole said, sounding irritated.

"Yeah, I agree. Let's meet at the bar," I told him. "I'll leave now."

I headed straight to the bar and met him there. He must've gotten there only seconds before me since he was still in his car.

"Hey," I said as I made my way up to his window.

Immediately, I could tell that he was bothered. "Hey."

I waited for him to get out, and we walked in together. We sat down at the bar and ordered our usual drinks.

"So, what happened?" I asked, maintaining my innocent facade.

"Well, the cops called and asked if I would come in to answer some questions. I thought it would be about Stacy. I was right...I just didn't know that it was because they thought that I *killed* her." He took a big gulp of his whisky and continued, "When I got there, they started asking me all these random questions, which I didn't know the answers to. They asked me where I was during the other murders. I was with my wife for all of the earlier ones, and then with you for hers. I don't know what would make them think that I did it."

"Wow, man. That sounds terrible. But maybe they only thought that you fit the profile of that person who's been seen with the other women," I casually said.

"I mean, I get that. But it sounded like more than that. Now I feel like I've relived her murder. That visit, them accusing me…it brought all those feelings up again."

Now I felt awful. I knew that he couldn't have been the killer, and it was insensitive of me to even think that. Luckily, Cole would never know it was me.

"But, you know, I've been thinking about something that I just can't shake," he said, staring at his drink but looking puzzled.

"What's that?" I thought for sure he realized that I was the one who called the police on him.

"Do you remember that gem?" he asked.

"What gem?"

"The one that was found in Stacy's clothes."

"What about it?" I pressed.

He briefly looked up at me, then said, "I didn't buy her anything that had that kind of stone in it."

"What does that mean?" I continued, not sure of where he was taking this.

"Tim. I mean that it was from someone else. Probably the killer. Besides, I checked every piece of jewelry that I've ever bought her, none of them have a *benitoite* gem. Whatever that even is," he said, emphasizing the word 'benitoite'.

"Oh, shit, man. What size was it?" I asked, my curiosity piqued.

"They said it was a quarter carat. You know, I looked this gem up after the police told me. It's rare, and definitely not Stacy's style," he said, sounding troubled.

"It's just something I think about, you know? But I realize that the gem won't be enough to find the killer. It might be rare, but not that rare. Plus, it's not like the killer deliberately leaves rare gems at their crime scenes. It might not even be from the killer. Maybe from one of Stacy's friends when she hugged them or something," he said, never once changing his tone or facial expressions.

Cole paused, taking a drink of his whisky, and then continued without a response from me, "It was stuck in the collar of her sweater, for God's sake. Her collar. The killer wouldn't be so stupid as to leave evidence lying around. Right?"

After a few drinks, and some good conversation, Cole started to feel a little better, so I decided to push a little further.

"Cole, are you ready to talk about what happened to Stacy?" I asked. I still hadn't heard his version of the story yet.

We'd spent so much time together during his grieving period, yet it was never the right time to discuss it. Each time I tried to bring it up, he just blew it off, or he was too drunk to make sense.

"Honestly, I think so. I haven't told anyone what the police told me yet, so I think I am ready." Cole gave me a slight smile, but it seemed to pain him. I didn't speak. Instead, I let him continue when he was ready.

"For starters, we all know it was the serial killer. But the police said that she was killed sometime on the morning of our return. The killer must've known that I wasn't home or something. Because, otherwise, she wouldn't have been killed on any other weekend. The killer must've been watching her. God, I felt terrible for leaving and having a good time," he said, shaking his head in disappointment.

"The police said that when they arrived, Rachel was broken down and in tears, sitting at the front door. They said that the front door was locked, so she went around the back to see if Stacy might've been back—" I stopped listening to process my own thoughts. Rachel had said the front door was unlocked. I distinctly remember her telling me that she went through the house and then went to the back. I made a mental note of it and continued to listen to him.

"They did the autopsy and found out that Stacy was dismembered postmortem. They're listing it as the work of the killer. They also determined that she was drugged but didn't suffer from dehydration like the rest of the victims. The killer changed his MO to allow for the time we were supposed to be gone." He shook his head again. "I'm just pissed that they haven't found the bastard."

I comforted him again, and he asked that we talk about something else. I spent the rest of the night distracting him with details of Rachel and Joe's upcoming trip to Chicago.

CHAPTER 24

I dropped Rachel and Joelle off at the airport two days before Halloween. They took an extra bag full of supplies for Joe's Halloween costume. This year Joe wanted to be a superhero, one of her own creation. I was a little sad that I would miss it, but I knew that I would see the pictures of her in her creative costume.

I went straight back from the airport to continue working on the big project we had at work. This time, it was vital to finish everything by the deadlines, which were a lot tighter than they had been in the past.

This project was for a client we'd dealt with a few times, and each time they'd been over-the-top demanding. I had requested to work from home so that I could focus on the project uninterrupted. After the trip, I returned to my office with a glass of whisky on ice – a necessity when dealing with a demanding client. I had to do some catchup for what I missed while I was driving Joe and Rachel to the airport.

In the middle of brainstorming a problematic risk, I ran out of my sticky notes. I liked to use sticky notes to problem solve with, then scan them into the computer. I hunted through my stationery cabinet and realized I'd run out. I went online and ordered a pack of them, but they weren't going to come for another day, and I needed them immediately. So, I went to Rachel's office to grab some from her desk.

I went to her desk and didn't see any sitting on top, so I rifled through her drawers and tried to find some. In the process of looking for a book of sticky notes, I discovered a binder. It looked familiar, but I couldn't put my finger on it. I picked the binder up and opened it.

I knew exactly what it was after opening it. The poetry book I bought for her some years ago. It was such a small gesture that I completely forgot that I got it for her. The first poem on the top was the first one she ever wrote for me. I closed it but decided to take it with me back to my office.

I kept looking for some sticky notes, and at last, I found them. I grabbed them from her desk drawer, took the binder, and headed back to my office. I went straight to work once I got to my desk, setting the binder on the floor. Frankly, there was not enough room for it on the desk anyway, and I needed it out of my head for a few hours.

It was nine in the evening before I was finally satisfied with my work for the day. I sat back and took a few seconds to breathe and appreciate the work I'd accomplished. It had been a long day, and I was sick of looking at a screen. Luckily, it was only seven in Chicago, and I was looking forward to video chatting with Joe and Rachel.

The call didn't last long since they were busy by the time I called, but it was nice to hear their voices nonetheless. After they hung up, I ate some food and sat down on the couch, remembering her binder. I got up and retrieved it from my office, then sat down in the same spot before opening it up.

I took a deep breath because I knew this would be an emotional roller coaster, going through these memories. Even the first poem she ever wrote for me was an emotional ride, but a good one, to say the least. I continued reading. Since they were going to be in Chicago for a few days, I figured I could read everything, and it would be nice to see how she saw the world through her eyes.

As I was reading each poem, I came across the ones she had written when she was having a hard time about not being able to get pregnant. Those ones were almost unbearable, and I had to stop reading them a few times. Everything I thought I felt about the situation changed when I understood how she felt. She was hurting much more than I was. But then again, it was her body that was the issue, not mine. I could see how frustrated and angry she was about it. While I was feeling bad about it, she was feeling terrible. I wished she'd said something to me about it; that might have made a difference.

Once I got past the diagnosis part of our relationship, I reached the part where we took Joe home. This was almost worth the pain she felt, and those were her words, not mine. She thought about how much better our lives got after Joelle arrived. It was almost as if all our issues were melted away by the warmth of this small baby's heart. It brought back many memories that I had myself, and I sat there for the rest of the night, thinking about one of the best days of my life.

When I woke up in the morning, I was still on the couch, in the same clothes I'd worn the day before. The binder was next to me, and the TV was still on. Luckily, I woke up before my shift started, and I was able to get a head-start on my very long day at work. I jumped right into it, preparing for our virtual meeting scheduled just a few hours from then.

As the project manager, it was up to me to create the meeting outlines and ensure all the points and objectives were met. Since we were nearing the end of the project, we needed to document all the potential risks, then find solutions to them, or advise the client so they could prepare for them after the software was released to them.

The meeting went very well, and afterward, I went to the kitchen to warm some leftover pizza. While I was eating, I decided to crack open the binder and continue reading. There was a pretty big break in time before Rachel wrote next. Most of the poems were just daily thoughts or random things. Then, the next big event was the move. She even mentioned how she felt when she got the letter in the mail from my biological family. She felt bad about it, but she thought it needed to be done.

I spent a lot of time forgiving her. Seeing how desperate she was, I could understand where she was coming from. It seemed like there was some kind of battle she had within herself about what she should do about the situation. She thought that I would leave everything to be with them, but that was never the case. After all, I found out about them, went to see them, and still returned at the end of the visit. Plus, I'd been talking to them weekly, so it wasn't like I had to choose one or the other. Not that she knew that in the first place.

That entire situation took her a lot of words, and it covered numerous pages. I told myself that I would go back to work after I finished this cluster of poems, and that's what I pushed myself to do. I spent the next few hours working half-heartedly. I wanted to throw in the towel for the day and keep reading her poems.

I'd only ever read the work she'd shown to me. I'd never looked at the writing she wanted to keep private. But now that I was, I wanted to read it all. It was almost as if the words she had down were mesmerizing or addictive. It also felt like I was inside her brain and finally able to see everything the way that she saw things.

At last, I was finished with work. I must admit, it took me a lot longer to get done than it did the previous day. My mind was clearly in the wrong place. After work, I cooked myself some dinner and video chatted with Rachel and Joe. They were getting ready to eat, but not at Rachel's parents' house. They were going to a fancy restaurant that Rachel and I used to go to when we started to get serious. I was a little jealous that I couldn't be there with them, but they both looked so beautiful when they were all dolled up.

Rachel had on a casual, yet classy, jumpsuit with a blazer. Joe had on a black tutu-like skirt, a red T-shirt with sparkles, and black shoes. They both looked like they belonged at that restaurant.

They couldn't stay on the phone long before they had to leave and make it to their reservations in time. This was honestly fine with me. I wanted to read more of her poems.

As I opened her book, it dawned on me that I'd seen more poems at her office when I was there the first time. I would have my work cut out for me if I wanted to read them all. But the temptation was there. I really wanted to read them all.

I decided to wait until I finished the poems that I had before I went over to the office. It was a good thing I was working from home. It meant I didn't have to factor in the drivetime and exhaustion I felt after a long day in the workplace. I would still have to go late at night to avoid crossing paths with the receptionist. If she was still working while Rachel was away.

That night, I let time escape from my grasp as I finished the rest of the poems. They were tear-jerking, hilarious, and thoughtful all at the same time. There would be one poem that swayed towards being funny. The next plummeted deeply into the depression she faced. Each poem seemed to be a different mindset towards life, and Rachel covered every possible emotion I could think of.

My day ended at two in the morning – time got away from me, once again. I closed the binder, feeling closer to Rachel than I'd ever felt before. But I was still curious. I hadn't gotten into any of the poems that would be from when we moved to Washington. I only knew this because there had been a few that she'd written for me over the past year, and they should be in there. The only logical explanation was that they would at her office.

With that, I fell asleep in bed, with the binder lying next to me. By the time I was finished, I was too tired to pack it away.

The next morning, I replaced the binder in its original spot. In fact, that was the first thing I did because I didn't want to forget to return it. I had no idea how Rachel would react to me reading what equated to her diary, but I was sure it wouldn't have been a positive reaction.

Rachel and Joe's vacation was half over at that point. They only had three days left. It was already Friday, but that didn't mean anything to me. I knew I would have to work through the weekend as well.

The only thing I was looking forward to was seeing my daughter and wife come home on Sunday. Actually, there was one more thing I was looking forward to. Going to read Rachel's other poetry. That night.

I must admit, I was slightly more excited to go read her other work. It also crossed my mind a few times that Rachel should really publish her work. Her words were soothing, and all the emotions were there. I was sure the things she said could really help other people feel related to. Some of them even hit home for me.

The rest of my shift dragged on for what seemed like two whole days. By the time I finished up, it was around nine at night. I told Rachel that I wouldn't be able to talk that day because I was behind in work, and to be fair, I was. I spent my entire day being pretty unproductive, regardless of how many cups of tea I had. I was too excited to get to the end of my shift, where I could spend the remaining night reading her poems.

After texting her, she responded and assured me that it was okay. She and Joe were pretty busy, anyway. She had said that getting candy was taking a little longer than she had expected, and Joe was having a good time. I didn't want to miss a moment like this, but Rachel promised to send pictures as soon as she got home.

I could finally head to the office and read the rest of her binder books. I sped there, not enough to get pulled over, but slightly faster than the fast cars were going. I got there in record time. I was thankful to see another nearly empty parking lot, especially in front of her office. I did the usual; went to the door, opened it, entered the security code, and then headed to the office.

I stood there, in front of her large office bookshelf. There were five binders, but they were all tiny compared to the one at home. I decided to start from the left and work my way right. I sat down in her consultation room since there was a comfortable couch in there.

It took me two hours to get through the first binder. It seemed like the theme to this one was all just positive thoughts. It was sweet and uplifting. Almost refreshing.

Then, I cracked open the second one. The first few were inconsequential, but then they started to get a little weird. There were even a few that I had to stop and re-read through.

Yes, I did it,

Nobody will know

But I must admit,

I enjoyed it a little bit

Did what? Enjoyed what? I was lucky enough to spot the date inside the cover. She started writing these when we first moved. It was clear she did something, something she shouldn't have. But what? Was she referring to the cheating? I was intrigued, so I continued reading.

As I kept reading, she mentioned in a few consecutive poems that there was a woman, but she didn't say what the deal was with her. Rachel just kept using pronouns like 'she' and 'her'. At first, I thought she might be referring to her receptionist. Then I thought she made a few mentions of what sounded like something sinful with her, which could have been when she started cheating on me. Then it dawned on me. Rachel was speaking about the receptionist. It sounded like she was admitting to cheating on me with Sarah, her receptionist.

I wanted to put it down and forget that I ever saw this, but my fingers wouldn't let me. I needed to know what she did and who she did it with, especially if it was about the cheating.

I am who they look for

Sometimes I still crave more

The words of the short poem halted me. After this poem, she talked about how there were five, how she stopped for Joe and me, and how a part of her missed it.

It didn't click in my head, not immediately. But then, as I kept reading, something didn't let me move on past this poem. I knew she cheated more than five times, and I knew that she didn't have five lovers. So, what did five have to do with anything?

CHAPTER 25

At first, I couldn't believe my suspicions. But then again, I was never one to make a quick leap of faith on something that I didn't have concrete proof of. So, I went home. I needed to gather evidence that would either prove the theory in my head correct, or it will debunk it.

It was the middle of the night, and I had so many thoughts running through my mind. I was struggling to remain calm. There was only one logical reason I could think of for why Rachel was harboring so much guilt. On the ride home, a whirlwind of details swirled in my mind.

Once I reached the house, I was too tired to think. I decided to head for bed and pick this up in the morning. My growing suspicions seemed too outlandish to dwell on any longer.

In the morning, I woke up in a daze. It hardly seemed like I slept. My alarm was blaring, and I rushed to press snooze. Today was going to be a long day.

I started by getting my laptop open and getting to work. However, I found myself distracted. I needed to do a few things that day that had weighed heavily on me since the night before. I told myself that I could continue my work later. My mind was completely elsewhere.

I picked up my phone while I got dressed. I dialed a number, and it rang three times.

"Hello?" a female voice answered the phone.

"Hi, yes. My name is Tim, Tim Cardington. I was in last December, and I bought my wife and daughter a gift for Christmas. I was wondering if you could give me more detail about what I bought them." I said to the lady.

"Oh, sure. Let me pull up that order," she said, then asked me for some more details about the specific order, along with information to confirm my identity.

She didn't respond for a second, but then said, "Okay! Here it is. What would you like to know? It looks like there were two items. Do you need to know about both of them?"

"Yes, if that's not too much trouble," I paused for a second, then continued, "Would it be too much trouble to get those item descriptions emailed to me?"

"Not a problem at all," she said, sounding like she actually enjoyed catering to my needs.

I gave her my email address, and she said she would work on it but wasn't sure when she would have time to send it over; she assured me that it would be sometime that day. I thanked her and hung up the phone.

That was one thing crossed off my list. Now I was able to move on to the others. The next few things were strictly suspicions, but I could work through them on my own.

I grabbed a piece of paper and started writing down incidents that had happened over the last year or so. I began to create a timeline.

Just as I finished, my phone notified me that I had mail. I opened the email from the jewelry store and scanned it for what I was looking for.

Gem: 0.25-carat benitoite surrounding

But Rachel was missing two; if one of them was in Stacy's clothes, where was the other one?

Then, almost shaking, I looked at the timeline on a large scale. Everything lined up. All the weird things that Rachel had been doing aligned perfectly with the killings. The strange night-time disappearances. The bizarre scratches and dirty clothes. The constant lies and secretive behavior. My worst suspicions were starting to look like they were true. My wife was the Mercer Island Murderer.

I started to pace the room. While pacing, I started to doubt myself. I didn't want to believe myself. Surely this could all be a weird coincidence?

The more I thought about it, the more all her actions started to make sense.

I had to do something.

I went to her office. Out of anger, I started pulling the books off her shelves. One after the other, till there were no more left to tear down. When I turned around to look at the mess I'd made, I wasn't satisfied. Still overwhelmed with emotion, I started to kick the books. When that wasn't enough, I began picking them up and ripping out the pages.

Minutes into ripping apart books, I picked up another, and several loose sheets fell out, along with five ziplock bags. Picking through the scattered pages and bags, a growing sensation of horror grew within me. With shaking hands, I examined the contents of those bags. Rose-pink identification cards with white borders. The donor cards. I'd found the victims' donor cards, Rachel's murderous trophies.

I dropped them, disgusted, still holding the papers I'd discovered with them. Sick to my stomach at what I was learning, I unfolded them.

The first page was a printout of an email conversation. It was from the donor clinic.

Dear Rachel,

Thank you for reaching out to us. We have tests that we need to complete. How does this coming Tuesday at 9:20am sound? You will need to get lab results, and after those get back, we can look into choosing the right donor for you.

The second one was from a few weeks after that.

Rachel,

We hope you are feeling well. Your results have come in. It looks like we're able to implant the eggs, but there's a low chance they will take. We do not want to get your hopes up. Please come in for a consultation, and we can go over the risk factors. We know this might be difficult. If you can have someone along for support, that would be good. We realize you are single and doing this alone, but possibly a relative could join. Please give us a call and set something up so we can discuss further.

The third and last message was stapled to multiple pieces of paper, making it slightly thicker than the previous ones.

Hello,

It was nice talking to you and clearing everything up. We are excited that you chose us to start your new journey. Since you have already paid, we are delighted to give you a list of egg donors you'll be able to choose from. Let me know if any of these appeal to you. Try to pick at least five, and we can go from there to determine which one might be the best fit for you.

Call us when you are ready to set up an appointment to talk.

Attached to the email were 12 profiles of egg donors. When I looked through them, they were all numbered. The first was victim one, Kathren Arnoldson. The second one was victim two, Sofia Jones. The third was victim three, Hannah Richards. And the fourth one was victim five, Carla Adams. The rest were numbered but not known victims. There was also a cardstock photo that looked to be printed from a regular computer. The picture was of Stacy.

Rachel knew the eggs wouldn't take; we'd tried it before. This is how she got the names of the victims and their details. But if Stacy wasn't on the list, why would she have killed her?

I stuck the 'trophies' in my back pocket and kept ripping up books, feeling even more emotional now that I found the proof that it really was her.

I had to confront my wife. The killer. The Mercer Island Murderer.

While I thought about what to do, I tried to get back to my scheduled work assignments. The constant thoughts of Rachel killing all those women made it almost impossible to concentrate.

I kept thinking about Joelle. If Rachel was the killer, Joe was still with her. She wouldn't be home for two more days. I had no idea what to do in this situation. I was sure that Rachel would never hurt Joe, but she might go MIA if I were to confront her about it at the wrong time. I decided to play this smart.

First, I needed to set up something for Joelle. I called Juniper's mom and asked if she would mind watching Joe for the night. I told her that I wanted to spend some time with Rachel when she returned. I also told her that I wasn't sure if Joe would stay there all night, but I would keep her up to date. Luckily, she agreed.

I texted Rachel.

> **I have a surprise for you when you get home. Also, Joe can go by Juniper's house this weekend. We can have some alone time. *wink, wink***

Did that sound like I wanted to confront my possibly murderous wife? I hoped not.

It was nearly midnight by the time I finished my work for the day. I told myself I would get some sleep, and somehow I did.

I tried to stay calm while I waited for Rachel to get home. She had texted me when her flight took off, and she had just texted again to let me know that she was landing.

The last days had left me in a state close to hysteria. It felt like a sick joke. My wife, being a killer. I felt like I was in a movie or a nightmare that I couldn't escape.

To help, I found a bottle of whisky and drank straight from it, not bothering to pour myself a glass.

I heard her car pull into the driveway. Then, I heard her walk inside. I couldn't bring myself to move. It was all I could do not to shudder as she set her bags down and embraced me in greeting.

"You smell like a distillery. Have you been drinking?" she asked, pulling back and looking disgusted.

"I think you have some explaining to do," I said, going to my office to retrieve the poems. "Follow me."

"Okay?" she questioned.

We got to my office.

"First, I want to start by asking you a question," I demanded.

"What's that?" she asked.

"Why didn't you tell me my family sent me a letter? Why did you try to hide it?" I asked her, holding up the envelope that I took from her office.

"What are you talking about?" she said, acting innocent.

"Damnit, Rachel. You know what I'm talking about," I said, throwing the letter and pictures at her. The photos fell at her feet.

"I don't know what you want me to say, Tim. It was a moment of weakness for me. I didn't want you to leave us, your true family, for those fakes," she said angrily. It sounded like I'd hit a nerve.

I was frustrated that she labeled my family as 'fake'. I responded to her, "They're not fake. They were my biological family. It would have been nice to meet them. That's why we moved, isn't it?"

"Yes, it is. I got scared, and I panicked."

"How long were you planning it?"

"Actually, I told my father about it, and he suggested that we move. Mom didn't know anything about it, though. I knew that she wouldn't understand how I felt."

I couldn't believe her. I expected this behavior from her father, but not from her. I sat down, putting my head in my hands, trying to work up the courage to ask her about the murders.

I grabbed the binder, pulling it out of the desk drawer. I laid it on the table. Before I had a chance to speak, she reached into her purse and pulled out a gun. She dropped her purse and everything else to the floor. I raised my hands in defense.

"Where did you find these?" she demanded.

"Does that matter?" I asked. I decided to be bold and continue, "Are you the Mercer Island Murderer?"

"Short answer, or long answer?" she asked.

"The yes or no answer," I said frustratedly.

"Yes," she bluntly replied.

"I don't know what to say. I should call the police and report you right now."

"It's not what it sounds like, Timmy. You know me. Just give me a chance to explain. Plus, if you move, I will kill you," she said. I nodded in response.

She went on to tell me that she didn't mean to keep the truth from me. She admitted to being the killer and killing all five of the women.

"So, explain this. While you were out cheating on me, when did you have time to kill people?" I demanded, knowing the answer before I'd finished asking the question.

"I didn't cheat. That was just my excuse to get you off my back. So that you wouldn't pursue the truth. I'm sorry, I didn't mean to hurt you; that was never my intention," Rachel stated, in an unrecognizable voice, one laced with menace.

"And what about everything you told me? The stress of the killings? The way you felt about it? Was it all a lie?" The questions just kept pouring out.

"Yes, I lied. A lot. But I won't lie to you anymore. I'm so sorry," she repeated herself, "but that was never my intention. I didn't want to hurt you. You just got caught in the crossfire."

"But you did, and you hurt others. In fact, you *killed* others. How can you justify that?" I asked, stressing the word 'killed'.

She looked down sadly, then responded, "I killed them out of spite." Her voice changed now, almost sneering, "Everyone loved them. They did all the right things. Volunteering to help the needy, donating their time to the less fortunate. Donating their eggs to poor, faulty women who couldn't make their own. AKA me."

I didn't say anything, and she continued. "I was just so angry at life. I didn't know what to do. I just wanted to talk to one of the girls, the first victim. But things got out of hand, and the next thing I know, I'm killing her," she told me as she pressed her bottom palm of her right hand against her forehead, with the gun still held in the fingers of the same hand.

"But *why* did you have to kill them?" I needed to know.

"Everyone has something that grounds them when they're facing fear. Mine just happens to be murdering people," she stated.

"What did you have to fear?" I asked, knowing, at that moment, that the killings weren't what scared her.

"You. You taking Joe and running off without me. Back to Chicago, back to your fake family," Rachel said, almost whispering.

Then, she went on to tell me how she felt bad about it, but it also felt so good. I asked her how Sarah, her receptionist factored into this. She said that Sarah was an ex-convict who had a record. The record made it hard for her to get a job anywhere. Rachel found her online, and Sarah agreed to help with covering up the murders in exchange for a job that looked legitimate. Rachel could provide that, and Sarah held up her end of the deal by helping Rachel cover her tracks.

"Was Sarah the reason those victims were decapitated and bruised up after they were killed?"

"No. I did that with the first victim before Sarah agreed to help. I wasn't strong enough to move a dead body. I had to cut them up to dump their remains. And the bruising? That was because I dropped their body parts a lot. You wouldn't believe how heavy a dead body weighs," she said, sounding almost happy to talk about what she did with the victims. It made me feel sick to hear it come from her.

It seemed like she was a bit manic as she was talking. She kept waving the gun around when she tried to explain things to me. Then, she would get upset again and point the gun directly at me. I wasn't sure what to do, but I was scared for my life. If she could kill innocent people, she could surely kill me.

"At what point did you stop killing?" I asked, not sure if that really mattered or not.

"When you asked for a divorce. I realized that I'd let this go on for far too long, and it started to mess up my daily life. I just stopped. I swear," she said with her hands up, as if in surrender.

"I thought that killers start by killing animals. Why did you bring home a dog, then? Did you think about killing Rufus, too?" I blurted.

"No, never. That's just a stereotype. That's not always the case."

"Okay, well what about those anonymous calls that the police were getting, that made them think it was a male?"

"Those were all me. I thought that you might put some pieces together. Remember that man we saw at the park that first day of Joelle's school? That rude man who just ran right into us? I thought that might've jogged your memory, and you would tell the police you'd seen someone looking like that. But, another part of me thought that you might find the missing piece of the puzzle when you heard about the 'suspect'." I got a shiver when she said that. I let my mind trail to that moment so long ago. We were happy. Life was perfect.

I sat down, my knees were weak, and I felt as if I might throw up. My mind was racing but stopped suddenly when Cole came to my mind again. *'Oh shit. Cole,'* my mind reeled. *'Cole's wife. Stacy.'*

"You killed Stacy, then?" I tried not to gag at the thought.

"Yes, but she was stuck-up anyway. She was always bragging to me about all her 'good deeds'. When she started on about donating eggs, it was too much. I killed her that day I was supposed to go to her house. I couldn't stand her." She spoke with anger in her voice. The gun still pointed towards me.

"Jesus, Rachel. What the hell am I supposed to do now?" I said with my hands on my head.

"Let's stay here and pretend nothing happened. Or we could move somewhere else," she said.

I thought about it for a second, then spoke. "Let's run away. If anyone ever comes to us, we can say the receptionist did it. Put everything on her, say you had nothing to do with it. But you'll have to get rid of all the evidence. You'll have to burn the books, everything," I told her.

"They're all at my office. Should I go there now?" she asked, lowering the gun.

"Yes, yes. Go now. Then come back here, I'll start packing, and we will plan our escape," I told her.

She put the gun back in her purse and kissed me, then ran for the door. "I'll be back in two hours, tops. Start packing. I love you."

I painfully responded, "I love you, too." It was the truth.

She was walking towards the door when I spoke again, "Rachel, wait. One last question. Why did you drop their bodies in parks?"

"Well, there were two reasons why, actually. I mainly wanted them to be seen. I didn't know what to do with the first one, so I just dumped her on the side of the road. But then I thought about it more. Why wouldn't I put them somewhere noticeable? The park just seemed like a fitting place," she said simply with a smile on her face. Then she turned and walked out the door.

"And the other?" I forced out.

"You and Joe were going to the park too often without me. I didn't think you deserved to be the highlight of her day. I guess you could call it jealousy," she stated, without an ounce of remorse in her voice.

I felt like I had so many unanswered questions, and I was asking all the wrong ones with what little time I had, but my mind was spinning, and I had no idea what to do next.

After she left, I did start packing. But I didn't pack anything of hers. Just things for Joe, Rufus, and myself. I packed the bare necessities. She was unpredictable, and I wasn't sure how much time I really had left. I was scared of her, and I wasn't sure I was making the right call. I called Juniper's parents and told her that I would be picking Joe up. After getting everything in the car, I called my bank.

I told the bank that I was going on a vacation and needed some cash for the trip, which was somewhat true. I told them I would be by shortly and asked them to have it ready. I jumped in the car and headed straight for the bank.

After the bank, which only took a few minutes, I went to get Joe. I pulled into the driveway of Juniper's house and stopped outside for a second. I tried to act as normal as I could, considering I'd just found out that my wife was a murderer. They kept talking too long while telling me that Joe was an angel. I tried to rush our departure without seeming anxious.

I made sure that Joe was buckled in her seat, and I told her what we were doing.

"Joe, I need you to listen to me for a second." She nodded. I continued talking and trying to sound calm. "We're going to go on a little trip, just you and me, like you did with mommy. We're going to go somewhere new, for both of us and spend some time there. I'm not sure when we're going to come home, though."

She smiled and nodded, not asking any other questions.

I rushed to the airport. Periodically, I glanced back at Joe. Each time, she looked happy, like she had no clue what was happening. It made me smile, knowing that she was still at peace with everything. But when I looked back to the road, the pain stung again.

How did I never realize it? The more I thought about things, the more it made sense that she would be the killer. All those phone calls to her receptionist; they must've all been for murder meet-ups, or whatever murderers and accomplices do. Then, there were the late nights at work. But when I started to think about that, a question began burning in my mind. I texted her. There's no way that she would've been back at the house yet to notice that we'd already left.

> **Did you ever even have clients? You told me you were very busy at one point. Was that a lie? Where did the money to pay the bills come from?**

It didn't take long for her to respond.

> **A few, yes. Just to make it look legitimate enough. Dad gave me money. I told him that I was having a hard time getting the practice going. But I told you, my heart wasn't really in it once the murders started.**

That bitch.

I wanted to call her dad that second but decided against it. I knew that Joe would want to talk to him, and I didn't want to say anything stupid to him in front of her.

I realized that this was my only chance to talk to him about anything that I wanted to, but I had to pass this opportunity up. Besides, we were close to the airport now. I needed to park the car, and we had to rush inside to get a flight that Rachel wouldn't be able to follow us on.

When we got to the airport, I paid to park the car for seven days. That should give Rachel enough time to realize that it was there and take it if she wanted it. Then Joe, Rufus, and I went up to the front desk and talked to one of the booking agents.

"Joe, why don't you take Rufus and go sit down over there," I said, pointing to a set of benches that were nearly empty. She headed over obediently, taking Rufus and a box of treats with her.

"Hello, how can I help you," the worker asked.

"Yes, we are planning a spontaneous trip. We do it every year," I lied to her, "whatever flight leaves first, we want it."

"Oh, okay. Let me find out," she said, the smile never leaving her face. She looked down at her computer and started typing and clicking.

"Alright," I said after waiting a few seconds.

"Okay. So, here's what I found. There's a flight to Hawaii, but that doesn't leave for three more hours."

"And that's your soonest flight?" I asked, feeling like that was a long time from now.

"Well, no. But that's more desirable than a spontaneous trip to Great Falls, Montana. It leaves in 35 minutes," she told me.

"I think Great Falls sounds good. We'll take three tickets. Assuming the dog can ride with us," I said, but I meant for it to come out as a question.

"Oh, okay. Well, yes. She—"

I stopped her right there. "He."

"Oh, sorry. He can ride, but he will need his own seat. Or you can pay to put him with the rest of the dogs," she said.

"No, he can stay with us. Can we get just regular economy?" I asked.

"Oops. Looks like only First Class is available for Great Falls," she said, not sounding too sorry.

"First Class it is."

She rang up our tickets and luggage. Everything was going smoothly. I just prayed that the flight would leave on time. She gave me my total, and I paid her with cash so that Rachel wouldn't easily locate us. I also blocked her number so that she wouldn't be able to contact me. I wanted nothing to do with her.

I went to Joe and explained to her what we would be doing. I told her that we needed to hurry because getting through security would take a few minutes, and we only had 25 minutes before the flight left. She understood and gladly got up to go to the line for security.

Since she'd just been through this process the other day, it was easy for her, and she took all the steps with ease. I, on the other hand, didn't have such luck. I forgot to take off my shoes, and then I forgot to take off my belt, which had metal on it. I was lucky that I didn't have to be searched; we would've missed the flight for sure.

When we got through security, we rushed to the gate that our plane was at. I looked around, and there was nobody seated. It looked like we'd missed the flight. I walked over to the chair and slumped down into it, wondering what steps we should take next. But, just then, the lady at the desk came up to us.

"Flight for Great Falls?" she asked.

"Yes. We missed it, though, right?" I asked in return.

"No, I just called last chance before you walked over here. The doors are still open. Let's get you on the flight," she told me. I nodded my head, and we all got up and boarded the plane.

The flight felt like every other flight that I'd flown. The plane had two seats per row in First Class, so I let Joe sit by Rufus for company, and I sat in the third seat that was a row behind them.

I spent the flight surfing the web after paying for internet access. I hadn't fully thought this through. I would have to leave my job, leave my house, and leave my car. I had no idea where we were going to sleep that night or how I'd be able to continue paying the bills. But in comparison to staying with Rachel, not having a car, house, or job was still a better risk.

I booked a hotel. We could stay there for a few nights to let me figure everything out. I also rented a car. That would be fine until I was able to purchase one in the next few days. The last thing I did was look at the bank account Rachel and I shared. In the moment, I almost felt bad for transferring over as much as I could, with the daily limit restrictions, to my personal account. I couldn't let her know where we were, so everything needed to go through an account that wasn't related to her. One that she couldn't track.

By the time I finished with my bank transactions, the landing announcement was made. We would be landing in Montana shortly, a place that I'd never been, a place that I had to build a life in.

When we landed, Joe was enthusiastic about getting off the plane. She often got excited to visit places that she'd never been to, and I was sure she'd never even heard of Montana before, much less Great Falls. I haven't heard of this place either, so we were really walking into the unknown. What had I gotten us into?

After the flight landed, we went to baggage and then to get our car rental. Once we had the rental, we packed up and went to the hotel. The hotel said that we couldn't have a dog, but there was a place a few blocks away that was a doggy hotel. Joe was torn that she would have to leave Rufus there, but we had no other option. I told her it would be temporary.

We left Rufus at the doggy hotel, which happened to be a vet as well. Then, we went straight to the car dealership. I needed a new car, as renting this one would suck up too much money. I let Joe help me pick one out, so she would feel better. I didn't think she understood that this was where we would be living just yet. I was just glad to see her having a good time. A much better time than I was having.

We went back to the hotel after returning the rental. While Joe took a little nap, I researched schools, jobs, and finally houses. I didn't really want my daughter to go to a public school, but it would have to do for the moment. I sent the school an email, letting them know that my daughter needed to transfer because we'd recently moved. It was the weekend, so I was not expecting a response.

As for the jobs, I couldn't find much for my profession. I definitely didn't want anything labor-intensive. I decided to call my boss, the head of the department.

"Tim! How are you?" he said by way of greeting after answering my call.

"Hey, hey. I'm fine. Are you busy?" I asked him.

"Not for you! What can I do you for? Working hard on that project? Deadline is coming up."

"Of course. I'm working on it right now; we're going to be on time for the deadline. But that's not really what I need to talk to you about," I told him, then continued to tell him about how Rachel and I had decided to split up, telling her she could have the house. I said that I was moving out of the state in a split-second decision. Then asked, "Do you think I could permanently work from home?"

"Tim, I like you, man. But that's a pretty big ask to spring on someone," he responded.

"I understand."

"But I'll tell you what, give me a day or two to think about it. Keep working on that project. We can talk about it Monday morning. I'll give you a call when I've made my decision," he said, then we exchanged goodbyes.

I had a good feeling about his answer. I was almost sure that he would be okay with it. I set my phone down and continued to look at houses.

I found a few that I really liked, and half of them were much bigger than they needed to be. One of them was in a great location, from what I could see, and it was a good price for what Joe and I needed. I decided to pick five different houses to look into. I called a local agent and gave her my requirements. Her name was Petra Hone, and she was more than polite. She told me that there was actually an open house for one of them that evening, but we could go and see the other four in the morning.

Joe and I got into the new car and went to the first house. It wasn't my first choice, but it was a lot nicer than the photos. It looked to be in my price range, more than affordable, and it had everything on my list of needs. I waited to put in an offer, though, since I might find better. Plus, there was a spark in Joe's eye that told me she was in love with the place. There was enough space for her to have her own bedroom and a toy room.

The next day, I didn't see anything that I liked more, and there wasn't a single other person at the open house while I was there. I put in an offer for $10,000 less than asking but offered to pay all cash.

They countered me with $6,000 less. I agreed to it.

Once again, I was a homeowner in a new city and state. Once again, I was starting fresh.

CHAPTER 26

It has been a full year since we moved to Montana, and things couldn't be better. Joe is excelling at the public school, and I've kept my job since they allowed me to work from home. I still have meetings over video chat every day with my team members, but it almost seems to be the same.

The house has been more than ideal for us, and a few weeks into summer, we built an inground pool in our large backyard. Almost everything else has stayed the same in the house, and I don't regret a thing about it.

I often think about my life in Washington, but it gets easier and easier with every day that goes by. I still talk to Cole, but he knows that I cannot tell him where I am or why I moved, and he's accepted that. He's now engaged to his girlfriend. I'm more than happy for him, and I told him that I'll try my best to make it to the wedding.

I haven't forgiven Rachel for anything she's done. The more that I've thought about it, the more I think

I should've realized the problem earlier. But, there's nothing I can do to change the past, and I'm still working on moving forward.

Today, Joe and I are celebrating our moving day by having a small party for anyone in the neighborhood who wants to come.

Living in a place like this is much different from the places I've been in the past. The small-town community lifestyle is meant for me, I've realized. As for Joe, she still complains about missing the city life, but she has a lot more friends here, and she seems to be much happier than she ever was in Washington or Illinois.

The best part about living in a small town is that almost everyone knows you. They know if you're lazy or hardworking, they know if you're single, married, or divorced. You don't have to constantly be telling your story to every person that you meet. I know some might see that as a bad thing, but I think it's wonderful.

Today, I walk into Joe's room to see if she's ready for the little celebration. She's sitting on the bed, crying, and holding a picture of herself, Rachel, and me at the park.

"I miss Mommy," she says, with tears streaming down her face.

"I know you do. I miss her too, dear." It isn't a lie. I missed the Rachel I knew before she was a killer.

"We live here now. We have a life here. And I promise that one day you'll understand it all."

"Will I ever get to see her again?" she asks.

I sympathize. "Possibly. She's getting help right now. Maybe once she gets the help she needs, she can come back into our lives," I tell her. "But dear. Your party is starting, and you don't want to be late!"

She smiles back at me, and her entire mood changes in a second. "You're right, let's do this," she says, hopping off the bed and leaving the picture in her place. She rushes out of the room, and Rufus and I follow.

I stand there for a while, letting Rachel's image form back in my head. Over the last year, I've had a lot of time to think about her and everything she's done.

I don't regret, in the slightest, leaving her and taking Joe with me. However, there are a few questions that I wish I could ask her. Questions that float to my memory every time I think about her. I wonder why she got me the expensive yacht in the first place. Was she trying to keep me preoccupied? Did she really just use that additional office space for storage, or was it for something more sinister? Lastly, the police never released, to this day, what the murder weapon was. I wonder if it was that gun she pointed at me. That seems the most likely weapon. What else do killers kill people with? Hopefully, I will never have the opportunity to find out.

When we get to the backyard, our first guest has arrived. Petra. My agent, but also my secret girlfriend. After she helped me get the house, we stayed in touch for a while, until the day she agreed to a date with me. We had a celebration that night and really got to know each other. It was one of the best nights of my life, something I will never forget. We've been together for the last three months, but I haven't told Joe about it yet. She still doesn't understand that her mom is an evil person, and it would probably upset her if she thought that I was trying to replace Rachel with Petra.

"Hi, Petra!" Joe says as she rushes past her to get to the table with food that was just put out by the local caterer.

"Hi, Joe," Petra says, then turns to me. "Hi, handsome. How are you doing today?"

"Hi, babe, I'm good. But Joe was crying about Rachel again. I don't know how to help her. Her mom isn't in her right mind, and I don't think that she's ever going to see her again, but I can't just say that," I confess.

"That's true. But some day. Some day. But what else can you do?" she says rhetorically, patting my back lightly.

One by one, people start to flock in. Everyone has either brought a dessert to pass around, a drink, or an appetizer. There are a lot more people than I had expected, especially for it being so chilly outside. For it being the end of October, it's definitely fall weather. Even the trees have almost lost all their brown, orange, and red leaves.

The rest of the day flies by. Eventually, the party starts thinning out, people start staggering home, and Joe is fast asleep on one of the outdoor chairs. Petra comes up to me, and we have an intimate talk while everyone else is leaving. Both of us are tipsy and talking about what we are going to do to each other once Joe falls asleep. The day really has been a good one, and everything ended perfectly.

The next morning, Petra and I wake up early so that she can leave before Joe sees that she's still here. I make us each a cup of tea, and we drink it while sitting outside on the front porch. Petra has changed her clothes, just in case Joe wakes up and notices that she was wearing the same clothes from last night.

After we finish our tea, Petra tells me that she has a busy day today with a few showings for a person who recently moved into town. She says that the person was pretty vague about what they want, and they only communicated through email. They arrived yesterday and are ready to view new houses, specifically in the higher price range. Petra isn't excited about this shady new client, but she has a job to do, and she leaves after giving me a kiss.

Joe is still in bed, so I do a few odd things around the house. I start to pick up a little from the party yesterday, but there's a cleaning service coming today to do most of the work. As I'm picking up bottles off the ground, I see the mailman doing his rounds, and I decide to get the mail.

I walk across the street to where the mailbox is posted in the ground. I open up the mailbox, and it seems to be a little fuller than usual. I sift through the mail on my way back to the front door. There's the weekly newspaper with all the specials and sales going on at the nearby stores. Then there's a bill for the water and refuse. I don't open it since it's already on auto-pay. There were a few pieces of junk mail, people trying to get me a new credit card, some coupons from a craft store, and lastly, a blank envelope.

The envelope is a classic white one, with no address, no name, no postage. It's just blank. I assume that it's from someone at the party yesterday just sending a Thank You card for hosting the party since there was no postmark. They must've just dropped it off on their morning walk or on the way to the store. I open it once I get back inside. My eyes are still adjusting to the light, but there's just a small note inside.

I get nervous reading it since it's in a typewriter font. The few lines seemed to be a poem. At that moment, I know who sent it. There's only one person I know who has a typewriter and writes poetry.

T. A. August

I know where you are
I've finally tracked you down
I even see you drive your car

Don't worry, I won't be wild
I'll keep my distance

ACKNOWLEDGEMENTS

Where to begin? I want to start off by giving thanks to my mother and father. Thank you for believing in my and supporting me along my entire journey. Thank you, Dad, for encouraging me to submit my short stories and poems as a young kid. Thank you, Mom, for listening to me as I worked through the story plot even though it meant spoiling the ending for you. Thank you to my editors, Brigitte and Becka, for perfecting my story and bringing out the full potential. Thank you, Alexander, my cover artist, for allowing me to make changes up until the very last second. Because of you three, I'm convinced this book will go farther than I ever imagined. Finally, the biggest of thanks goes to Torrence. Thank you for constantly listening to me talk about how excited I am to publish. Thank you for listening to me complain about not knowing where to end this story. Thank you for doing everything for me while I sat on the couch, in my office, or in the dinning room writing my heart out. Because of you, it finally happened.

ABOUT THE AUTHOR

T. A. August has been writing short stories and books since she was a young child. It has been her lifelong dream to become a published author. Her debut novel The Mercer Island Murderer is just the start of her career as an author.

For more books and updates from T. A. August, visit www.taaugust.com.

Made in the USA
Las Vegas, NV
09 February 2021